A NOVEL

KEITH DAVID McCOY

WILD IRISH HUMOUR

ISBN (Ebook): 978-1-9163652-0-9
ISBN (Paperback): 978-1-9163652-1-6

Edited by Charlie Wilson
Design by Vanessa Mendozzi

CONTENTS

This is dedicated to all those who dream and hope and do their best minute to minute, hour to hour, day to day to make their lives, the lives of those around them, and the world a better place. Well done and thank you.

Nota Bene

'Sometimes life sneaks up behind you and gives you a big kick.'

CONFUSION

CHAPTER 1

People hurry to make their way to their place or, if they aren't a creature of habit, a place. Some are just entering the room, some have been seated for up to twenty minutes, and others are issuing 'excuse me's as they either squeeze past people who are already sitting or use it as a code to get them to stand so that they can pass. There's a collection of differing noises: jackets being zipped open and off, seats being moved from the vertical to the horizontal, other seats springing up as people rise, mobiles being turned off, other mobiles being put on vibrate…

At the front of the lecture theatre, Lena Maguire is seated facing the class. She isn't opening her bag; she hasn't got a pen out and she doesn't look like she's going to use the whiteboard. The door at the back is closed, everyone is in and seated, and silence falls as the forty or so men and women stare down at her. She watches the second hand on her wristwatch count down until it is officially nine-thirty a.m. and she looks up at her audience.

'Wow,' she says, smiling. 'Finally. It's taken me a full three years to get you all into this room on time.'

The audience giggles. Standing and moving beyond the desk, Lena looks at them and it feels like she makes eye contact with each and every one of the students.

‘First of all, congratulations. As you know, you got your results yesterday and you all passed.’ Mutters of excitement descend around the lecture hall. ‘As I said previously, I was never in doubt.’

‘I believed you, Lena, but I wouldn’t have bet on it,’ says the Glaswegian, Ross.

‘I was panicking,’ advises Rita from Zimbabwe.

Then there’s a bit of bravado from Liverpool Dean. ‘I knew it would work out,’ he says with a smile, and accepts a couple of jeers from best friends Robert and William, natives of Bolton and Burnley.

Lena, from Ireland, continues: ‘It’s been a privilege and honour to be your lecturer for the past three years. I’m so proud of you all. As of tomorrow, you will be qualified mental health nurses, though, as you know your registration number from the nursing and midwifery council won’t come for another month or so, and obviously, the graduation, which will take place here in Manchester, isn’t for another few months. So, this is it, our last day together. Life has taught me that things change, and I can guarantee that we’ll never all be in the same room again together; that’s just how things work out. Therefore this is a special day, and as such I have deliberately kept it blank, so that we can decide how to mark the day and fill it together.’ She pauses. ‘So, what do you want to do?’

Someone jokes, ‘Let’s go home early – like, now,’ and that raises a few giggles.

Someone else says, ‘Let’s all go to the cinema together.’

Seamus from Mayo, whose wife has just given birth to a baby girl, lays his head on his desk. ‘Rest,’ he calls out.

Irene, a highly organised twenty-something from Chelmsford, asks, ‘Would you tell us about your favourite patient?’

‘I can’t really – that’s too hard,’ explains Lena. ‘I never had a favourite; there were so many I adored.’

‘What about your most dangerous?’ asks William.

‘Not on our last day, please,’ Lena responds.

‘What about your most annoying?’ smiles Liverpool Dean.

‘That would be you,’ she throws back at him to great applause, including Dean’s.

‘Well,’ says Irene, ‘if it can’t be any of the above, can you tell us about your most interesting patient?’

Without thinking, Lena immediately responds, ‘That would be easy, very, very easy indeed.’

‘Go on then,’ say a number of her newly qualified students.

‘Are we in agreement?’ she asks, and forty hands rise.

‘Okay,’ she says, ‘I will. The usual rules apply: no recording the talk, for reasons of confidentiality, and whatever is discussed stays here.’

The forty students give a well-rehearsed response: ‘Agreed.’

‘I’ll try to tell it as much as I can, how *he* saw it, his perception, and the bits he didn’t know, I’ll fill in,’ she says. ‘So, to Ireland.’

CHAPTER 2

The droplet is elongated, over eighteen inches in length, and progressing unbroken from Lawrence Barry's mouth to the worn carpeted floor like the Angel Falls of Venezuela. He has become so used to this happening that most of the time he doesn't even notice it. When it first occurred, he immediately thought of the Angel Falls. He hadn't heard of them until a drunken night out in his late teens with college friends, when the acquaintance of a friend, Mickey O'Rourke, urinated from a railway bridge onto the incoming Dublin train, a mile from Limerick's Colbert station, whilst shouting out, 'Angel Falls'. O'Rourke is no longer with us, killed stone-dead in a car accident in San Francisco. There are no waterfalls in Limerick; maybe there's one in Killaloe; but there is a small and gorgeous one in Killarney, Torc, which Lawrence visited as a ten-year-old with his parents.

Lawrence is giving his undivided attention to the tie that his psychiatrist, Dr Ciaran Noel Best, is wearing. Best, also known as *Ciaran Knows Best* by colleagues, is a studious type who wears Mickey Mouse socks and other novel but incongruent items of clothing in an attempt to create an identity of a cool, trendy, weird, fun, academic-type nerd. Best is talking, but Lawrence is miles away, staring intently at the tie. He recognises it from a previous meeting some months ago. The Daffy Duck on it insulted him and, as he remonstrated with the tie, Lawrence failed to take any notice of the fact that it was bound to Best, and he, Daffy and the good doctor crashed to the floor as Lawrence gave Daffy the old Mike Tyson one-two.

If Lawrence were a nobody, he would have been moved to a secure unit, but there are some perks to being a senior Garda (Police) detective, albeit one who's on sick leave. Rather than keeping Lawrence at St. Patrick's Hospital, Dublin, the Gardai (Police) and the health service came to an arrangement that, with Lawrence and his wife's agreement, he would be treated in isolation at Desmond House, Monagea, County Limerick. This eighteenth-century pile was a nursing home in the 1960s and '70s, but is now in the possession of the state, more notably the Gardai and more specifically the Special Branch. Best continues to oversee Lawrence's care and drops down from Dublin every fortnight. The day-to-day care is provided by a qualified nurse and occasionally a Garda, with support from some prison officers picking up easy overtime. It's a very unusual arrangement, but one that the Gardai commissioner signed off on himself: 'I give it my blessing' was the line he used, which is strange in itself as he's a self-confessed atheist.

Lawrence's eyes don't leave the tie.

'You're unwell,' says the doctor.

‘I am?! How do you mean?’ enquires Lawrence.

‘You had a breakdown. You were very psychotic – you still are. I mean, some of your symptoms still remain.’

Lawrence is confused; he doesn’t understand what the doctor is talking about and he explains this.

Best gives a sympathetic sigh, leans forward and speaks kindly, quietly and slowly. ‘You hear voices that aren’t there. You see things that aren’t real. You get paranoid. In a nutshell, you…’ He smirks. ‘That’s funny, get it?’ Lawrence, of course, doesn’t. ‘Never mind,’ says the doctor, waving it away. ‘Anyway, you’re as mad as a brush.’

And with that, having given his expert opinion based on twelve years of training and ten years as a consultant, Best leans back in his chair.

Lawrence breaks eye contact with the tie and turns his head sideways in response to someone shouting words of encouragement. ‘Hello, Larry, stick up for yourself!’

Lawrence is a bit shocked and scared by the fact the speaker is a brush, but he engages it in dialogue anyway.

‘What did you say?’

‘I’m not mad, and neither are you, Larry,’ reports the brush.

Lawrence concurs. ‘That’s right, I’m not mad either.’

‘What’s that?’ asks Best.

Lawrence had momentarily forgotten that he was with the doctor. He apologises, explaining that he didn’t mean to be rude but had been conversing with the brush, and that both he and the brush are of the view that Lawrence isn’t unwell.

With a more serious demeanour and whilst shaking his head, the doctor explains that this isn't normal, as brushes, inanimate objects, don't speak. Lawrence looks at Best and at the brush and just doesn't know what to think or say; he is bemused and confused and feels like crying.

Best leans forward again and assumes a more comforting tone. 'You've made seriously good progress, Lawrence. However, I'm not going to change your medication just yet. I have you on a more traditional antipsychotic, in part because I was concerned about your levels of aggression following your assault on me. I'll put you on something more modern soon, but before then I'd like you to start having sessions with a counselling psychologist. Her name is Majella Quinn and she's excellent. Be careful, though: she's also a psychotherapist, so she'll probably tell you the breakdown happened because you wanted to ride your mother.'

Best laughs, but he can tell Lawrence isn't in on the joke and he offers a hollow explanation: 'It's an industry joke. Freud. Anyway, I think you're well enough to leave here during the day, as you're no longer a risk to others. I received your letter about returning to work, but I don't think you should go back just yet. Take some time for yourself during the day – but you must still return here at night.'

'I just need to come back at night?' enquires Lawrence.

'Just so we can monitor things and ensure you don't relapse. It's been a tough journey, you have been with me nearly a year. Also, some people find it helps to keep a diary of their thoughts, feelings, colours they feel like and so on,' says the doc.

'Okay, that should be easy enough. I've always kept a diary,' Lawrence says.

Best waves a small see-through plastic bag containing spheres that catch the light. 'C'mon,' he says, 'let's play a game of marbles.'

CHAPTER 3

Flashes of light totally overpower the small room, and as the blinded trio make their way to a desk, they use their feet and hands to feel out where exactly the chairs and table are, so that the leader doesn't fall on his arse like he did the previous week. The leader has his hand up to try to block the flashes and is blinking so quickly that if he were lying down you would probably nudge him to disturb his rapid-eye-movement (REM) nightmare. He sits down squished in tight between his two aides, as if scrummaging in what would be the most undernourished Irish front row ever against a pack of baying journalists.

They shout at the leader, the Taoiseach, the Irish Prime Minister (PM), demanding to know what he's going to do about the current economic crisis. From a distance it looks like a pile of dogs jostling with the kennel owner to ensure they'll get their Pedigree Chum rations, and if you closed your eyes, you would firmly believe that this was so, as all you would actually hear is barking. This is probably deserved, as this Taoiseach has proved to be a complete and utter eejit who's unbelievably out of touch with the realities of the country.

As the storm waves crash against the table, at the centre is the Taoiseach and his thoughts, which are, *Oh shit, oh shit, oh shit*. Finally, he composes himself, and on cue silence descends. Then the Taoiseach declares that he loves all his people, all of them, including those with big noses.

This completely turns the tide. For a long moment, the members of the media look startled and out of it, as if some sort of cannabis haze has descended, or as if they're sharks that have been flipped onto their backs. Then they begin snarling, demanding that the Taoiseach voice his opinion on American foreign policy, specifically with relation to the Middle East.

Again, the Taoiseach freezes as he thinks, *Oh shit, oh shit, oh shit. I need a thought; I need a thought.* This thought arrives and reminds him: *Must smile, must smile, always smile.* He opens his mouth, postures like Martin Luther King and declares to his audience, 'I must smile.'

The journalists fall about in laughter at what they agree is utter incompetence, but the Taoiseach isn't giving up and he follows up by declaring that he loves his people, especially those with big wallets.

Now the journalists are incredulous and can hardly breathe they're laughing so much.

'What's he on?'

'He's totally out of his depth.'

Then one of them, who has neither barked nor laughed, quietly acknowledges, 'But we got him elected.'

Eventually, the room calms and a journalist politely asks the

Taoiseach if he has any information on the missing accountant, Mike McCarthy.

The Taoiseach hasn't moved on from his previous thought process and again poses and bleats out, 'I love all my people, big hearts, blah, blah, blah.'

'But what about Mr McCarthy? It's been a year,' someone shouts from the floor.

The startled Taoiseach puts his finger in the air and declares that he will get his minister onto it straight away. With that, he stands and walks to the exit, accompanied by the skinniest props in the world, and looks to the heavens, thanking God for blessing him with such excellent oratory skills.

Outside the room, aide number one slimes sycophantically all over the self-absorbed Taoiseach, trying to sow seeds that will grow into promotion opportunities. Not to be outdone, aide number two adds that the Taoiseach's performance brought a tear to his eye.

The Taoiseach hardly hears any of this, as he has started to quietly sing to himself, 'All you need to do is smile, na-na-na-na, all you need to do is smile, na-na-na-na,' to the tune of the Beatles' track 'All You Need Is Love'. He turns to aide number one and states that he, the Taoiseach, is in the wrong job and that Tom Hanks isn't good enough to stand next to him. As the Taoiseach daydreams about winning an Oscar, aide number two exclaims that he is indeed better than Hanks.

CHAPTER 4

Lawrence is pleased that he will be allowed to leave Desmond House during the day, but he hasn't been fully open with Best: he intends to get back to work immediately. Unfortunately, he has been out of action for about eleven months, and during that time, he discovers, professional decisions were taken concerning him. Lawrence is no longer working from Dublin; he is no longer the leader of the Special Branch and he is no longer the detective chief superintendent. He will now work as an ordinary senior detective in a special task unit set up a number of months earlier and based in Limerick city.

It hurts Lawrence that his boss and friend, Reggie Pearse, the assistant commissioner responsible for the Crime and Security Branch, didn't fight Lawrence's corner against the Garda commissioner, Hugh O'Sullivan, who designed and executed his transfer to the southwest.

Lawrence's wife, Eileen, isn't pleased about the move either. Originally from Galway, she was happy in Dublin and had adjusted to life there. Now she's stuck living with two young children in a rented house in Annacotty on the outskirts of Limerick, while her husband is treated for bipolar disorder thirty miles away in Newcastle West. On the positive side, she was able to get a job transfer to a local private hospital, she only has to work two days a week and they continue to own the house in Dublin. But it's still a strain.

So now, on top of the hallucinations and mood fluctuations, Lawrence has to manage guilt. *All this change*, he thinks, *it's hard.* Isn't that what he learnt doing his MBA? That's what John Kotter says – not the John Kotter who played on the school's Gaelic football team with him; a different fella, a guru. Lawrence supposes it helps that his new boss and one of his new colleagues visited him, though he can't remember their names or what they spoke about, just that one of them was very heavy and the other kind of tall.

Lawrence drives slowly down the narrow lane leading from Desmond House to ensure he doesn't damage the electric wire on both sides that's supposed to keep the sheep in the green fields. After about half a mile, the lane widens and there are a few houses either side. Three hundred metres on, it's a left turn onto an actual road. A three-mile drive from here will take him from deepest Monagea to the town of Newcastle West; a right turn at the church, and then it's a straight drive to Limerick city. *Good directions*, he thinks.

As he drives, he decides that his priorities now have to be to get out of hospital, support Eileen and get his old job back. All of this can be achieved if he can show the hierarchy that he's back and winning; therefore, he needs to do an excellent job in Limerick.

What went wrong? he wonders. *How did I end up having a breakdown?* He has no answers.

THE ACCOUNTANT

CHAPTER 5

John O'Shea is seated in his office and speaking on the phone. He listens intently, nodding without uttering a word. He's a tall man, a lean man – slim, probably close to being skinny – a highly intelligent man, and an extremely frustrated and angry man. To date, he's never quite lost it, though; his conservative and reserved nature, nurtured by the priests at Rockwell College, prevents him from physically assaulting others, regardless of the provocation. From Rockwell College to Templemore Garda Academy: not a well-travelled route and one his uncle – a now-deceased gay dentist who found love in Rio de Janeiro and who paid O'Shea's fees at Rockwell – tried to talk him out of.

O'Shea regrets the career choice now. There were years when he loved the work, and he was marked out early in his career for the top police job in Ireland, but it all went wrong. Despite his academic brilliance and his detective knowhow, he's never been able to figure out who put the ten kilos of heroin in his garage. The fallout was huge. The media had a field day: 'Drug Mule' they called him in one paper, 'Captain Coke' in another, but the one that hurt the most was

'Smackhead', as at the time he was the head of the main organised-crime intelligence unit for the country.

O'Shea knows it wasn't the paramilitaries. He's wondered if it was a crime boss, but usually they aren't looking to out you in the media – they look for some way to get leverage over you, so that you indirectly assist them with running their operations without too much interference from the authorities. What O'Shea doesn't know is that it was a prank by one of his junior officers that went wrong. Mickey O'Rourke (of Angel Falls fame) took the heroin from Garda storage following a drugs bust and put it in the garage with the intention of winding O'Shea up with a few of the lads when he got back from his holidays. However, the discovery was made when the ten-year-old twin boys from next door accidentally broke the window and then entered the garage with their mum to retrieve the ball. It was the scoop the mum, a journalist who was new to the area, needed, and her career immediately rocketed north as O'Shea's sank south.

O'Rourke would have remedied this on his return to Ireland, as O'Shea was someone he liked and admired, even if he was a bit anal, but fate intervened and when O'Rourke returned, it was a week later than planned and in a wooden box. (A driving error, caused by his confusion over driving on the other side of the road, brought him into terminal conflict with a huge truck. He died instantly. The truck driver suffered shock, but was more upbeat a few weeks later when he found out the deceased driver was a cop, allowing him to chuckle with his mates that he'd smoked bacon.)

Unfortunately for O'Shea, O'Rourke hadn't told anyone about the prank, and even though the incident was managed through the correct channels and O'Shea didn't face any charges, his career nosedived. He was moved around from backwater to backwater in meaningless middle-management roles: Mayo, Carlow, Westmeath and, for the past year, Limerick. This latest post is his least favourite to date, running a unit of the most useless bunch of cops Ireland has ever produced. These misfits have been shoved together in out-of-the-way Limerick, unknown to the general public but laughed at by everyone on the force and nicknamed the Extra-Special Special Branch. The unit, not quite understanding that they're the butt of a joke, take some pride in this, calling themselves the Specials. But O'Shea knows the truth: they're a laughing stock and this is his purgatory. He should have been a doctor like his uncle wanted; he was certainly smart enough and had the grades to get in and all the right connections. But no, he wanted to help society in a different way.

Eventually, he speaks into the phone. 'Yes, Deputy Commissioner Clarke,' he says, and puts the phone back on the receiver.

O'Shea sighs. He sighs a lot these days. He never used to sigh, but now this is probably the thing he does most, apart from breathing, and he has every reason to do so. He looks through the internal glass window into the other room. *How do they expect me to get results with these clowns?* he thinks. He's no ringmaster and this isn't supposed to be a circus, but it is. He rests his head on the table and then bangs it a few times, not hard enough to harm himself, small taps, like he's involved in a game of charades and his word is 'woodpecker'. Lifting his head, he acknowledges that results aren't really what his superiors want and that his team are usually given nonsense cases, ones that don't matter to the top brass. He stands up to his full height, giraffe-esque, takes a deep breath and walks towards the door.

CHAPTER 6

Mooney, Noddy and Big Mac are sitting at their desks. Mooney is crying and Noddy is gazing at Big Mac, who is devouring a doorstop sandwich.

Big Mac, real name Seamus O'Bese, is a big man. Life and soul of the party, renowned for his charm with the ladies. Quick-witted, jovial and sarcastic. He wears an out of date mullet hairdo, and is also wide and fat, with some of the unfortunate physiological consequences of being that size. He struggles for breath and sweats profusely; he could walk fifty metres and look like he had just stepped out of the shower. He deals with his problems by throwing himself into consuming food and more food: his appetite is vast, mostly triggered by blood sugar drops caused by the shite food he favours. He's also fond of the booze, but it's food that will kill him – a stroke or heart attack most likely.

Mooney is considered by most to be an attractive woman, but a little neurotic at times. With her high energy and excitability, she's very easily distracted and doesn't get a lot of work done. Inappropriately nicknamed Miss Moody by Boss, she's very bright: she studied computing at Trinity College,

Dublin, before joining the police force. One of her sisters is an architect and the other an ear, nose and throat specialist. Her parents are extremely proud of the three of them. She was knocked unconscious during a hockey match, aged twenty, and suffered a very minor brain injury, but enough for those that know her well to recognise that she had a small change to her personality and no longer understood the subtle nuances of social interaction, and as a result, sometimes people felt she was a bit odd.

Noddy is a complete moron, as dumb as you can get, but with a heart of gold. His uncle, a senior police officer, was able to pull some strings and bypass the usual channels to get his dunce nephew into the force. The priesthood was also an option, but no one was training to be a priest anymore, most of them were quite old, a dying breed, and his uncle realised Noddy would never remember the words to a single prayer and was very likely to fail in Maynooth, the priest college, so he placed the lad where he had sway instead. Of course, once the uncle passed away, Noddy was moved to Limerick.

Big Mac, munching away, advises through a mouthful that his sandwich is gorgeous. Noddy, who isn't eating anything, states that his sandwich is gorgeous.

Big Mac lovingly licks his lips, following this with the words, 'The relish.' Again, Noddy does and says the same.

'Oh God, the tomato,' says Big Mac, and Noddy replicates these words. At once Big Mac puts his sandwich down, stares at Noddy and tells him to stop copying him.

Noddy says, 'Stop copying me.'

Irritated, Big Mac yells, 'I'm serious!'

The parrot-esque Noddy responds with his own, 'I'm serious.'

O'Shea – known collectively as 'Boss' – enters and asks for everyone's attention, then quickly turns to the men and asks why Mooney is crying. Big Mac tells Boss he doesn't know. Noddy, who isn't listening, copies Big Mac. Big Mac threatens him, and Noddy echoes the threat.

Boss shouts at them to shut up, and then turns to Mooney and calmly asks her, 'What are you crying about this time?'

Mooney blows her nose, goo leaking from her tissue onto the desk, and through her tears tells her boss that she had to dump her boyfriend again.

Big Mac makes a motion with his hands as if celebrating a World Cup-winning goal and whispers to himself, 'I'm in with a chance.'

Big Mac loses his temper when Noddy mirrors him again, and he rushes over and starts to fight with Noddy. Boss takes no notice of the men, keeping his focus on Mooney.

'What did he do this time?' Boss asks. 'Forget the sugar in the tea?'

Mooney doesn't notice Boss's sarcasm and slowly describes through her crying that, 'He-he-he-he belched and didn't excuse himself.'

Boss tells her to get a grip and then belches at her. Out of shock, she immediately stops crying.

Noddy asks Big Mac why he attacked him, to be told it was because Noddy was copying him. A confused Noddy pleads with Big Mac, saying, 'But you said I should try to be more like you.'

Big Mac wipes the sweat from his face and brow using his shirt sleeve, meaning his elbow is now an island as a massive sweat stain reaches down from his armpit. He gives Noddy a pitying look and explains that he meant Noddy should copy him in a cool, intelligent, sophisticated way. He lifts his leg ever so slightly and his face tightens as he squeezes out a fart. He then opens his arms to meaningfully communicate with Noddy, asking, 'Do you know what I mean?'

Noddy looks at him for a few moments and appears to be having a real good think, then follows up Big Mac's question with a 'No'.

Big Mac shrugs his shoulders and tells Noddy not to worry about it.

Boss walks to the centre of the room, puts his hands on his hips and says, 'Well, now that I've got your attention, I've got some news for you all. Detective Lawrence Barry will be joining us today. I've been aware of his transfer into the unit for some time, but the start date was only agreed a few days ago.'

'Where was he, sir?' asks Mooney.

'The bin,' says Boss.

Noddy looks in the dustbin and says, 'I don't think so!'

'The loony bin,' Big Mac clarifies, 'the nuthouse, the

madhouse, the mental hospital – he lost it, had a breakdown, cracked up.'

Noddy still looks like he doesn't understand. Mooney is wiping up the snot on her desk and Big Mac is looking like he wants gratitude from Boss for providing extra understanding for his colleagues.

'Anyway,' says Boss, 'when he arrives, could we just act normal? Please don't mention his absence or the bin.'

Mooney and Big Mac agree, but Noddy looks in the bin again and appears confused.

Boss approaches him. 'Do you understand that, Noddy, do you? Do you?'

Noddy nods in confirmation.

Boss frowns. 'Don't nod if you don't understand.'

Noddy shakes his head from side to side.

Bemused, Boss asks, 'Do you understand or don't you?'

Noddy nods and shakes his head in an alternating pattern.

Boss sighs and mutters to himself, 'For fuck's sake.' Then he composes himself and addresses them all. 'As well as that, Deputy Commissioner Clarke has asked that we take on the case of missing accountant, Mike McCarthy.'

Lawrence slowly walks into the room as Boss delivers this news, head down and appearing distracted and pressured. There is a pregnant pause while everyone looks at each other, unsure how to break the ice.

Lawrence keeps his eyes on the floor and says, 'Hello.'

Noddy immediately responds with a fast few sentences.

'Heard you were in the loony bin. Cracked up – did you crack up? Was it like being in Vietnam? The average age of a combat soldier in World War Two was twenty-six; in Vietnam it was twenty-two–'

This volley of words is broken by Boss kicking Noddy on the posterior and shouting, 'For fuck's sake, you eejit, what did I tell you?' Then, turning to Lawrence, Boss calmly and with great sincerity apologises to Lawrence.

Another awkward pause.

Eventually, Lawrence straightens up, looks at his colleagues, opens his mouth and utters, 'No, it wasn't like Vietnam. It was just like being in a mental hospital.'

Boss hurriedly intervenes, trying to reset the tone. 'I just want to welcome you back and let you know that nut, nut, nut, nut, nut thing, I mean nut, not nut, nothing, nothing – that's it, nothing will prevent you, us, from working together.'

Mooney cheers and Boss forces a very exaggerated smile. Noddy again looks in the bin and Big Mac pretends to puke. Lawrence just stands there, eyes down, almost statue like.

Again, a pause.

Lawrence squeezes out an almost audible, 'Thanks.' He appears perplexed and a little frightened, which is understandable given that, when he looks at his colleagues, he is hallucinating and sees they all have ant heads. He muses to himself that this can't be real. The doctor told him he wasn't fully ready for work. As frightening as this is, maybe it is psychosis, in the same way the tie was talking to him yesterday.

He reaches into his pocket, takes out some medication, bursts the blister packet and swallows the tablet. The others don't quite notice this.

Boss steps forward and, in a manly, macho, caring way, pats Lawrence on the shoulder. He starts to depart the room whilst issuing directives to everyone: 'Anyway, Lawrence, Mooney will brief you on our current case. Noddy, Big Mac, I want you to see if you can get any leads on Mr McCarthy's disappearance. Mooney, I will organise for you to get a job at the firm whose accounts he was working on. Lawrence, just support Mooney on this one. I want to ease you back in slowly; I want you to be semi-supernumerary on this case. I don't want nut, nut, nut, nut, nothing to hinder your progress – health-wise, that is.'

CHAPTER 7

Fingers slide through the oil-soaked hair of Jesse McCarthy. He has competition from James O'Sullivan, who has enough grease on his head to comfortably fry bacon and eggs for the entire Munster rugby team. Like a pair of practised synchronised swimmers, they attempt to style their hair into the form that creates their confidence. Samson may have got strength from his hair, but for these guys the hair is transformational – they don't become ruthless estate agents and auctioneers until the gel is on and every strand is exactly where it is supposed to be; only then can they rival a cokehead for confidence.

Jesse turns to James. 'I sold him this tiny box room. I told him it was a studio flat, told him there was no chance he'd ever be able to afford anything else, bargain of the century.' He laughs. 'Anyway, then I started lying, saying other people had put in bids when they hadn't. I stretched him to the max. Once the interest rates go up, there's no way he'll be able to afford to keep it.' Again he laughs. 'He'll lose it to the banks.'

James, with his hair in place, is now fixing his tie and suit. The suit is so shiny that it could be used as a landing light at Shannon Airport. He volunteers, 'That's a good one – stretch them, bleed them, take their money, sell, sell, sell, get our commission, our percentage, and screw the lot of them.'

The door to the agency swings open and in walks an attractive woman. Composed, orderly, professional – this is a different Miss Mooney to the one we previously encountered. No tears, and her makeup is immaculate.

The agents are momentarily thrown off-guard by Miss Mooney's good looks, but quickly compose themselves. The power of the hair gel. Jesse wasn't always this confident. He sometimes wonders what might have been if he had started applying the gel sooner. Surely he would have done better in his exams at school. But it wasn't until he got the estate agent job that James introduced him to oils, creams and gel. Jesse read somewhere – he can't remember where; must have been a lads' mag, as he doesn't read books or papers, or maybe he overheard a conversation – that success in life is all about connections. He now appreciates that this is the case, and wishes he had met James when he was about fifteen. He would have started using gel for sure, and then maybe he'd have done a business degree.

The agents get ready to strut their stuff, to use the well-worn lines that have seduced many a buyer and messed up many a bank account. James smiles, displaying his whiter-than-snow teeth. Feigning helpfulness, he asks Mooney if he can help her. She explains that her name is Michelle Mooney and that she is here to secure the job working with them.

James' and Jesse's thought processes are also closely

synchronised. Their heart rates instantly increase by twenty beats a minute as they think, *This lady is a ride and a half and being around her every day would be fucking amazing.* Their confident demeanours lapse for only a nanosecond, and then their initial thought is replaced by a mental slideshow of them cheering as if they'd just won the lottery.

'Thank God,' says James. 'I thought you were a customer for a second there. I was afraid I was going to have to act nice. Ha-ha!'

They all laugh.

CHAPTER 8

Walther Matthau and Jack Lemmon were the odd couple, but Big Mac and Noddy could rival them. Noddy trots in front, stops, lifts his head, looks about like a meerkat until he is joined by Big Mac, receives his directions, trots on again, does the meerkat, trots on again, ad infinitum. Big Mac plods forward, out of breath, shifting his torso forward. He's almost like an amoeba in shape, carrying an awful lot of weight, well over thirty stones. True, he arrived at this size by using food as a coping mechanism, but he also comes from a long line of fat people. As far back as anyone can remember, the O'Beses were wide. Even those who survived the famine of 1845 were supposedly big boned – well, according to Seamus Big Mac O'Bese anyway, and he takes great pride in how the family name has become a medical condition, fame of a kind, but it is still a huge struggle for him to walk anywhere.

Big Mac urges Noddy to stop. 'Hold up, I need a break. That's at least a hundred and fifty metres.'

One of the problems that comes with being this huge is biochemistry. Big Mac eats a lot of junk food, far too much, meaning that his blood sugar quickly spikes, but then plummets again, leaving him craving sweet food.

'Let's go into that café,' he says. 'I'm starving, and we're due a break anyway.'

Noddy appears perplexed and totally unable to even consider making a decision. He stops, raises a finger as if he is about to say something poignant and delivers the line: 'Have a break, have a Kit Kat.' He smiles, taking great pleasure in having for the first time in his life said something funny, or so he believes.

Big Mac offers him a congratulatory clap on the back, but when Noddy turns away he raises his eyes to the heavens and mutters something to himself.

They sit at a table for two, which is dwarfed by Big Mac's girth, and pick up two menus. Big Mac recognises that Noddy has his menu upside down and duly corrects this for him. Noddy thinks this is hilarious; shaking his head, he gives his friend a thankful smile. The menus are laminated and contain the usual standard greasy-spoon meals – all-day breakfast variables and a few lunch specials.

The waitress is relatively slim, with a leathery, Sahara-dry face that is heavily creased and stains on her fingertips. Big Mac concludes that this heavy smoker, who looks to be in her late sixties, is actually more likely fifty-five. She moves at a snail's pace and speaks slowly, drawing out each word.

'What would you like?'

Noddy orders a coffee and Big Mac chirps, 'I'll have bacon, beans, bangers, burgers, chips, black pudding, white pudding, shepherd's pie, cottage pie, peas, liver, sausage, onions and broccoli.'

The waitress doesn't initially respond, as she is waiting for Big Mac to say he is only joking, but enough time passes for her to realise he is genuine. She responds by asking if he is hungry, and Big Mac returns her serve sarcastically with, 'Just a little peckish.'

CHAPTER 9

Lawrence is in a different part of the city, in the vicinity of the railway station. He looks suspicious and distracted as he walks, constantly glancing over his shoulder to ensure he isn't being followed. He makes his way down a side street, cuts over a block and steps into a small park. He sits on a wooden bench, and waits.

The bench is at least thirty years old and has various symbols and names carved and painted onto it: 'Mike was here', 'Mary', a heart shape with an arrow through it, 'Kevin'. This park is off Perry Square, and in the '80s it was the place to go for men who wanted to pay for lust, being physically warmer than the wind-drenched and run-down Dock Road. But now men tend to use younger, good-looking types who prefer to be known as escorts, all lipstick and hair. That raises a question for Lawrence: what has happened to those women, tidy but worn, beaten by life, known as hookers? Where are they now and how do they earn a crust? He trails his finger across some of the names; vandalism or art, he asks himself, and agrees that it is both.

Once he is satisfied that he hasn't been followed and isn't

being watched, he crosses the park towards a small building. 'To let' reads the sign on the facade, but in truth, who in their right mind would want to rent this old place? No one, of course, and as Lawrence enters through the door with the small outline of a man on it, he recalls that he has been to other establishments without the 'I' in the sign.

He quickly closes the door to the men's room and jams it shut by placing a dustbin under the door handle. He walks past the three toilet cubicles. They are empty, the doors ajar. One has a broken lock with the tag stuck on 'engaged'. Each toilet is low with a long pipe at the back that extends up to a water tank from which hangs a steel pull-chain. There's an overwhelming stench of urea, and as he steps nearer to the urinal, the sharpness of the smell increases to such an extent that it pinches the inside of his nose. The urinal is on a tiled wall, and where the tiles are missing or cracked some sort of green fungus has sprung up. Mushrooms are fungi and mostly edible, but this green gunk… Lawrence can't ascertain its purpose in life.

At the end of the room is a wall, and attached is a closed cupboard. Lawrence opens the cupboard, steps back from it, folds his arms, stares in and, after a moment, says, 'I knew I'd find you here.'

'Hello Larry,' comes the reply. 'Look, I haven't done anything wrong. I'm going clean now. You can see that – you can't bust me for nothing.'

Obviously, Lawrence is psychotic, as there is no one in

the room and no one in the cupboard, but Lawrence sees a bottom and he continues to hold a conversation with this average-looking male bottom.

'I'm not here to bust you. I'm here for some info,' he says.

'I know nothing, and even if I did, I wouldn't tell you,' scowls the bottom.

Lawrence calmly replies, 'Now, now, don't push it, or I might just organise a little trip for you back inside.'

Panic-stricken, the bottom says, 'Look, Larry, honest, I'm going straight now. I don't deserve this.'

'We don't always get what we deserve. And you know, jail wouldn't be a good place for someone like you,' says Lawrence.

The bottom shouts, 'I'm no grass!'

Lawrence laughs at him and gently pats him on the left cheek. 'Sure you're not. But you are sixty per cent of the way there, aren't you, Mr Ass?'

CHAPTER 10

Jesse sits at a distance to the side of Mooney, while James conducts the interview sitting across the table from her. She maintains a standard interviewee position, sitting upright, hands on her lap, legs together, while James shifts about in his chair, occasionally leaning forward with his forearms on the desk. He is someone who talks as much with his hands as with his words, a serious waver, and in another life he would surely have been a competent crew member on any aircraft carrier.

'So, tell me, what are the most essential skills and qualities for an estate agent?' enquires James.

Mooney considers her response and then replies, 'Well, we've got to be good liars, bare-faced, two-faced. We have to be willing to say and do anything to get a sale. And… oh yes, keep trying to push the price up. Make them bleed.'

Jesse cheers from the sideline, raising his arms as if he has just tackled Paul O'Connell and won turnover ball. 'Brilliant, you're going to be brilliant!' he shouts excitedly, but has to quickly calm it, as a customer appears to be just about to open the door to the office. Quietly, he motions to Mooney. 'We have our first customer – he's yours.'

Before the customer can choose whom to address, Mooney takes ownership of the space and offers assistance. The man explains that he is looking to buy a five-bedroom house.

Mooney forces a ridiculous, over-the-top smile and says, 'You've come to the right place. I think I've got what you're looking for – in fact, I know I have.'

The buyer is pleased.

'I hope you don't mind my asking,' Mooney goes on, 'and I'm sure you get asked this all the time, but aren't you that guy from the TV, the actor? Peter something.'

Without expression, the man confirms that he is. Mooney tells him how much she adores the character he plays and tries to impress him by sharing that she was once in a play. Despite his professional abilities, Peter is beginning to feel slightly uncomfortable.

Mooney continues, 'Yeah, I can still remember some of the lines. Like riding a bike, I suppose – some things you never forget.' She places a hand on her forehead with the palm facing outwards and shouts, 'Ah, ah, ah, ah, ah, ah, ah, ah!'

Alarmed, Peter jumps towards her, with every intention of assisting her, and asks, 'Are you alright?'

Mooney's expression switches to confusion and then to frustration. She points at Peter. 'Please don't interrupt. I'm acting. You wouldn't like it if you were interrupted when you were acting.'

Peter freezes and, without emotion, apologises.

Again, Mooney places her hand to her forehead and expels, ‘Ah, ah, ah, ah, ah, ah, ah! Run – it’s the big, bad wolf!’

She stops and looks at Peter. He is frozen. She motions to him, but he is still confused. Eventually, he twigs that she wants to act out a scene with him.

Getting all grand, he exclaims in a very theatrical way, ‘I’ll huff and I’ll puff and I’ll blow your house down.’

Whilst this has been going on, Jesse and James have been sitting at the same desk, eyes glued on Mooney and Peter, heads moving from side to side in synch as if they are on the sideline at a tennis match.

Jesse volunteers, ‘She’s doing a brilliant job.’

James adds, ‘She’s a natural.’

• • •

Back at the toilet, Lawrence is all ears, as the bottom now appears to be eager to share intelligence.

‘Very interesting; very, very interesting. Needless to say, if what you’ve told me turns out to be a pile of crap…’

‘It’s not, I swear. Cross my heart and hope to die,’ the bottom responds.

‘Fair enough,’ Lawrence says, and he turns and walks towards the exit.

‘It’s unusual, Larry, don’t you think?’ the bottom calls after him.

Larry stops, but doesn’t look back at the bottom. ‘What

is?' he asks.

'That someone as bright and as senior as you, with no family history of mental illness, could have such a severe breakdown.'

Lawrence thinks this is a good point, but he doesn't want to acknowledge it. He removes the dustbin and opens the door. But before exiting he has to have the last word, so he half-turns and tells the bum that his breath stinks and that he should probably see a dental hygienist.

CHAPTER 11

Back in the café, there are several empty plates on the table. Noddy appears vacant and Big Mac is rubbing his tummy. He has a look of satisfaction, which shifts to pensiveness. As the waitress passes, he raises a hand with one finger pointing to the ceiling. The waitress stops and looks at him. He keeps his hand raised but the finger descends to join the others.

'Same again, please,' he says.

'Sure,' says the waitress.

While this has been going on, Noddy has started to look confused. 'Shouldn't we be doing some work?' he asks.

Big Mac sits upright, and his whole being shakes like a gigantic plate of jelly. As the wobbles end, he agrees with Noddy. 'You're right.'

He puts his hand back in the air, much higher than before and this time with all his fingers straight up towards the ceiling, like a schoolboy wanting permission to go to the toilet or alerting the teacher to the fact he has the answer to whatever the testing question was.

The waitress comes back to the table, and again Big Mac lowers his hand. Now when he speaks his tone has changed and he looks serious. 'You know that accountant who's been missing since last year?'

'Yeah.'

'You haven't seen him?'

'No.'

'Thank you.'

As the waitress heads off to serve another customer, Big Mac turns to Noddy and says, 'There you go. We've been working.'

Noddy is relieved. Then he has a light-bulb moment and queries whether he should ask questions of people too. Big Mac opens his palms, as if he were a priest at mass about to make an offering up to the Lord, and pulls a face, signalling to Noddy that he doesn't have any issue with Noddy doing this.

Noddy walks over to a male customer who is pretty much minding his own business, munching his eggs, beans and chips in his own unique way. He cuts the eggs, dips the chips in, and swallows the forkful. He stabs some more chips, places the fork curved side down next to the chips, pushes beans onto the belly of the fork using the knife and again devours the nourishment. Then he puts the cutlery down, sips some tea, picks up the paper, reads for about thirty seconds, puts the paper down and begins the ritual again. The drinking of the tea is very precise, expertly executed with the skills honed through experiential learning, no doubt the trial and error that comes with having to adapt your everyday living when you have one of the biggest noses ever. Big enough that if the man were standing on some parts of the Alps, he could be in both France and Italy at the same time.

Noddy politely presents himself. ‘Excuse me, mister, sir…’ His eyes almost pop out of his head as he stares at the gigantic stalactite reaching outwards and downwards from the man’s face.

With some annoyance and without looking up from his paper, the man asks, ‘What?’

Noddy is flustered. ‘Um, um, um, um, um, you’ve got a big nose.’

The man puts the paper down and looks up at Noddy. ‘What’s that supposed to mean?’ he says incredulously.

Noddy appears perplexed but gets a line out: ‘Um, you can smell things, a lot.’

The man is having none of this; he is aggrieved. Finger pointing at Noddy, he says, ‘You’re harassing me for having a big nose. Let me tell you, having a big nose puts me in a minority group. I’ll sue you for this through the European Court of Human Rights. I nose my rights; I nose all my rights.’

Big Mac sees there is a bit of a commotion and tries to calm it. But after receiving the insult ‘What are you going to do about it, lard ass?’ he changes tack and says roughly, ‘Shut it, hooter.’

The man quickly assesses the situation and appears to calm down. Noddy sits down next to Big Mac and thanks him for the intervention. Again, Big Mac opens his palms and he makes a face that communicates there is no need to thank him and they are a team.

Big Mac's phone starts to ring and vibrate. He would prefer it not to vibrate, but he has only had this phone for three days and he hasn't figured out how to turn off the vibrate feature. Big Mac realises it is their boss calling, so he feigns total professionalism as he answers it, while presenting his milkshake to Noddy and whispering to him, 'Hold the shake.'

Boss kind of hears this and asks, 'What are you talking about?'

Big Mac tries to reverse out of the situation. 'Sorry, Boss, I thought you were someone else.'

Boss asks where he is, and to try to reclaim the high ground Big Mac lies. 'Down-, down-, downtown. I'm just about to finish interrogating someone. Hold on, sir… So you definitely didn't see him?' He whispers to Noddy, 'Say no, say no.'

The dutiful Noddy complies, parroting with some volume, 'Say no, say no.'

Boss is a highly intelligent man and Noddy's execution was very clumsy, so Big Mac isn't going to get any leeway. Boss shouts down the line, 'Do you think I'm an idiot, O'Bese?'

'No.'

'Well, don't treat me like one then, do you hear?'

'Yes, sir.'

'Anyway,' Boss goes on, 'I have some intel for you. Get yourselves out to some parkland in Newcastle West called the Demesne. Detective Barry believes there's a lead to be found there. Make it a priority.'

Boss hangs up, and Big Mac puts his phone away and

stands up, motioning to his partner to join him.

At that moment the waitress puts several plates of food on the table. Concerned that Big Mac is now leaving, she asks, 'What about all the food?'

He points to the man with the gigantic nose and tells her, 'Give it to him. He can hoover it up.' Big Mac then starts laughing, and after a few moments Noddy realises this and, as usual, copies him.

The man fumes and swears and declares that he will see them in court.

Big Mac retorts, 'Not with that nose blocking your view, you won't.' He laughs again, and after a short delay Noddy joins in.

CHAPTER 12

Mooney is showing the potential buyer, Peter, around a property. It is a very grand house, once owned by an English lord. He never lived in it – his main residence was a few miles outside the city – but his sister did, with her husband and their children. That was well over a hundred years ago. The house has retained its grand features, but is now a modern, high-specification property.

Mooney maintains her professional 'estate agent seller' approach. She brings Peter through to the kitchen, which has a modern AGA cooker that impresses him. All the usual white goods exist, she shows him, but they are hidden from view by counters and cupboards – modern, shiny and blue. The colour can be changed, a simple matter of clicking panels in and out.

The wide glass double doors are already open, and she leads Peter out into the enormous garden. The flowerbeds are in full bloom, and she advises that the garden has been arranged so that there is nearly always something in bloom, no matter the season. Peter spots a huge horse chestnut tree in the corner, which makes him return to a well-tucked-away memory of growing up with his brothers, climbing horse chestnut trees and trading conkers as if they were a priceless commodity. He returns to the garden when Mooney points out that the trees at the far end are actually apple trees.

Peter is nearly there; he recognises that the house is an immense property, a stunning place. He is very excited, but is conscious that he doesn't want to appear interested, as he can negotiate a lower price if they believe he's nonplussed. *I am an actor, after al*l, he thinks. *I played Hamlet at drama school. I'll make her believe whatever I want.*

They return to the house. As they make their way up the grand staircase Mooney tells him that there is a second one in the house, a spiral. They cross a landing and step into the vast master bedroom. There is a walk-in wardrobe to the right and an en-suite bathroom to the left, and at the far side of the king-size bed are huge Georgian windows that afford a panoramic view of the garden. Mooney sells all this whilst launching herself onto the bed to test the mattress. She observes that Peter isn't quite interested in the property. *Maybe he can't afford it*, she thinks. A shame, as it is an amazing property; she is taken aback by its beauty.

She starts to roll about on the bed in a seductive manner – which catches Peter's attention; Mooney is gorgeous, after all. 'This is a luxury king-size bed, big enough for any king and his queen,' she says. 'It's really spacious, massive, grand. Try it out.'

Peter has been caught off-guard. 'No, it's okay, I don't need to,' he replies.

Mooney insists: 'But you must, you have to, it's vital, it's essential.'

'No, it's not,' he responds.

Mooney had great success as a teenager playing netball; she played for her school, province and, aged seventeen, for her country. As a child she was quite the gymnast, but as she developed and became more athletic in stature, she found some of the manoeuvres more difficult, and then boobs arrived, adding other complications, so she stopped. Her dexterity and body control meant she quickly became an expert in self-defence whilst training for the Garda, and over the years she has become proficient in various martial arts. Peter is within range, and she expertly extends her leg, hooks him and tips him onto the bed. By the time he has his bearings, he is lying on his back, arms pinned down, with her straddling him.

Looking down at him, she exclaims, 'I've loved you for years. I have your poster on my bedroom wall. This is our destiny.'

'But I'm married!' is his extremely fearful response. He realises he is trapped; he doesn't know this person and he's in a situation that worries him – he is used to being in control, but here he is being controlled. His bowels are rumbling, but thankfully he has been on the Atkins for a few days and therefore there is nothing to come out; otherwise, his boxers would be ruined.

Mooney starts her response slowly, but quickly gathers momentum until she's speeding through the words. 'It doesn't matter – I'll be your bit on the side, your starter, your after

– maybe in time you might want me as your wife and I could become the main course – we could be so brilliant together, ooooooooooooh, ooooooooooh.'

She gets off him and, with huge excitement, jumps up and down on the bed, singing out, '… and I'm single, I'm single, I'm single.' She stops, sits down and starts crying.

Peter has come to the conclusion that this lady is not well. Or perhaps this is a prank and he is being filmed for one of those silly candid camera programmes. With that in mind, he needs to protect his image.

'What's wrong?' he asks sympathetically.

'I had to dump my boyfriend this morning,' she tells him.

'Why? Was he cheating on you?'

She shakes her head.

'Was he beating you?' he enquires, placing a supportive hand on her shoulder.

Again, she shakes her head.

'Then why?'

Mooney raises her head and meets his eyes, and in a low voice she says, 'Because he belched and didn't excuse himself.'

Peter continues to feign genuine concern, but in his head he is doing cartwheels. Y*es, yes, yes*, he thinks, *this is a candid camera show. I'm going to come out of this looking great. Did these fools really think they could catch me out?* 'You poor thing,' he says, and holds her hand.

CHAPTER 13

In single file, the black ants march along a well-worn path in the dried mud. There are brambles all about and large trees everywhere. From an ants' perspective this landscape is gigantic; if they were collected and dropped in the deepest, darkest African jungle, would they notice a difference, apart from the heat? The ants have reached their destination for now, a melted pool of liquid that once belonged to an ice lolly, discarded by some person who is benefiting from being in the forest but doesn't actually appreciate it.

The two individuals who were sauntering alongside the ants on the path now overtake them. They are in the Demesne. Big Mac is, as usual, out of breath and sweating as he slowly trudges along. Noddy has a smile larger than an HGV; this is an adventure, after all.

'I'm wrecked, knackered, tired,' grumbles Big Mac.

With a very serious contemplative look on his face, Noddy turns to his colleague and expertly advises, 'Well, we have walked over a hundred and fifty metres.'

Big Mac lumbers into a small grass clearing. He makes sure that there are no animal droppings, or indeed friendly black ants, and slowly lowers himself onto the ground. 'I'll just lie here for a little while. Gosh, that does feel a lot better.'

Noddy stretches out too, lying on his back, hands behind his head and with his knees off the ground and crossed. He removes the lengthy piece of grass sticking out of his mouth for a moment so he can engage with his work mate. 'To think we get paid for this.'

Looking up at the Columbus clouds, Big Mac wonders to himself, were the clouds named after Christopher, and if so, why? He can't see a link. 'Yeah! Great, isn't it,' he replies. 'We're the elite of the Special Branch. We're the Extra-Special Special Branch. We solve the crimes that no one else can.'

Noddy gets all serious, rolling onto his side to face his colleague. 'Cool, and to think we do all this just by eating, resting and walking… it amazes me.'

Big Mac has a subtle giggle to himself and adds, 'Most things do, I'm sure. Anyway, I'm going to have a snooze. While I'm snoozing, see if you can rustle me up something to eat. God, I'm starving.' He closes his eyes and very quickly drifts off.

CHAPTER 14

Jesse and James are both sitting in their high-back leather chairs in the office, Jesse slightly rocking and James slouched down.

Looking into the distance, Jesse says to James, 'The thing I like most about being an estate agent is that you can wear suits and gel your hair and walk around being cool.'

James validates this: 'Yeah, I know what you mean. But for me I think it has to be about being two-faced. Watch this,' he says and then puts on his sales act: 'This is a bargain! The best deal you'll ever get. Honest to God.'

They both get the giggles, Jesse a sniggery, saliva-moving sound and James deeper and slower. While Jesse has been focusing on the distance, James has been keeping in touch with his surroundings, and he's noticed a man observing the properties they're advertising in the window. He sees that the chap is about to enter. He addresses his slouch, returning to an upright position, and warns his friend: 'Hold up, we've got a customer.'

James stops rocking and returns the chair to its usual position. The customer pushes the door open, looks at the agents and smiles, but then turns back to the door and ensures that it closes behind him; he doesn't want it to slam, so he gently places it in the frame. The man steps towards the agents. It is Lawrence.

Jesse asks, 'Can I help you?'

Lawrence appears to mishear and says, 'What?'

Jesse repeats, 'Can I help you?'

Lawrence appears bemused. 'Are you a psychiatrist?' he questions.

'Of course not, sir, we're an estate agency,' comes the reply.

Lawrence remains bemused. 'So how could you help me?'

James intervenes. 'I'm sorry, sir, what can I do for you?'

'I'm looking for a flat,' Lawrence tells them.

'You've come to the right place,' James says at once – his usual patter.

Lawrence is experiencing a mixture of confusion and annoyance, but he knows he needs to apply pressure on this pair too. Raising his voice, he says, 'What?'

James is wary now. He realises this is no ordinary punter; somehow there is an issue here. He studies Lawrence quickly. He doesn't recognise him at all. Maybe he is the relative of someone they tripped up with a deal from hell? He responds slowly and calmly, 'I just said that you've come to the right place if you're looking for a flat.'

Lawrence steps closer to the pair and lays into them. 'I'm not stupid, just ill. I've come here because I'm looking for a flat – that's why people come to estate agents. If I was looking for vegetables, I would have gone to a grocer; if I was looking for petrol, I would have gone to a garage, and if I was looking for paracetamol, I would have gone to a pharmacy. I think I'm smart enough to know why I'm here.'

There is silence, a tumbleweed moment. Both agents have their heads bowed.

Jesse raises his head. 'Sorry, please keep your hair on. We were just being salesman-y and charming.' A bad choice of words, and they completely go over the head of this once-leading detective.

'What the fuck are you saying about my hair? This is my hair. It's real – touch it, go on, touch it,' Lawrence roars. He is deliberately being hard on them to get what he wants, answers.

Jesse quickly complies, and as he returns to his seat he says, 'Very nice, thank you, very nice, very, very, very nice, extremely nice hair, sir. I didn't mean nut-nut-nut-nothing by it.'

Lawrence points a finger at him angrily. 'Did you call me a nut?' He rushes toward Jesse, catches him by the front of his shirt and holds him close to his face. 'How did you find out? Tell me. Tell me!'

James, who is cowering, can see his friend is in over his head. Trying to help, he points at the pictures of houses they are selling and says, 'No, sir, we don't know anything. We're just trying to sell properties. I've got some lovely flats, see, see.'

Lawrence doesn't understand him. The communication between them and him has started to become more difficult for Lawrence as he has started to struggle with auditory hallucinations of some kind.

‘Of course I can see. Did someone talk to you about me, did they? Say I was blind or something? Tell me what they said. Who are they? Don’t they like my eyes?’ Lawrence shouts. He appears genuinely distressed – but he is also acting for effect. He wants success, after all, he wants the big job in Dublin back.

He still has a hold of Jesse. Jesse has his head bowed and his eyes shut. He exclaims, ‘Of course they like your eyes. You’ve got lovely eyes, great sight.’

This soothes Lawrence a little. ‘They are good eyes, great eyes. Touch them, touch them, touch them.’

Jesse doesn’t follow the instruction but meekly says, ‘I believe you, I believe you, I believe you.’

James still has his hand outstretched, pointing at properties. Lawrence looks at him and says, ‘I want to see that one.’

Without opening his eyes, Jesse quietly replies, ‘Great. I’ll take you there.’

CHAPTER 15

Noddy is busy foraging in the woods. He is collecting things. He has a number of items already, such as leaves and twigs. He sees some dandelions. What an extremely yellow colour, much more vivid than the daffodils under the tree to his right. Some of the dandelions no longer have their yellow thatch, though, replaced by an afro-like wig of grey that will disperse in the breeze, spreading seeds to grow elsewhere. Noddy can't resist: he snaps the stem of the largest dandelion. *It's like a mini stick of candyfloss*, he muses as he lifts it toward his mouth and blows. If it were a birthday candle he would have made a wish – what for he is unsure, but that is typical of Noddy: he certainly isn't a thinker.

The seeds disperse and are caught by the breeze. One in particular soars through the air as the majority descend to the ground. Noddy follows it, and eventually it parachutes down onto a patch of ground that has some unusual-looking sticks. He inspects them, picking up a few and wiping the forest from them. He smiles, extremely pleased, a little ecstatic, as he tells himself that these will help make the perfect stock.

• • •

Back at the estate agents' office, Mooney and Peter are sealing the deal. 'I'm glad you like the house, and I'm glad you want to buy it,' she smiles.

'I really like it. I'll pay the asking price. I really like it,' is his offer.

Lowering her tone, to try to avoid being overheard by her colleague, Mooney says, 'That's excellent. And I'd like to thank you for not taking advantage of me when I was in that vulnerable state.'

With a sincere look on his face – which may be authentic or may not; who knows with actors – Peter opens his hands and then his mouth. 'Don't mention it. Look, I'll phone you later to sort out the nitty-gritty. Bye for now.'

Mooney nods her agreement, they shake hands and she says goodbye. Peter paces across the office in a reasonably relaxed manner and is preparing to reach out and open the door when Mooney releases an 'Oh, Peter'. He turns to respond, but instead focuses on Mooney's lips, which are moving.

'I love you,' she silently mouths.

Peter panics. *Oh Christ*, he thinks. He quickly turns to the door, but his coordination and dexterity are off and he hasn't slowed, but he also hasn't got a proper grip of the door handle. As a result, he ends up walking straight through the glass door, shattering it, and stumbling face first onto the concrete footpath outside the office.

Mooney is concerned and leaps up to go and assist him, but he immediately bounces to his feet and, without glancing behind him, removes himself from the area with the rocket-like ability of Ben Johnson after a one-litre steroid injection. Mooney's shock is quickly replaced with pleasure as she accepts James's appraisal.

'That was brilliant, absolutely excellent. Congratulations, well done.'

CHAPTER 16

Society really is a disgrace. Pollution, plastic, chemicals, litter – mankind should be ashamed and probably renamed to reflect their disastrous behaviours to something more appropriate such as man*un*kind. Of course, on this occasion someone's fly-tipping has benefitted Noddy, as he's acquired a pot into which he's placed his ingredients. The stew-like concoction is boiling away over a campfire expertly created by Noddy. This is the first time he's been successful. Several years as a Boy Scout and hundreds of attempts at creating a fire – Noddy believes this was his five hundred and first attempt. He is delighted; he is pretty cool now, 501, just like Levi's jeans. He stirs the concoction to the left and then to the right and very occasionally dips in a spoon, places some in his mouth and then adds some more leaves. He doesn't know why he is doing any of this, but he has seen everyone from Jamie Oliver to Gordon Ramsay do it, so he's doing it too.

He thinks it is ready. Really pleased with himself, he walks over to Big Mac and gently nudges the sleeping giant. 'Big Mac, wake up, I've cooked you something. Wake up, it's ready, the soup is ready.'

Big Mac rolls onto his back and stretches out, then rolls onto his front, gets onto his hands and knees and slowly rises with the grace of an elephant. He rubs his eyes and makes his way over to Noddy, who presents him with a bowl of soup. Big Mac hesitates to do anything other than blow on it, as he understands it is very hot, and he is still half-asleep and not fully functioning and therefore not yet ready to indulge. After about a minute, he starts to eat the soup.

'Brilliant. God, it tastes gorgeous. You have outdone yourself. Well done, Noddy, you've surprised me.'

'It was nothing really. It's a Delia Smith recipe – herbs, leaves, get a stock going.'

Big Mac continues to demolish the concoction. 'Good man. What did you use for the stock?'

'Bones,' Noddy replies.

'Excellent. What kind of bones – chicken, rabbit?'

Noddy shakes his head. 'I don't really know, I'm not sure.'

'Well, where exactly did you find the bones?'

Noddy points. 'I found a load of them over there in a shallow grave. I didn't boil the skull though.'

With that, Big Mac stops eating. He has a hundred and one thoughts running through his head. *Holy fuck*, he thinks. *I know I have a binge-eating disorder, but me, a fucking cannibal! God help me*. His stomach starts to churn. He has never vomited before – the constitution of a horse, he always says – but his stomach is constricting, his mind, obviously disgusted with this act of cannibalism, is ordering the stomach to expel its contents. Big Mac bends over a little and vomits for the best part of thirty seconds without breaking stream, which reminds Noddy of a film he once saw on the TV called something like *Exorcism*.

Big Mac stands upright and looks to the heavens. ‘Oh Jesus, forgive me, forgive me, Christ, forgive me.’ Then he bends over again and pukes three more times in a minute.

Noddy says to Big Mac, ‘Strange that.’

‘What?’ is the reply.

‘Your puke. It looks like carrots, but I didn’t use any.’

Big Mac doesn’t engage with this, as he already has his phone in his hand. He types a number and puts the phone to his ear. ‘Hello, Boss. I think we’ve found the body.’

CHAPTER 17

A large articulated lorry makes its way through the centre of Limerick city. It's the type where the cab and the trailer are two separate entities, so the driver can leave the trailer at a factory for loading and drive off in the cab. The cab is unusual in that it isn't one of the vertical flat-faced cabs that you encounter on the roads of Ireland and the UK, but the type most associated with the United States of America. It moves with grace through the city and comes to a stop on O'Connell Street, one of two main streets in Ireland named after the great moderate and orator Daniel (a man born in 1775, not to be confused with another Daniel O', the country singer Donnell).

The lorry parks up just short of Arthur's Quay. The sides of the trailer are rolled up, and there on the trailer are several men. They all have musical instruments of one kind or another, mostly traditional ones: banjos, fiddles, guitars, tin whistles, button accordions, mandolins etc. On the trailer behind the musicians is a large green banner with orange writing: 'THE MAGIC BAND'.

A crowd of people stop and stare. 'This looks interesting,'

some say. Others are delighted at the unexpected entertainment. Soon, hundreds of people have gathered. They just stand there, saying nothing, not moving, just breathing. The musicians are also still. Then the musician in the most central position, who may indeed be the leader of the band, turns to his band mates.

'Right, lads, let's play.'

As they play, the hundreds who have gathered involuntarily start to dance in River Dance style. Everyone is in synch, making the same moves and steps (albeit some execute these better than others). This continues for a good five minutes – not just on O'Connell Street, though. It is happening all over Ireland, everywhere, and everyone is in synch – teachers, students, accountants, doctors, nurses, prisoners, politicians.

Then, after 300 seconds, the band stop playing and the people of Ireland carefully lie on the ground where they danced in some sort of sleepy trance. The side of the lorry is rolled back down and tied. The men make their way to the cab and climb in, and the driver slowly drives the articulated lorry out of the city – where to is uncertain.

After ten minutes, everyone slowly rises to their feet, initially a little groggy, but the haze lasts no more than thirty seconds. Then they get on with their day with no recollection of The Magic Band, the lorry and the fact they all danced like crazy and then rested.

CHAPTER 18

Lawrence is obviously struggling with his mental health condition, which is hugely traumatic for him, but behind this major obstacle is a highly intelligent and brilliant detective. He and Jesse are inside a modern, spacious, open-plan loft apartment that would be more fitting in downtown Manhattan than downtown Limerick city. A converted warehouse, made with Celtic Tiger money.

Jesse remains very wary of Lawrence. He knows something isn't quite right, but hasn't the intellect to figure it out. Jesse thinks his best bet is to try to impress Lawrence.

'It's a special flat. Spacious, quite a lovely kitchen, large bedroom. It's really a steal. It's a bargain. What do you do for a living, Mr Barry?'

Lawrence senses the young man's anxiety and fear and decides to up the ante. 'I'm an undertaker,' he says.

This has taken Jesse by surprise. *Fuck*, he thinks. *How am I supposed to respond to that?* 'Gosh, I've never met an undertaker before,' he says.

Lawrence looks him straight in the eye and says soberly, 'Great job. Dead people everywhere. Never cause you any bother, dead people. Do you know why?'

'No,' Jesse replies.

'Because they can't talk, that's why.'

They remain looking straight at each other for about ten seconds, until Jesse breaks the stare and looks down.

'I suppose so,' he says.

Lawrence walks towards him, slowly, deliberately. 'Ever seen a dead person, boy?'

Jesse gulps. 'No,' is his reply.

'They stiffen up,' says Lawrence. He cracks his knuckles. 'Sometimes you have to break their bones to straighten them out.'

Jesse is about to shit in his underpants with fear.

Then, without warning, Lawrence becomes very distracted. He is staring at a specific spot on Jesse's tie, at the small tie tack of a honeybee that has started talking to him. The bee eggs him on: 'Hello Larry, keep it up. You've got your man, it's him.'

Lawrence walks ever closer towards Jesse, staring at his chest. His tone is very different now, dark and serious, as he talks back to the tie. 'It's him – are you sure it's him?'

Poor Jesse doesn't know what is going on, and in the most timid of voices he asks, 'What?'

Enraged, Lawrence turns his gaze upwards from the tie to Jesse's eyes. 'Shut up. I'm trying to talk to your tie.'

'My tie?' Jesse says. 'Are you crazy?'

Lawrence catches hold of him and, with about six inches between their faces, claims, 'Certifiable, pal. But you might be able to help me. Being an undertaker and all that, I'm looking for a dead body.'

'Please don't kill me,' Jesse begs.

'I'm not looking for your body, Jesse. I'm looking for the body of the accountant Mike McCarthy. Tell me, where is the body? It was meant for me,' Lawrence shouts.

Jesse cowers and, in tears, cries out, 'I don't know, I don't know, it has nothing to do with me, it's James, you really need to speak to the other estate agent, he has all the answers, he knows everything, it was him.'

• • •

The local radio station makes a certain amount of its income from advertisements. Between those, it offers a sports coverage show, some local political discussions, a slot that discusses art in its many forms, and of course music. Coming through the speaker in the estate agents' office at this moment in time is the beautiful voice of Dolores O'Riordan with The Cranberries. Mooney and James listen, making the odd slight body movement in time with the tune.

James can see that Mooney likes the song and tries to impress her. 'That's my favourite song, that is.'

Mooney states, 'I like it as well.'

'My favourite film is *Dumb and Dumber* with Jim Carrey,' James tells her. 'I love the faces he pulls.'

'I like a good romantic comedy, like *Leaving Las Vegas*,' Mooney contributes.

This catches James off-guard, and he says seriously, 'But that was a sad film about a dysfunctional couple, a whore and an alcoholic.'

Mooney is laughing uncontrollably. 'Yeah, it was very funny, don't you think?'

The song ends and James is about to further the discussion when the radio announcer advises that there is a news bulletin for listeners. He reports that today the Gardai found the remains of missing accountant, Mike McCarthy; that his remains were found in parkland known as the Demesne in Newcastle West; that his skull was intact but the rest of his body was in the form of soup; and that the remains have been taken away for forensic testing.

James looks extremely worried and bangs his hand on the desk. 'Shit, shit, shit.'

Mooney warmly responds, 'I know how you feel. I am disgusted. How could someone kill another person and then make them into soup?'

James's worry turns to confusion as he realises the announcer and then Mooney both said 'soup'. 'Soup,' he mutters.

'What kind of sick, weird, twisted person would do that?' Mooney says, energised by this news.

James shakes his head as he contemplates his answer. 'I don't know.'

'What kind of sick, two-faced, bandy-legged, gimp-headed person would do such a thing?' she throws out.

Deep in thought, James replies, 'I don't know. I'm confused.'

Mooney says, 'Soup.'

James says, 'Soup.'

Mooney says, 'Soup.'

And then Lawrence enters just as James once again says, 'Soup.'

'No, thanks, I ate earlier,' Lawrence replies.

James attempts to compose himself and get his sales face back on. 'Sorry, sir, just thinking out loud.'

Mooney interjects: 'We just heard that some sicko killed a man and made him into soup.'

James is completely composed now and he asks where his colleague, Jesse, is. Lawrence advises that he has gone for lunch.

With a deep nasal laugh, Mooney says, 'Hope he doesn't eat the soup.'

Neither James nor Lawrence laugh.

Two more customers enter the establishment. With consummate professionalism, James makes eye contact and greets them with, 'Good afternoon. What can I do for you gentlemen?'

Big Mac replies, 'Wouldn't mind something to eat.'

That makes Noddy laugh. Annoyed, Big Mac asks what he is laughing at, and Noddy, as per usual, responds with a shrug of the shoulders, a smile and an 'I don't know'. Then he laughs again.

Lawrence walks towards James. 'Sir, I have to inform you that we four' – he points to himself, then Big Mac, Noddy and Mooney – 'are Special Branch.'

James sits down, puts his head in his hands and says, 'Shit.'

An insulted and defensive Noddy responds with, 'No, we're not.'

With more hope than desperation, James refocuses. Maybe this is a prank. 'You're not Special Branch?' he asks.

'No, we are,' Noddy says.

James sits back down, head in hands, and swears again. 'Shit.'

Again, an aggrieved Noddy bites back. 'No, we are not.'

Big Mac massages Noddy's shoulders. 'Calm, calm, calm. He's not saying *we* are shit. I think he's saying, shit, I'm caught.' Big Mac walks towards James. 'Why did you do it?'

'You wouldn't understand,' comes the reply.

Big Mac points at Noddy. 'He wouldn't, but the rest of us would.'

James sits upright. Perhaps by cooperating, he thinks, he may get a more favourable sentence. 'I had gambling debts, online gambling, and I just couldn't get away from them. I started overcharging everyone – the vendors, the buyers. All illegal, of course. The accountant found out. He was going to turn me in. I panicked, we fought… I didn't mean to kill him, but he died.'

'But why did you turn him into soup?' asks a confused Mooney.

James stands and, with emotion, defends his honour. 'I didn't, I didn't, I swear I didn't!'

Noddy has become quite sheepish, and Big Mac takes the moral high ground: 'Sure you didn't. Nobody believes you, you sicko.'

CHAPTER 19

Boss is on the phone. He appears to be pleased – happiness at last radiates from his face, success. He might get out of this hellhole after all; he might just get his career back on track. He nods and nods and nods as he fixes the knot on his tie. At the other end of the phone is the Taoiseach, speaking in the bizarre way that only his close aides understand, a fusion of speech and verbalised thoughts.

'Smile, smile, well solved, yes, yes, smile, bye,' the Taoiseach says, and puts the phone down.

(The Taoiseach's aide advises him once again, 'You don't have to smile when on the phone, sir, because there isn't anybody watching.'

The Taoiseach puts his finger in the air as if this is a eureka-moment and makes a motion that could be interpreted as, *Good point, very good point.*)

Boss makes his way into his subordinates' office. There, Mooney is very relaxed and radiating love – much to the disappointment of Big Mac, she has made up with her boyfriend. Noddy raises the issue of the boyfriend farting, but is corrected by Mooney, who explains that the farting wasn't the issue, it was the belching, but now that he has apologised, all is okay.

Boss assesses the room and asks where Lawrence is. 'Appointment at the hospital,' is the response.

'Alright, well, we just had the Taoiseach offering us congratulations for solving the case, so congratulations. How did you do it?'

They all shrug their shoulders.

'Thought as much,' he says and turns to leave, and as he passes Mooney, he belches at her.

'Word Up' by Cameo is on the radio, and Boss's news is enough to get Big Mac and Noddy to show off their dancing party pieces by way of a celebration. Noddy does a very decent robotic dance and Big Mac demonstrates that he is a top-class break-dancer.

'What a happy chappy Boss is,' muses Big Mac.

'I suppose,' says Noddy.

'I suppose not. Sarcasm, Noddy, sarcasm,' educates Big Mac.

Noddy nods his agreement but doesn't know what Big Mac means. He remains confused as they keep dancing.

• • •

Lawrence is drawing invisible circles on the glass table with his left index finger. Majella Quinn is very relaxed. He has been doing this for about five minutes and she hasn't intervened. Eventually, Lawrence returns to the conversation.

'Yes, I am finding it hard to cope and I've been minimising it to my work colleagues and to Dr Best.'

'Wow, thanks for sharing, Lawrence. It's taken three sessions. Progress – well done, you are brave.'

'Thanks,' he says. 'I was thinking about something you said in a previous session.'

'What's that?' asks Majella.

'I think you might be onto something with regards to my hallucinations.' She gives him a supportive nod and he continues. 'I think you're right. The hallucinations call me Larry, though no one else does – everyone in real life calls me Lawrence. And yes, it does appear that the voices and hallucinations, as scary as they are, are generally positive and appear to be trying to help me.'

• • •

Lawrence's diary reads:

I'm doing okay. I don't think I'm as unwell as Dr Best thinks. I've fallen a long way professionally though. I do feel alone. Some strange things are happening. Maybe I was unwell. Eileen isn't talking to me – if I phone her during the day, she won't pick up, and she never returns my calls. I'm worried about the kids. I'm still upset Reggie didn't stand up for me; I thought he was a friend. I haven't heard from him. Dr Best is insane, and I just don't trust him. I've met Majella Quinn and I'm getting psychology input from her. I've been told she is good. I think she is good. I like her.

The new team have their idiosyncrasies. I like them. They are trying to make me feel welcome, but I also know they think I'm mentally unwell, and incapable. I need to, as much as I can, hide my symptoms, I don't want to get sacked. I was ever so slightly upset by Noddy when I first met him. I know he didn't mean it. I'm confused. Fear, hurt, loneliness, confusion. Dark brown, very dark brown, dark brown. The Doors, 'People Are Strange'. The Verve, 'The Drugs Don't Work'. Radiohead, 'Paranoid Android'. Genesis, 'Land Of Confusion'. Lily Allen, 'Fear'. Queen, 'Radio Ga Ga'. Electric Light Orchestra, 'Mr Blue Sky'.

• • •

'That's an introduction,' says Lena to her students in the lecture hall.

'Which is the one with the mental illness?' jokes Liverpool Dean.

'They all seem unwell to me,' says Robert.

There is some laughter.

'The Big Mac guy is just greedy,' says William.

'I think he has a binge-eating disorder,' says Rita.

'No way,' says William. 'He's just a joke.'

Lena interjects: 'From tomorrow you will be out there as

registered professionals, you need to be extra-careful. Don't make assumptions and don't be too quick to diagnose. Yes, they're an odd bunch, they have their peculiarities, but only one has a severe and enduring mental illness. Keep an eye on gambling, look what happened to that guy, it can be a terrible addiction for some.

All things considered, Lawrence is doing well, remember most people with mental illness have a mild or moderate illness – anxiety or depression related – but Lawrence's is quite severe, in the top 1%, and of course there's an obvious strain on his relationship, which you can understand. He's exploring what his priorities and objectives now need to be: *I need to support Eileen, win her over; this can be achieved by me getting my old job back; if I do a good job and deliver here…* As you know, one of the challenges with mental illness is the recovery journey. Frequently, it's a case of taking two steps forward and then, unfortunately, one step back.'

SHE

CHAPTER 20

A man known as Ratty scurries into the bookies. He quickly scribbles something on a docket and hands it and some money over to a teller. There are about twenty people in the bookies, all doing their own thing. Some are watching the races on the TV; others are monitoring the football scores. Some are studying the form via newspapers that have been sellotaped to the wall. Two are heading out the back for a smoke.

A guy in a cowboy hat tells a guy in a beret that he had an accumulator and he got to the seventh race, and if his chosen mare had won that particular race, he would have won a million, all from a one-euro bet. The beret man shakes his head and placcs his hand on the cowboy's shoulder in a show of support.

A selection of faces – those swollen from too much beer, those extra-wrinkly from undernourishment and smoking – turn towards the screens to watch the three p.m. from Leopardstown. Ratty moves from the teller and receives a nod from Glenda the waitress, and then she turns to focus on the race.

• • •

Back at HQ, Lawrence, Big Mac, Noddy and Boss are glued to the box. The race has started and they are cheering on their favourite horses in their own idiosyncratic ways: Noddy smiling; Boss making very small, agitated, sharp moves; Big Mac doing some sort of continuous Mexican-wave-type motion; and a pressured Lawrence staring at the screen and heavy-breathing as if his life depends on the outcome.

The commentator talks them through the race, moment by moment:

'… and in this much-anticipated Tampax Hurdle, it's Red Rag from Once a Month, and Angry Cow is coming up on the inside. Can't Cope Won't Cope is in third position, and then Without Wings. As they come around the second corner, Flying Tampon moves into third place. Once a Month appears to be making a move. She's closely followed by Red Rag, who's closely followed by Angry Cow. At this stage, it looks like Can't Cope Won't Cope and Flying Tampon and Without Wings are out of the race. As we come to the last corner, it's Once a Month in the lead, then Angry Cow and Red Rag. And Red Rag has overtaken Angry Cow and is closing in on Once a Month. It's gonna be a tight finish. Angry Cow is closing in on Once a Month. They're neck and neck. It's anybody's race. What a climax to the Tampax Hurdle! It looks like it might be a photo finish. But here's a resurgence from Once a Month… and Once a Month takes it, with Angry Cow in second place, then Red Rag, Can't Cope Won't Cope and Without Wings, and Flying Tampon coming in at the rear.'

• • •

Nearly everyone at the bookie's leaves, spilling onto the street, a losing team. It is better to be on your own at times like this. It hurts too much when those around you know you are a loser. You just can't save face. Lying to yourself is easy, but it can't be done in the company of those who know the honest truth.

Glenda hasn't budged; she never bets. Ratty has remained too, and he is all smiles: he picked the winner. The teller gets to see all his pointy teeth as he hands in the slip.

• • •

Boss is pissed-off. He kicks a cardboard box, sending it flying across the office. 'Damn!' he screams.

Noddy hasn't picked up on the cue. 'That was one great match,' he says.

'That was a race, you eejit! A match is when you have players and most often some kind of ball.'

Noddy nods, and with an index finger raised and a look of new-found knowledge on his face, he replies, 'Gotcha.'

Boss says dismissively, 'Sure you have. I bet you didn't understand a word I said.'

Before this conversation can progress, Big Mac enters the fray. He has switched from the Mexican wave to a belly dance, and he's waving a betting slip. 'Speaking of bets, gentlemen, I believe I won, again. The takeaway is on me.'

CHAPTER 21

Through the keyhole and another day, we are at Boss's house. His hair is combed and in place, he has his suit jacket on and he is in the process of tying his tie. We can see that he has had his breakfast: on the table is a glass with remnants of orange juice and a bowl with a few drops of milk and a very small amount of some sort of cereal paste, too small to make it onto the spoon. The box on the table reveals that it is a cousin of Weetabix, Oatibix. Boss has been eating this for four months now, as he thought he might be suffering from Irritable Bowel Syndrome, or maybe he was a coeliac or wheat intolerant; anyway, he feels better, whether from the oats or some placebo effect, he doesn't know or care.

Knot complete, he calls out to his wife, 'I'm off to work, darling,' and he heads towards the door, slowly, as his wife is clasped around his right leg, making his departure a little difficult. He continues to make progress, slow progress, but she is hanging on like a koala bear on a tree.

'Don't go. Don't go. Don't go!' she cries out.

'I have to earn money, pay the mortgage, treat you like a queen,' he explains lovingly without breaking his momentum.

'Please stay. I need you, I love you, I need you, I love you.' She digs in, hugging the tree trunk more tightly.

He stops moving, looks down. 'I have to go. My department needs me.'

She sobs, '*I* need you. Please don't go.'

He considers that for a few moments, and then untangles himself from her vice-like grip, with a few shakes to break the shackles, and does a hop, skip and jump to avoid the desperate tackle she makes. He sprints out of the house and is almost into the car when she calls out, 'John.'

He turns. She is at the front door. 'Yes?' he says.

'I love you, I love you, I love you, even if the heroin was yours.'

He gets into the car and drives off. He is gone, long gone, but his wife still remains at the front door, looking into the distance and constantly repeating, 'I love you, I love you, I love you.'

• • •

Lawrence is sitting at the breakfast table, dressed and ready. There aren't any cereal bowls or other items on the table to suggest he has had anything for breakfast. He looks perplexed and is staring at the wall. He has been sitting there for an hour, and the upper-left side of his gluteus maximus is starting to get sore. He is fixated on the clock. Round and round the second hand goes.

The big hand is now at six and the small hand at eight: time for work. He stands up. He knows his wallet is in his left trouser pocket; he can feel it. The house keys are in his left jacket pocket, the car keys are in his right jacket pocket and his gun is in its holster fixed on the left side of his chest so that he can reach in with his right hand to draw it should the occasion require.

He heads into the hallway and towards the front door. He doesn't need to check on the kids; he checked earlier, and if they were awake, they would have come down. He assumes Eileen is asleep or awake upstairs but avoiding him. She requested some time ago that he sleep in the spare room and he obliged.

As he puts his hand on the lock, he hears her.

'I love you,' she says.

He pays no attention and opens the door.

'I love you,' she says again.

He turns and is surprised to see her at the bottom of the stairs. She hasn't spoken to him for weeks. 'Did you say you love me?' he asks in a very hesitant way.

'Yes,' she says and smiles.

Lawrence's eyes start to well up, but he doesn't cry. He says, 'I wasn't sure. I thought it was a voice.'

'No, it was me. I love you, and your voices.'

A moment or two passes. Lawrence wants to get his response right before he opens his mouth. 'Eileen, I know it hasn't been easy for you…'

She smiles the most beautiful of smiles, that smile he used to know so well, that smile that can make everything golden, and she says, 'Don't worry. Bye now. I love you, I love you, I love you.'

Lawrence closes the door behind him and starts to cry. *Thank God. I thought I lost her*, he thinks. He sits in the car and wipes his eyes before driving off.

• • •

Mooney parks her car and totters off in her Jimmy Choos, blue open-toed sandals with two-inch red heels and white ankle straps. No stockings today, and her colour-coordinated toenails are on display: two blue toes, two red toes and a white middle toe on each foot.

Mooney really doesn't think about the impact she has on others. She is an extremely beautiful creature, sculpted by God himself – or herself, depending on your viewpoint. Male and female heads turn all round, females with admiration and frustration in equal measure, males with desire. The men gawp at her, their mouths open as if catching flies. Today, Mooney is ecstatically happy, and she mouths an 'I love you' to every male she passes. Some men just smile, some are hypnotised, others walk straight into poles.

She walks over the quay and alongside the Shannon. The tide is out and this is a very pretty part of the river and city, close to where the tide stops impacting the river. She enters an office block and takes the lift, which opens into a hallway. She has her access card in her hand and she swipes it at the door – and enters the office of the Specials.

She's confronted by the sight of Big Mac throwing paperclips at the back of Noddy's head. Noddy hasn't realised that Big Mac is the culprit and is looking up towards the ceiling with an accusatory stare.

Mooney looks directly at Big Mac, but only to deliver her line: 'I love you.' Then she makes her way to her desk.

At low volume, to ensure she won't hear, Big Mac says passionately, 'I'd love to make love to you.'

Noddy turns to Big Mac and says, 'Thanks.'

'Not you, you fool. Her.'

'Oh,' says Noddy.

Boss walks in and notices Big Mac throwing a paperclip at the back of Noddy's head.

Noddy points at the ceiling and informs his boss, 'I think there's a leak.'

Boss nods. 'Brain fluid probably,' is his response.

Big Mac sniggers, and Noddy laughs. 'What are you laughing at?' asks Big Mac.

'I don't know,' says Noddy and then he continues to laugh.

Boss goes over to Mooney and speaks to her in an almost private way. 'Miss Mooney.'

She looks up at him. 'Good morning, Boss. I love you.'

Boss is surprised by this. Mooney doesn't usually pay him compliments, so declaring love for him is startling. He holds his ground, because he wants to get her expert view on something.

'Thank you,' he says. 'I was just wondering whether you might be able to help… My wife, she never pays me much attention, but then today she's all over me like a rash.' He makes a face to convey he's confused by his wife's behaviour.

Mooney stands. 'Sounds normal to me. You're a wonderful man. She must be crazy about you. My God, look at you! You're good-looking, fun. You all are.' She looks around her team. 'Big Mac, you hunk of beef. Noddy, so endearing. Lawrence…'

However, before she can compliment Lawrence, he shouts out in fear, as he is hallucinating and sees her as a witch. 'Leave me alone, leave me alone!'

Everyone stops what they're doing to stare at Lawrence. There is a tumbleweed moment in the office for at least a minute.

Boss breaks the silence. 'Okay, okay, back to work, everybody.'

• • •

The day passes. It's a very busy one in the various boutiques, as women all over the city of Limerick buy clothes, maxing out their credit cards. Mooney buys shoes, shoes and more shoes, Eileen tries on several dresses and Boss's wife purchases eight new outfits.

CHAPTER 22

It is breakfast time at Boss's house again. He is someone who doesn't keep the Oatibix in biscuit form; once the milk is added, he turns it all into mush. As he scoops the last bit up and into his mouth, he uses his free hand to lift the half-full glass of apple juice. The spoon is returned to the bowl, and once the last of the mush is swallowed, he opens his mouth and empties the glass with three gulps.

His wife is sitting opposite him at the table, wearing her navy silk pyjamas. Boss places the glass on the table, and before he can decide what to do next, she intervenes.

'I bought lots of clothes yesterday.'

Boss nods as he says, 'I noticed.'

With a look of disappointment, she follows up with, 'I don't think I can wear any of them.'

Boss, who has seen the outfits and thinks they mostly look good, is surprised. 'Why not?'

'Because I'm fat,' she says.

Warmly and genuinely, Boss responds, 'You're not.'

She starts to cry. 'I am. I know you're just being nice. I know that I'm really, really fat and I've got a huge bum.'

• • •

Lawrence hasn't had breakfast again. He has been staring at the clock, doing the usual countdown. With sixty seconds remaining before he would usually stand and prepare to go, Eileen enters the kitchen and starts putting different dresses on the table.

'I bought this and this and this and this, and I'm fat, I'm fat, I know I am. Does my bum look big in this?' she asks.

Lawrence can't quite make up his mind. 'Yes, no, yes, no, yes, no, yes, no,' he dithers.

'Come on, give me an answer,' she demands. 'I can't handle it when you're like this.'

He steadies himself. 'Yes, I mean no, I mean yes, I mean no, I mean yes, I mean no, I mean yes.'

Eileen is in tears. 'I wish you didn't have a split personality,' she blubs.

Lawrence tries to reassure her. 'I don't, I do, I don't, I do, I don't, I do, I don't, I do, I don't.'

• • •

Mooney cards her way into the office.

'That's a nice outfit, Miss Mooney,' Big Mac compliments her.

'Thanks. I got new shoes, a bag and a jacket as well,' is her smiley response.

'Very nice,' says Big Mac. 'Special occasion?'

Mooney puts her handbag on her desk and sits. 'I was just in the mood.'

Big Mac nods. 'Fair enough.'

There is a period of quiet apart from a little typing.

Mooney stands. 'Can I ask you guys something?'

Both Big Mac and Noddy say, 'Sure.'

She steps towards them. 'You will be truthful?' she says.

In unison, the duo sing, 'Cross my heart, hope to die, stick a needle in my eye.'

She nervously bites her lip and then declares, 'I'm fat, I know I'm fat, but does my bum look big in this?'

She scrutinises her colleagues closely, ready to determine whether their response is the truth. In sync, both say the opposite: Big Mac says no, whilst Noddy says yes.

Unsure, Mooney says, 'What?'

Big Mac gives Noddy a 'C'mon, get wise' look, and again they deliver their answers in sync, but the responses are unchanged: Big Mac says no, whilst Noddy says yes.

Mooney jogs back to her desk in tears. 'I've got a big ass. Oh God.'

Big Mac moves close to Noddy and, in a low voice, tries to educate him. 'Don't you know anything? If a woman asks you if she's got a big bum, you say no, and if a man asks if he's got a big knob, you say yes.'

With a sheepish look, Noddy says, 'Sorry. I keep mixing them up.'

At that exact moment Boss enters. 'What's that?' he asks.

Quick as a flash, Noddy reacts. 'You've got a big knob, sir.'

Boss stops dead in his tracks and shakes his head. 'I do wonder about you, Noddy.' He points at Noddy's head and verbalises what many before have thought: 'I do wonder what goes on in there.'

CHAPTER 23

Boss is asleep. The alarm goes off and has the desired effect; he reaches out to turn it off. He scratches his nose, covers his yawn and opens his eyes – to see his wife at the end of the bed, wearing green silk pyjamas this morning. She is staring at him.

Slowly and without energy, he declares, 'Good morning, darling. Another day, work, work, work. How did you sleep?'

She crosses her arms and sniffs. 'As if you care.'

This is a bit odd, he thinks. Sitting up in the bed, revealing that he is wearing a Freddie Mercury-style vest, he says genuinely, 'I love you.'

Pulling a face, she shoots back with extreme sarcasm, 'I love you, I love you, I love you. Is that supposed to make me feel content, happy? Well, it doesn't. I hate you. I hate you more than anyone else in the world. More than Hitler, Stalin, the Devil.'

Boss knows she isn't joking; he knows her well. He quickly tries to recall whether he has done something wrong or forgotten an important date. Nothing computes for him, and he softly asks, 'But what have I done?'

With an 'as if you don't know' look on her face, she

screams, 'You've done nothing, nothing! That's the problem. You've done nothing, and for that you'll have to die.'

She reaches down to reveal she is in possession of the axe that Boss uses to chop wood. She rushes towards him, swinging the weapon. He dodges and it cuts into the pillow.

She swings it vertically next, but he slips out of the bed onto the floor at the opposite side of the bed to her. She climbs onto the bed, but the softness of the mattress means she is off-balance and can't quite get the power or accuracy into her swing, and she falls onto the floor where Boss had been standing.

He rushes from the room, slamming the door behind him, and runs down the stairs. He grabs slippers, the car keys and a coat, and exits the house without checking whether the slippers and coat will match his pale-blue pyjama bottoms, and attempts to put them on.

He's backing the car out of the drive when he sees she's given chase. He keeps the car in reverse and manages to accelerate away from her. She stops the pursuit. As he switches from reverse to front drive, he hears her shouting in the distance: 'And don't come back!'

• • •

Lawrence is on his sixty-second countdown when he notices Eileen has entered the house through the back door. He leaves the table with forty-five seconds to go to avoid the axe head that was on a trajectory to hit him in the chest. He has no idea what is going on, but he quickly decides not to draw his gun and instead makes a run for it. Slamming the doors shut behind him, he is able to buy himself enough time to get into the car, start the engine, put the car in gear and lock the doors.

Eileen appears at the window beside him and threatens, 'I'll get you! I'll get you if it's the last thing I do.'

Without waiting for the follow-up sentence or indeed the next swing of the axe, Lawrence floors the accelerator (glad he took the time yesterday to back into the drive so the car is facing forward) and makes a quick getaway.

The neighbours across the street who are both out collecting the milk have witnessed all this. The redhead says, 'I used to feel sorry for her, having to put up with a lunatic like him.'

'Yeah,' says the blonde.

'Now I think they're probably well suited,' says the redhead, to another 'Yeah' from the blonde.

• • •

Big Mac and Noddy are already at work. Big Mac is still enjoying taking the piss out of Noddy by chucking paperclips at the back of his head. Noddy continues to look up at the ceiling.

Boss bursts in.

Noddy greets him with, 'There's definitely a leak, sir.'

Walking past Noddy, Boss says, 'No, there isn't, you idiot. He's throwing things at your numbskull of a head.'

Noddy turns to Big Mac. 'Who?'

Big Mac whispers, 'I don't know.' He points at Boss and then twirls his finger around his temple to indicate that their boss has a screw loose. Eying the slippers, blue pyjama bottoms and Freddie Mercury vest, he calls, 'Groovy look, Boss.'

But Boss isn't engaging; he is making a beeline for Mooney. He approaches her with speed and comes to a sudden stop.

'Miss Mooney, hi, I was hoping you might be able to explain something to me. It's my wife. She was all lovey-dovey the other day, but she's never really like that. Then today she was just different – aggressive, violent,' he blurts out.

Mooney doesn't respond at first, but puts down her nail file and looks up at him. Then she launches into: 'What am I supposed to do about it? Do I have "agony aunt" written on my forehead or something? Don't you think I have enough problems without having to listen to yours, you snivelling, hatchet-faced goon-back.'

Big Mac slaps his thigh as he guffaws. 'Hatchet-faced goon-back, nice one.'

Mooney continues her tirade. 'I hate you, hate you, hate you,' she screams at Boss.

Big Mac can't resist having a craic at his boss's expense. He interjects: 'As popular as ever, sir. A definite candidate for Boss of the Year again, I'm sure.'

Mooney doesn't allow Big Mac to enjoy his jibe, but venomously berates him: 'Shut your mouth, you lipid, cos I hate you as well, all of you.'

'Surely not me,' smiles Noddy.

'I said all of you, you brainless gorm. I hate all men equally.'

Noddy shrugs his shoulders. 'Fair enough. Seeing as it's all of us, there's no prejudice there.'

Mooney shouts at him, 'You fool!' and jumps over the desk and runs at him. She grabs him by the throat. He's laughing, though she has him half-killed.

Big Mac and Boss restrain her. Noddy picks himself up and starts clapping; he thinks this is great fun.

'This is great craic. Tag me, tag me, Miss Mooney. I can't join in if you don't tag me,' he states as he reaches his hand out, welcoming her touch.

Big Mac, struggling to hold Mooney, says, 'This isn't World Wrestling Entertainment, Noddy.'

Boss, who is equally struggling, says, 'It's for real.'

Noddy's face shows he is seriously apologetic. 'Oh! Let me hold her leg then.' And he joins in the melee.

They struggle on for a few minutes. Mooney is wild.

'What can we do, Boss?' asks Big Mac.

'Noddy, cuff one of her wrists to the radiator,' orders Boss.

Noddy, of course, messes up and makes the situation worse by cuffing Boss to it.

'For fuck's sake!' yells Boss. 'That's *my* wrist. Unlock me – the key is in my pyjama pocket.'

Noddy has a rummage.

Boss squeals, 'Ah! Don't squeeze those! What are you trying to do?'

Noddy says, 'Oops, sorry, Boss. I took a wrong turn. I've got it!' He pulls his hand out of Boss's pyjamas and excitedly shows everyone his catch, the key.

They manage to cuff Mooney to the radiator. Boss crawls a few feet from the scene and sits on his bum with his legs crossed.

'Thank God,' he breathes.

Big Mac just rolls onto his back, gasping for air. 'I'm not as fit as I used to be,' he says.

'Were you ever?' says Boss with a dry laugh. He notices that Noddy is now holding rosary beads and is mumbling to himself. 'What are you doing? Yes, you, Noddy.'

'I'm thanking God,' says Noddy.

'Why? You aren't religious.'

'Correct, sir, I'm not, but you ordered me to thank God.'

Boss sighs. 'And I suppose if I told you to jump off a bridge, you would.'

Before Noddy can respond, Big Mac intervenes: 'Sir, I think you know the answer to that.'

'Yeah, you would.' Smiling to himself, Boss adds, 'I'll try not to forget that.'

Mooney is back on her feet, trying to pull herself free from the radiator with no success. She turns to her colleagues. 'I'll kill you all.'

Boss tells the guys, 'That's what my wife said to me this morning.'

Big Mac is on his feet and taking a closer look at Mooney. He circles her and then delivers his expert opinion: 'Worst case of PMT I've ever seen. Isn't that right, Miss Mooney?'

She tries to break free; she tries to hit him. 'I'll kill you!' she screams.

'How can you be so sure?' asks Boss.

'I'm an expert in women,' Big Mac says, and he blows on his nails and polishes them on his sweater.

'And what makes you such an expert?'

'Eight marriages and eight divorces,' jokes Big Mac.

Noddy thinks he is being serious and asks, 'What did you do with your eight wives?'

Mooney shouts out, 'He probably ate them!' and laughs hysterically, then follows up with, 'I love the gallows humour, boys, love it, but I'm still going to kill you.'

'I like the wit, Miss Mooney, it suits you,' says Big Mac. Turning to Boss, he says, 'This is definitely PMT.'

Curious, Noddy asks, 'What's PMT?'

'Pre-Menstrual Tension,' explains Big Mac.

A vacant-looking Noddy says, 'Sounds bloody awful.'

Big Mac nods. 'It is.'

'So, what is that exactly?' asks Noddy.

Big Mac sidesteps this. 'Over to you, Boss.'

Boss takes his hands out of his pyjama bottoms and makes a vague motion. 'It's menstruation – you've heard of menstruation?'

Noddy nods whilst saying no.

Boss continues with the direct approach. 'You know what a tampon is? Heard of the expression "on the rag"?'

Noddy shakes his head.

Mooney claps sarcastically. 'Ha-ha, on the rag. Well done, Boss.'

Frustrated, Boss looks back at Noddy. 'Just ask your mother.'

Noddy nods obediently.

Big Mac has stepped away from all this and is paying attention to the TV. He calls out, 'Boss, look at this.'

The TV is showing images of apocalyptic weather – tidal waves, hurricanes, earthquakes, erupting volcanoes. There are also scenes of rioting. This is a report of some kind. They all listen to the male voiceover.

'From tomorrow we can expect more changes in females all over the country, and these will be negative in nature. Yesterday you may have noticed women were tearful and anxious, the day before, quite loving, and today, threatening and violent. Scientists are predicting more damage than El Niño and are calling this natural disaster El Periodo.

'If you look at the chart for China and the Far East from two days ago, you will see utter devastation. It spread across the Middle East and Central Europe yesterday. We can expect this situation to continue for some time. Scientists believe that the last time an epidemic of this magnitude occurred, it brought about the extinction of the dinosaurs. We are strongly advising men to stay indoors. Don't make any unnecessary ventures outside. God bless you all.'

Big Mac and Boss look at each other and say, 'Shit.'

Noddy starts to look around at the floor. 'Where?' he says.

Big Mac and Boss ignore him, as the TV news has switched to a press conference with the Taoiseach. No doubt he will bring a sense of calm and control to this situation of biblical proportions.

CHAPTER 24

The Taoiseach walks into the press conference with an aide. For a change all is quiet and there is a much smaller turnout than usual; there are no women present. Everyone stays seated. There is no jostling, and the journalists look anxious.

'I've got some news for you,' the Taoiseach announces.

A single, well-mannered voice from the floor responds: 'What's that, sir?'

The Taoiseach says, 'From today, income tax is going up to eighty per cent.'

Panic and pandemonium set in on the floor. After about twenty seconds of hysteria, the Taoiseach points at the journalists and says, 'Gotcha. Only joking.'

Relief spreads across the hall and everyone sits down to several mutterings of 'Thank God'.

A reporter stands up. 'Mike Murphy, *Woman's Every Week* magazine, sir. Could I ask what your views are on the PMT situation?'

The Taoiseach senses he has a moment to deliver something quite meaningful. He leans into the microphone and says with sincerity, 'I'm totally against all terrorist organisations, and the Polish Movement for Tea is no different.'

There is silence once again in the hall. The members of the press don't know whether this is another *gotcha* or if the Taoiseach is just back to his true form.

After thirty seconds or so, Mike Murphy tries for some clarification. 'But sir, that's not what PMT stands for. It means Pre-Menstrual Tension. Women get it.'

The Taoiseach jumps at the opportunity to appeal to female voters. 'Women are great. My mother was a woman, and her mother before her was a woman. There is a tradition of women in my family. John Lennon said, "Woman, you are forever in my debt."'

Another reporter intervenes. 'No, sir. "I'm forever in your debt."'

The Taoiseach smiles at him. 'Well, if you say so, young man.'

Mike Murphy tries to help again. 'No, sir, you got the lyric wrong. Lennon said, "I'm forever in your debt."'

Quick as a flash, before anything more can be said or done, the aide shouts out, 'That's all the Taoiseach has time for today. Thank you.' And he escorts the Taoiseach back out of the room.

• • •

Lawrence has seen the TV reports, and in this time of difficulty he realises he can only trust one person: his oracle, the arse – whose name, he has learned, is Tom. Lawrence listens with great interest as Tom tells him how he sees it.

'Larry, having viewed this from a number of perspectives, I think your only option is to convince the professor of feminology at the university to help you come up with a cure.'

Lawrence slowly paces up and down the bathroom. Again he has used the dustbin to keep the handle up, so he won't be disturbed. He turns a tap on and the water flows; it might help him think, he figures.

After a few minutes of slow pacing, he returns to the tap, turns it off and walks back to Tom. 'I hear you,' he says. With kindness in his voice, he adds, 'You could get rid of those spots, you know. I had spots when I was younger. Clearasil worked for me.'

Tom responds, 'Thanks for your support, Larry, but I've been to a dermatologist and tried everything, and nothing has worked. I've accepted that this is who I am. And besides, I get my fair share of women anyway. I think they're more interested in intelligence and humour, and I prefer to be wanted for those qualities really than, say, for my good looks.'

Lawrence nods, and then asks, 'Can you take a compliment, Tom?'

'Sure,' says the arse.

Lawrence says, 'Tom, I think you're a bona fide smart arse, the real McCoy.'

They laugh.

CHAPTER 25

Big Mac's mobile rings. He puts it to his ear and immediately hands it over to Boss. 'It's for you, sir.'

Surprised, Boss takes the mobile and says, 'Hello?'

'Boss, it's me, Lawrence.'

'Where are you?' asks Boss.

'It's better I don't say; the line won't be secure. Use the radio. Go to the channel that's the length in inches of an average man's appendage.' And with that Lawrence hangs up.

Boss walks over to a desk and picks up a radio. He turns to Noddy and Big Mac. 'Men, how big are your knobs?'

Big Mac looks surprised, but after a few moments he realises Boss is serious. 'Well, mine is twelve inches, sir,' he lies.

'Same,' says Noddy.

Boss is a bit shocked; he wasn't expecting the number to be so high. Without much confidence he says, 'Of course, mine too.'

Mooney lets out a big cackle. 'Fucking liars.'

• • •

Several women are in some office somewhere with a range of communication tools including transmitters. They are monitoring all communications across the country. They have similar radios to Boss and Lawrence.

One of the women says to the others, 'It has to be either Channel 3 or 4.'

They all nod in agreement.

Lawrence is out on the street, trying to keep out of harm's way. He sees groups of women chasing after men. Some of these men are caught and beaten up. Lawrence knows he can't intervene, even though he has a gun; he has to stay focused on the big picture, the macro. He is nervous. His radio vibrates and he opens the line. Lawrence has obviously chosen Channel 12 too, and as expected it is Boss.

'Aren't we a bunch of big dicks,' says Boss.

Lawrence gives a half-smile, but time is of the essence so he cuts straight to business.

'I've had a tip-off, sir, that the only person who might be able to help us is a professor down at the university, some guy from Amsterdam. I'm going to go down and see if this is the case.'

'Okay,' Boss says. 'Big Mac and I will head down as well to support you. Noddy has to remain here and keep watch over a prisoner – Miss Mooney, I'm afraid. We'll hang outside the university.'

'How will I recognise you?' asks Lawrence.

'We'll be in a van.'

'What kind?'

'Trust me, you'll know.' Boss closes the line.

• • •

There are thousands of women around the University of Limerick. They're burning cars and looting, and torturing men. There are dead men on the streets. Women are marching and chanting the words on their banners: 'KILL MEN' and 'MANARCHY'. Soldiers have managed to kill some of the anarchists, but soon a group of women use bras as slingshots to hurl grenades that blow them to smithereens.

Lawrence is in the group that is chanting, 'MANARCHY.' He is disguised as a woman, wearing a big blond wig straight off a mannequin and a dress that is too short for him, and walking very awkwardly in high heels. The eyeshadow suits him, but he has slapped on the lipstick as only a man can: clumsily.

One of the women turns to him. 'Hey, sister, I've killed ten men today – high-five.'

Lawrence gives her a high-five and says, 'Way to go.' He immediately panics that his manly voice will get him caught, so he coughs and in his best attempt at a high, feminine tone says, 'I mean, way to go.'

He stays with this group for about five minutes and then casually steps away from them. He enters a university building and makes his way down to the basement. After walking for ten minutes through a labyrinth of passageways, he eventually reaches what he hopes is the door he is looking for. He knocks and knocks and knocks, but there is no response.

There is a small letterbox. He opens it and whispers loudly in his feminine voice, 'Professor Femidom, Professor Femidom, let me in. I'm here to help.'

He is surprised by the response. Tom told him the professor was a man, but the voice is that of a woman. 'Who are you?' asks the professor.

'I'm police,' says Lawrence.

'You don't sound like the police,' says the professor.

'Sorry, but I am police,' says Lawrence in his normal voice.

Now the professor speaks in his normal, manly, voice too. 'I can't let you in if you're not a man.'

'I am a man,' says Lawrence, pointing to his crotch.

'In that case, what is the password?' is the professor's response.

Lawrence hasn't a clue, but with nothing to lose, he throws out, 'Swordfish.'

The professor laughs. 'A fan of the Marx Brothers, I see. But it may be a trick to fool me into believing you're male. I have a few more questions for you. Do you like shopping?'

Lawrence scowls. 'Definitely not.'

'Very good,' is the response from behind the door. 'And can you explain the football offside rule?'

'If the attacker is behind the defender in the defender's half before the attacking side kicks the ball forward, then the attacker is offside.'

'Very good. And one last one: sausage or kebab?'

WTF? thinks Lawrence. *I like sausages and kebabs. What is the answer here? Maybe it's sausages – most men like sausages, and women like salad and you generally have salad with a kebab.* He is about to say sausage, but then he has another thought. *Men constantly think about sex. There'll be a sexual connotation to the question. It isn't really about food at all. Women would say sausage.* 'Kebab!' he shouts out.

The big, heavy steel door opens and Lawrence is greeted by the Dutch professor, who is the spitting image of Albert Einstein, obviously it is not him, but the resemblance is so strong. *Maybe a relative*, thinks Lawrence. The professor closes and locks the door and Lawrence scans the room. There are the dead bodies everywhere.

'Come in, come in,' the professor says in a thick Dutch accent. 'Obviously, the flaw with the last question is that if you were a lesbian, you would also have said kebab and I would now be dead.' He gestures to the dead women. 'Please forgive the mess.'

Lawrence is taken aback and is still scanning the room, estimating the body count – at least fifteen, he reckons. Slowly, he utters, 'Okay, I'm here to help.'

The professor gesticulates wildly with his hands as he speaks. 'I don't know how you can. I tried some experiments on these women here, to come up with a cure, but they died. And it's too dangerous to try to capture another one. They're so wild it's likely one of us would get killed.'

Lawrence sits on one end of a three-seater sofa. There is a dead body at the other end. The professor sits on an armchair. He points to the dead woman on the sofa and says, 'This is Mary. She was my assistant, but I killed her.'

Lawrence looks at the body and says, 'Hello, Mary.'

They sit there in silence for five minutes, the professor closely observing Lawrence, who is deep in thought.

Eventually, Lawrence says in a low voice, 'Think, think, think.'

'Are you talking to me?' asks the professor.

Lawrence says, 'No, sorry, I'm talking to myself. I might be bipolar or schizophrenic.'

The professor sits back in his chair, crosses his legs and says, 'Interesting. The best of us probably are.'

Five more minutes pass, and then Lawrence half-heartedly volunteers, 'We've got a woman back at base you could test on.'

Whilst considering this, the professor moves his tongue against his teeth, but his mouth remains closed until finally he says, 'Very well, but it will be a hazardous journey.'

CHAPTER 26

Lawrence and the professor have made their way outside the building and are on the university campus. They are disguised as women and trying to keep a low profile. They attempt to enter a car park to take a shortcut, but it is completely full of women and they decide it will be easier to go around rather than risk being caught and killed. Executions are still taking place.

'Where are your friends?' whispers the professor.

'They said they would be in a van,' Lawrence tells him.

Worried, the professor says, 'But there are many vans. Which one do you think is theirs?'

Lawrence looks around and he has no idea. There are quite a few vans, some burning, some empty. He is beginning to worry that this is his end.

There are cheers in the distance. The mood of the female crowd is lighter; there is still hatred and aggression in the air, but also a sense of pride and celebration. The crowd is going wild and appears to be parting to let a vehicle through. Lawrence can see that it is a van, and as it gets nearer, the cheers get louder. In the driver's seat he can make out a tall nun, and taking up the other two front seats is the fattest nun he has ever seen.

'This is them,' he tells the professor.

The van continues towards them, and as it parks alongside them they read the big banner on the side of the van: 'GOD IS A WOMAN.'

The professor turns to Lawrence and declares, 'You have very smart friends.'

With no time to waste at this dangerous rendezvous, they get into the back quickly and are about to drive off when the mood of the crowd changes. It has become violent again, the mob baying and surging towards the van.

'Fuck, what's up with them now?' says Boss.

'Shit!' says Big Mac as they all see that the banner has blown down the street, revealing that it is actually a Garda van.

The women hurl missiles at the van, and a petrol bomb explodes in front. Big Mac starts to have what appears to be an epileptic fit, and Boss isn't able to help him as he appears to have succumbed to a fit too. There is considerable noise in the back of the van, but the professor and Lawrence aren't having a fit, they are dancing – and on closer inspection, so too are Boss and Big Mac, it's just that in the confined space of the front of the van, it looks like a fit.

Outside the van, across the campus, across the city of Limerick and indeed the whole of Ireland, everyone is dancing, the same dance, all in sync. The Magic Band have saved the day.

It happened like this: Initially, when The Magic Band lifted up the side of their truck, the women all around noticed the men on the mobile stage and they charged at them like warriors in *Braveheart*. The band looked a bit panicky, but the lead singer, smiling and calm, said to his men, 'Hold.' The women were getting closer, wild, murderous, but again the leader said to his men, 'Hold.' And then, just as the first lady was about to step onto the stage, he shouted at his men, 'Play!' They played their instruments, and at once every woman danced.

When the band finish playing, everyone lies down. Boss lies across the steering wheel, which sets off a continuous horn blow. The band depart, as they always do. Everyone remains lying down. What we never realised before, but do now, is that the music impacts women for longer than men, meaning the men in the van come round about thirty seconds sooner than the women who are intent on killing them. They are groggy, but the professor quickly reminds them to get moving.

'Fucking move, fucking move! They're waking up – they'll kill us!'

Boss hears a horn. It stops, but he doesn't realise the reason it has stopped is because he's lifted his head off the steering wheel. He puts the van in first and, looking to his left, thinks, *Who is the fat nun?* Then he realises it is Big Mac.

They snake their way out of the university at about ten miles per hour, leaving behind what appears to be a whole load of hungover women heading home from the greatest and wildest music festival of all time.

CHAPTER 27

Back by the Shannon, Boss drives the van through a rear entrance that automatically opens for them, and they are back on secure ground. They card their way into the office.

Mooney notices the four women. 'Sisters, sisters!' she shouts. 'There's only this numpty here' – she points to Noddy. 'Break me free and we can rampage through the world.'

One of the women approaches her and, in a masculine Dutch accent, asks the other three ladies, 'This is the guinea pig?'

Mooney starts to realise that she kind of recognises the two nuns and the other civilian female, and it dawns on her that they are her male colleagues. She sits back down on the floor, de-energised.

Noddy has taken zero notice of any of this.

Big Mac and Boss disrobe and begin to dress into the clothes they were wearing earlier in the office. Lawrence has a spare at the office. Boss advises them not to chuck their female disguises away. 'We may need them later.'

The professor had his shirt and trousers on under his lady's dress, so he completes the change back to normal very quickly. The others are only halfway through the task when he says, 'Faster, gentlemen. Time is of the essence.' Turning to Mooney, he utters, 'I think if I can bring about a molecular change in the plasma levels of particular neurotransmitters, it may be possible to return females to normal, and thus save the human race from disaster.'

Boss has kept the female shoes on, better for running than slippers the thinking. He turns to Big Mac. 'What's he talking about?'

Big Mac still isn't fully dressed and is munching on a doughnut. 'Damned if I know,' he mumbles.

With a look of disgust, Boss says, 'How can you eat at a time like this?'

Big Mac gulps down the last mouthful and replies, 'Comfort eating, I guess.' He sits down to start on some takeaway leftovers.

The professor is walking around Mooney, but staying out of her reach so she can't attack. 'So this is the female specimen,' he states.

Mooney attempts to strike at him while snarling, 'I'll kill you, I'll kill you.'

The professor strokes the small half-goatee on his chin. 'Let me see if this works,' he says, and then he picks up a chair and hits her over the head with it.

Mooney is knocked to the floor, but she gets up immediately and tries to smack the professor. He hits her with the chair again, and before she can rise from the floor, he hits her another four times. Then he steps back. She immediately springs back to her feet, full of anger.

The professor puts the chair back. 'This is not effective,' he says.

He rushes at Mooney and kicks and punches her repeatedly, but again it has no effect. She continues to snarl like a wild beast.

He walks over to a computer and messes with the electrical cord. He keeps it plugged in but takes the end that inserts into the computer and uses a penknife to strip the plastic back and reveal the wiring, which has a live electrical current running through it. He picks up the sweeping brush and breaks off the brush bit, giving himself a four-foot handle. He ties the electrical cord to the pole with the exposed wires at one end to create a kind of cattle prod.

'He's a genius,' says Big Mac.

Noddy says, 'Thanks,' mistaking the false compliment as a genuine one for him.

The professor holds one end of the handle and directs the other end, with the live wires exposed, towards Mooney. He electrocutes her. She screams an unusual scream, one of pain, but also joy – the joy that comes from the knowledge that this won't defeat her. The professor electrocutes her again. She screams again. This continues.

After a few more electrical instalments, Big Mac turns away from the desk and wipes his face, meal over. Facing his colleagues, he asks, 'Anyone want to play famous faces?'

Noddy agrees. Big Mac starts. He makes a strange face

and movement and sings, 'It's electrifying!' Then he stops and says, 'So, who am I?'

Noddy considers and says, 'Someone fat.'

'No, not in real life, Noddy, in the game, in the game. What famous person am I?' Big Mac repeats his performance. 'It's electrifying!'

Noddy makes a guess. 'Um, an electrician.'

Big Mac says, 'No, come on, think: movie, seventies, musical, electrifying.'

Boss crosses his arms across his Freddie vest. 'I'm not playing this stupid game.'

Noddy tries again. 'Um, um, Dirty Harry?'

Lawrence says, 'I don't know.'

Big Mac waits for a few seconds and then says, 'So, do you give up?'

A weary Mooney says, 'Yes.'

The professor laughs. 'He's not talking to you,' he says and pokes her again with the broom handle, delivering another electric shock.

Big Mac looks at his colleagues with contempt. 'I can't believe you didn't get it. I'm John Travolta from *Grease*.' He sings a little of 'You're the One That I Want'.

Noddy gently punches himself on the quadricep with his closed fist. 'Damn, I should have known that one.'

Somehow Mooney gets her hand on the broom and yanks it. The professor loses his footing and comes flying towards her. She meets him with a head-butt, knocking him five feet backwards and out of her reach. She snaps the broom handle and pulls on the cord till it comes out of the socket. As she starts to reel it in, it catches on the plates, mugs and cutlery that Big Mac had been using and they come clattering to the floor, within her grasp. She reaches out and pulls the cutlery and crockery towards her, and quickly uses a fork to unpick her cuff.

The professor has groggily sat up, and as he tries to get to his feet, he shouts a warning to the other men: 'She's picked the lock and she has a knife. Run!'

The men make it through the door and jam it shut, putting their weight against it, to stop her leaving and to keep them safe. They wait and wait, but the hurricane that is Mooney doesn't arrive. They look through the glass panels in the door and see that Mooney is much calmer. She is carrying out an action of some sort with the plates.

Boss points out the obvious: 'She's calming down.'

The professor stops pushing and steps away from the others. He performs a pirouette and shouts out, 'Eureka! It's the act of cleaning, it's grounding her. Her primary instinct as a woman is to clean. This supersedes any need she may have for violence. Get more dishes,' he orders.

The men find lots of dirty dishes and cutlery. They go back into the office and put them before Mooney, and calmness descends.

'This is ground-breaking research,' declares the professor, and he excitedly jumps up and plants a kiss on Noddy's head.

Noddy smiles.

Boss is all serious, as usual. ‘We have to let the outside world know,’ he says.

Noddy puts his hand up as if he’s at school. ‘Sir, we could broadcast it over the radio.’

Stunned, Boss agrees.

They get the radio and open all channels. Lawrence raises the radio to his mouth. ‘Hello, this is Lawrence Barry of the Special Branch. We’ve had a breakthrough. To calm down the violent symptoms of PMT, you have to put dirty dishes in the path of the women. They won’t be able to resist cleaning them and this very act will calm them down. Shake and vac. Over.’

• • •

All around the world, men put dishes in front of crazy women. The women wash them, and calm down.

Later that day, on the evening news, the newscaster reports: ‘The world has been saved! Not since Moses parted the Red Sea to save the Israelites from Egypt has a miracle of this magnitude been performed. Thank you, Special Branch.’

CHAPTER 28

It is almost home time. Mooney hugs her colleagues and the professor individually and then addresses them as a group.

'It was so scary, but you saved me. Thank you all. I love you.'

They all head home.

• • •

Boss receives a hug from his wife. 'Thank God you're back to normal,' he says.

'It was so scary. I'm glad to be back,' she says.

• • •

Lawrence is nearly home. He is ecstatic: after his achievements at work, he will most certainly get his old job back in Dublin. He'll probably win the Scott Medal, the highest award a Garda in Ireland can get. And, more importantly, Eileen will be happier.

He parks the car and gets out, noticing that the kids are waiting in the backseat of Eileen's car. He gives them a little wave and heads to the front door, which is open. Eileen is in the hallway as he walks in the door.

He says, ‘Hi, honey. Thank God your PMT is over. That was scary. I’ve missed you.’

He moves in to hug and kiss her, but she pushes him away. ‘Lawrence, I’m leaving you. I love you, but we can’t go on like this. It’s like *you’ve got* PMT all the time.’

He is shocked, stunned. There is an uneasy pause, and then his eyes start to well with tears and he says, ‘I’ll try washing the dishes.’

Eileen walks past him and out the door. Glancing back, she says, ‘Sorry, Lawrence, it’s over.’ Then she’s gone.

It’s crazy, thinks Lawrence, *my memory*. He can remember the first time he saw Eileen; she was an Accident and Emergency nurse. The most beautiful brown eyes. They were fast dancing to ‘I Useta Lover’ by The Saw Doctors at Copper Face Jacks, a hangout for many nurses and cops in Dublin. Same again the following week, but he didn’t have the confidence to talk to her. The third week, he asked her for a slow dance to a Bryan Adams’ track, ‘Heaven’ – and it was heaven for many, many years. *Why can’t I remember much about our relationship over the past two years or so?* he asks himself. *The session with Majella tomorrow is badly needed, the timing perfect.*

• • •

The next morning, in Majella's office, Lawrence relays everything to her. There is a long pause as she gives very serious consideration to everything she has heard.

Eventually, she says, 'Lawrence, do you want me to be honest with you?'

'Yes,' he says.

'And I want to be honest with you, but I'm not sure that you can handle it.'

Another big silence, which is broken by Lawrence. 'Let's just go for it.'

'Okay. A lot of that "Shemageddon" story, I'm really sorry, Lawrence, but it just isn't true. Some of it is based on reality, but your mind has somehow exaggerated it.'

'How do you mean?' asks Lawrence.

'Well, there weren't riots across the world involving women. But there was a global liberation movement that highlighted inequality in corporate pay. There were peaceful marches and legal challenges against companies that had discriminated against women who took maternity leave.'

'But there were problems out at UL.'

'There weren't, Lawrence. It was a peaceful demonstration.'

'But what about Professor Femidom? I met him. He helped us,' states Lawrence.

'I googled him. He doesn't exist.'

'And The Magic Band?'

'There is no magic band, Lawrence.'

'But how would you know? They knock everyone out with

their music. You wouldn't remember,' he challenges.

'Exactly, Lawrence, and you would be knocked out too, so how would you remember?'

He knows she is making sense, but it is still hard. He feels really stupid. 'So how and why has all this happened?'

Majella thinks for a moment and then says, 'Well, there's a very sexist tone to what you told me. It could be something to do with being angry with Eileen. She's left you on your own and taken the kids off to her mother's in Galway. It could be that, but I'm unsure, I don't know. Could you tell me a little about your relationship with your mother, Lawrence?'

He is incredulous and a little incensed. 'For fuck's sake, Majella, I don't want to ride my mother.'

'I've no idea what you're talking about,' she replies.

'That Freud stuff. Best warned me.'

'That's just nonsense,' she says. 'It plays no part in my practice or my thinking.'

• • •

Later, Lawrence writes in his diary:

I'm on my own in Annacotty. Eileen is gone with the kids, to stay at her mother's in Galway. Things are getting worse. I figured out that I don't know the difference between my thoughts, my hallucinations, reality and maybe what I dream. I'm so confused. This is difficult. Did I dream up a whole situation about women or am I very unwell, or both? Christ it was so real. It's a living nightmare. Thought I was a hero, ended up minus zero.

Maybe I am angry with Eileen. I hate life. I wish I was dead. I can't tell work how bad things are, I might get sacked. Majella Quinn is a decent person. Big Mac looks troubled. He is holding something in. I'm struggling. I'm convinced that the country is corrupt, but it's hard to be sure. I'm probably paranoid.

I'd like to die. Loathing, distain, self-hatred, useless. Black. Red. Black. Red. Black. Red. ACDC, 'Highway to Hell'. The Doors, 'The End'. Nirvana, 'Smells Like Teen Spirit'. Michael Bolton, 'How Am I Supposed to Live Without You?'. Roxette, 'It Must Have Been Love'. Justin Timberlake, 'Cry Me a River'. Roy Orbison, 'Crying'. Jimmy Cliff, 'Many Rivers to Cross'.

CHAPTER 29

Lena sits on the desk, facing the group.

'For all his bravado, Big Mac doesn't have much success with women; it is all an act. He has been dating a lady called Joan O'Rourke for a couple of months. The chemistry is magic, and things are moving really fast – they've had a lot of dates. She is the first woman he has been with in quite a few years. There is a huge shadow that hangs over Big Mac, something he never talks about: he was once married and had a daughter, but a tragic accident removed both from this world and he hasn't been the same since. Now he is literally twice the man.

'He really does like Joan, but there is one thing that keeps eating away at him, an itch he has to scratch, a scab he has to pick. Her brother was Mickey O'Rourke, the cop who died in the San Francisco smash. She is adamant that it wasn't an accident; she is totally convinced that it was suicide. She says that Mickey was very desperate for a long time because he was being blackmailed – something to do with false evidence against him of a paedophilic nature. Mickey once mentioned to her when drunk that the blackmailer was someone known as Bull. When she raised it with Mickey on another occasion, he flew into a rage and told her to never repeat that name again, that her life depended on it. This keeps nagging away at Big Mac. He does know of a dirty cop known as Bull, a big fella, a corrupt fella, a dangerous fella, a very dangerous fella. Probably just a coincidence?

'Bit of a dark time in a number of ways, wouldn't you say?'

No one responds.

'A real tough time for Lawrence. Eileen is gone, and let's face it, she isn't coming back – and who can blame her? And Lawrence has now got something else, something potentially very dangerous: he now has insight. He knows his mind is shot to pieces. He knows he can't tell the difference between dreams, reality and hallucinations. He knows Eileen is unlikely to return. He knows he is struggling in the job. He knows he is a bit doomed, and maybe better off dead. There is always hope, though, isn't there? He needs to hold on tight, hold on to what he has, and at the moment all he has is his job and his team.'

Rita pipes up, 'They're not a team.'

Lena considers this. 'They are. You've all been on placements where you joined teams for a short period of time. You all had different experiences, you said – good teams, bad teams, strange teams. Maybe I've misrepresented the Specials a little, but they are a team. Dysfunctional with a capital D, but a team. And they're all Lawrence has now. He needs to hold on to the job. It's keeping him occupied, which is good, a form of therapy.'

• • •

At this juncture Lawrence reviews his objectives and resets his goals. He decides he needs to keep trying to get well, and that means getting better at recognising the difference between reality and his psychosis.

His major objective is to get Eileen back. He is convinced that to do that he needs a promotion, and therefore he needs a big success story to get recognition from Dublin. He focuses on the whole organised crime and politics thing. He is convinced the Taoiseach is crooked in some way, and that if he could make a breakthrough and nail the Taoiseach, he would be at the top table again – he would be on the up, he would be the man, he would be back, and Eileen would want him.

Nota Bene

'Sometimes you just have to go for it, grab hold of life, hang on and see what happens.'

COCAINE

CHAPTER 30

There wasn't an igloo in sight, nor an Eskimo or a polar bear, though there were some Fox's Glacier Mints in a pot on the round table. Lawrence may well have been in a Nordic region, though, judging by his uncontrollable shaking, which if it were a cold day and he were in summer clothes would easily be mistaken for the shivers.

'I've been getting the shakes a lot, Doc,' explains Lawrence.

'Anxious about anything?' Best asks.

Lawrence shakes his head. The truth is that he is very worried about several matters, but he doesn't believe he can fully trust this medic.

'It's a side effect of the medication,' Best tells him.

'Can you reduce it?' asks Lawrence hopefully.

'I can't. You're far too unwell. You told me yourself that the hallucinations are strong. But I'll change it to a modern antipsychotic; that should do the trick.'

Lawrence breaks eye contact, looks at the floor and releases a shallow but lengthy sigh. 'Okay,' he says, nodding.

Best recognises that he needs to motivate Lawrence, give him some positivity, something to hold on to. 'You're still improving, Lawrence. You'll need medication for some time, maybe a couple of years, but you're progressing well.'

Lawrence looks at him. 'Fair enough.' Then he wonders if he is hallucinating, as the good doctor starts leaping around the room like a frog whilst singing Paul McCartney and the Frog Chorus's 'We All Stand Together'.

As Lawrence leaves, he's glad he doesn't have to drive down that long lane from Desmond House anymore. These days he meets the various health professionals at a private clinic called Big River Practice in the city. *Progress perhaps*, he tells himself on the way back to work.

CHAPTER 31

Lawrence is sitting in the corner, trying not to draw attention to himself; his shakes haven't subsided yet. Big Mac is eating a sandwich, which he holds in his left hand. In his right hand is a tomato slice. As he chews, he moves his right hand from side to side like a conductor leading his orchestra, though the only person paying any attention is Noddy. His eyes never leave the tomato and his head turns north, south, east, west, following every hand movement of the maestro.

Big Mac throws the tomato high into the air and Noddy leaps, salmon like, arms to his sides, and expertly captures it in his mouth like a champion canine. He swallows it and licks his lips.

Big Mac sniggers, then becomes all serious. 'Good boy. Now sit.'

Noddy obliges.

Mooney enters with a Mediterranean-looking man. He is wearing a worn, baggy suit and is tieless with the top two buttons of his shirt open.

Mooney stops in the middle of the room. 'Hello, everybody. Can I introduce Señor Habitaz. He is a detective on exchange from Madrid.'

Lawrence says nothing, Noddy stares at Habitaz and Big Mac says something incomprehensible, waves and then points to his full mouth as a non-verbal communication to explain his incomprehensibility.

Mooney walks Habitaz over to Lawrence. 'This is Lawrence,' she says.

Unfortunately, what Lawrence sees is a man with the head of a crocodile. He reacts quickly, putting his arms up to protect himself and shouting out, 'Ah! Go away.'

Smiling, Habitaz makes the same gestures as Lawrence and shouts out, 'Ah! Go away.' He laughs and turns to Mooney. 'You have some strange greeting ways in this country.'

A confused Mooney agrees. 'Yes, we do.'

She introduces Habitaz to Big Mac next. Big Mac is trying to swallow and motions that he needs a moment before he can engage in conversation. Eventually, he swallows the last of his sandwich, wipes his dirty paws on his sweater and then offers his hand to Habitaz. As they shake hands, he says, 'I'd just like to say that Spanish omelettes are one of my favourite dishes.'

Habitaz gives a beaming grin and responds, 'Thank you, Big Mac.'

They move over to Noddy. 'This is Noddy,' says Mooney. 'Noddy, Señor Habitaz is from Spain.'

'No, he's not. You can't fool me,' says Noddy. 'He's from Mexico. I know what Mexicans look like and he's a Mexican.'

'Noddy, he's from Spain, not Mexico.'

‘Well, how come he looks like a Mexican then?’ queries Noddy.

Mooney steps into teacher mode. With both feet planted firmly on the floor and using her hands to accentuate her point, she explains, ‘Lots of people from around the Med have a similar look about them to people from South America. Isn’t that right, Habitaz?’

‘Sí,’ comes the reply from Habitaz.

‘But I assure you, Noddy, Habitaz is from Spain. What’s your problem with Mexicans anyway?’ asks Mooney.

‘They’re the bad guys,’ Noddy states.

Confused, Mooney points out, ‘But you’ve never met a Mexican in your life.’

Noddy nods. ‘True. But I’ve seen loads of Clint Eastwood movies. They love nothing better than killing us gringos.’

Big Mac joins in. ‘Good to see you’re living in reality, Noddy,’ he laughs. ‘A twin for Lawrence.’

Mooney tries to diffuse the situation. ‘Habitaz won’t harm you.’

‘Fair enough,’ Noddy replies. ‘But I still think he’s a Mexican.’

Mooney turns to Habitaz – who in truth has poor English and has no idea what is going on. ‘Don’t worry about him. He’s not the brightest, God bless him,’ she says.

Habitaz says, *‘Sí.’*

CHAPTER 32

The team and Habitaz are in the office watching TV. Lawrence is in the corner, distracted. An advert comes on. A good-looking man is talking while walking through beautiful green fields to a soundtrack of inspiring but calm music.

'Here at Honesty Bank, we give people the best deals. We care about you and your loved ones. We want you to achieve your goals; we want you to prosper, advance in life, be the best version of you that you can be. We will help you get there. We have loans and mortgages to get you on your way.'

• • •

Cut to the bank executives responsible for the advert discussing it.

'That's perfect,' says one. 'Excellent PR, makes us look caring.'

'Indeed,' says another. 'Those fucking plebs only exist to make us rich. Fodder, that's all they are, fodder.'

Another nods. 'They've forgotten about the 2008 crash now. We don't need to run these positive adverts anymore, but we do need to start thinking up new ways to capture these people – I mean, get their business.'

The head banker speaks: 'We're only repossessing a thousand homes a week. This is clearly not good enough. Frank, get your team on it. I want this doubled within ten days or I'll sack you. Feed the greed, feed the greed.'

• • •

That advert is followed by another, which the team watch. The focus is a beautiful twenty-something woman in a swimsuit.

'Hi, men,' she says. 'I'm beautiful. You should buy a car like this – then you can pretend to yourself that you have the potential to go out with a gorgeous girl like me. Go on, get deluded, buy the car.'

This creates an office discussion.

'Do they really think men are stupid enough to buy a car because of a hot chick?' argues Big Mac.

Mooney counters, 'Some men feel they have to, for their egos, their sense of security.'

At this moment Boss enters the office. He is whistling and appears to be in a joyous mood.

'Hi, Boss,' says Mooney. 'You're in a good mood today.'

'I sure am,' comes the response.

'Why's that, sir?'

'I've just bought a new car, one of the ones advertised on TV by that gorgeous chick.'

Mooney turns to Big Mac. 'See!'

Habitaz says, *'Sí.'*

Boss sits on a desk and looks around the group. 'Anyway, just because I'm in a good mood, that doesn't change anything. I dislike you all. Don't forget that. Do you understand me, Big Mac? Do some work.'

'Yes, sir,' is the response.

'Lawrence, do you need a blanket?'

'It's the side effects of my medication, sir.'

Under his breath, Boss says, 'Still psychotic, are we?'

Lawrence hears and nods.

Boss turns his attention to Noddy, who is staring at Habitaz.

'Noddy, Mr IQ, what are you doing, and who the hell is this?'

Noddy doesn't respond, so Mooney intervenes. 'Sir, may I introduce Señor Habitaz. He's our exchange detective from Spain.'

'Mexico,' says Noddy.

'Hello, Señor Habitaz,' says Boss. 'Who's been exchanged for you? Because looking around me I see all the usual idiots.'

Mooney says, 'He's swapped with Robert Hanley at HQ, but HQ felt Habitaz would fit in best here.'

Boss nods, looks at Habitaz and says, 'So you must be pretty shit at your job then for them to do that, Señor?'

Habitaz is unsure what is being said and replies, *'Sí.'*

Boss says, *'Ça va? Combien de frère et de soeur?'*

Mooney says, 'That's French, sir. Habitaz is Spanish.'

'Mexican,' says Noddy.

'French, Spanish, Brazilian, Mexican – it doesn't really

matter to me,' says Boss. 'They're all the same. They look the same, they talk the same, and I just don't understand them. Poor English – might as well be dealing with someone from the Gaeltacht. Why aren't we able to attract the Swedes, the Dutch or the Germans? For perfect English, give me a Pole any day, and I'm not being racist here, no, and do you know why that is, Miss Mooney?'

'No, sir.'

'Because I dislike everybody equally, including the Irish, and especially the fools that I have to manage here at Purgatory HQ. Isn't that right, Señor Habitaz?'

Habitaz straightens up, composes himself and says, '*Sí*. I am honoured to be here.'

'Brilliant, excellent, obviously very intelligent. You would have to be, to get placed here. Back to work, everybody,' Boss yells, and he strolls into his office, slamming the door behind him.

CHAPTER 33

The Taoiseach has made a number of attempts to get the knot in his tie right. Eventually, he concedes defeat and waves his aide into battle. The aide expertly creates the desired knot.

'There you go, sir,' he says and steps to the side.

The Taoiseach admires the knot in the mirror and then breaks into song.

'I really feel like taxing, yes taxing,
I'll tax them all that's right,
I really fancy taxing,
I feel like taxing,
The young and the old,
The warm and the cold,
Tax, oh just tax,
Gorgeous tax, uh, uh, uh, uh…'

His aide intervenes. 'Sir, they're waiting for us. We have to go out there, remember.'

'Yes, yes, yes.' The Taoiseach sniffles, takes a couple of large breaths, shakes his head a few times and then stares at himself in the mirror. 'Okay, show time. Elvis is ready.'

The Taoiseach and his aide walk into the news conference.

Like a pack of rabid dogs, the reporters are champing at the bit. To a background of barking, the Taoiseach takes a seat and his aide stands a few feet behind and to the right.

A journalist stands up. 'Taoiseach, Mr Taoiseach. Brian O'Brien, *RTE*, sir. The cocaine crisis, sir, what are you going to do about it?'

Brian sits and the room breaks into a cacophony of barking. The Taoiseach looks across the room without making eye contact with any person. He thinks, *Oh shit, oh shit, oh shit.* Then he opens his mouth and the room goes silent.

'Yes, 'Cocaine', Eric Clapton. Good song.'

An incredulous Brian O'Brien stands up. 'No, sir, Taoiseach, you seem to have missed the point.'

The Taoiseach nods and thinks, *What would Bill Clinton say?* Then quickly he stands. 'I never inhaled it,' he says, and sits back down.

The journalists are stunned. Brian O'Brien has sat down and a colleague quietly says to him, 'I can't believe we so fervently supported his campaign. What were we thinking?'

The aide nervously intervenes. 'That's all for today. Thank you.' Quickly, he scuttles the Taoiseach out of the room, which is as still as a morgue.

Once through the door, the Taoiseach turns to the aide. 'I was brilliant today. I worked that room; I had them eating out of my hand.'

The aide is unsure what to say. He knows that what happened was a disaster, that the Taoiseach is a disaster, and that he, his aide, is constantly having to save this man's bacon.

He smiles at the Taoiseach and says, 'Yes, sir.'

CHAPTER 34

Mooney is painting her nails. She likes to change the colours, but the changes are sometimes subtle. She generally favours red, pink and lilac, but has several shades of each. What would Henry Ford think? He was famous for painting every car black, and now there are several different shades of red nail polish.

Lawrence is in the corner, perplexed, under strain, uncomfortable and still suffering from tremors. Big Mac is in his own world and doesn't realise that every move of his pen, every drum roll, is being copied by Noddy.

Big Mac puts the pen down, sits back in his chair and announces to the room, 'I'm starving. I could eat a horse.'

Immediately, Lawrence springs to his feet, hurtles over to Big Mac and pulls out his gun. 'Leave the horse alone. Horses are our friends.'

Obviously, Big Mac isn't ecstatic to have a loaded gun pointed at his face from only a few feet away, but he doesn't seem overly concerned. 'Chill, Lawrence, relax. It's only a figure of speech to describe my hunger. I wouldn't eat a horse,' he says.

Lawrence looks twitchy and is staring Big Mac down. 'Yes,

you would, I know you would,' he says. 'You've eaten a lot of things in your time and I believe you would eat a horse.'

Big Mac tries to calm the situation. 'C'mon now, I'm your friend, your colleague, I'm on your side. Lower the gun.'

Boss has heard the commotion and he swiftly enters the room and shouts out, 'Shoot him, Lawrence, shoot him.'

Mooney continues to paint her nails. Without looking up from her artwork, she calmly interjects, 'Don't do it, Lawrence, don't do it.'

Boss is animated, like a Munster fan with only minutes to go in the game and a five-metre scrum underway. He passionately urges, 'Do it, Lawrence, you chicken, do it.'

Mooney pauses her painting and looks up at Boss. 'Why should he?' she asks.

Excitedly, Boss explains: 'If Big Mac is dead and Lawrence is in jail, there won't be a team to lead. HQ will have to find me another job. I don't really want to be here, Miss Mooney. Do you actually think I enjoy working with you morons?' He turns back to Lawrence and screams, 'Shoot him!'

While this has been going on, Noddy has been watching as if this is an episode of *Sesame Street*. He isn't expecting what happens next, though.

Lawrence turns to him, keeping the gun trained on Big Mac, and says, 'Noddy, what should I do? I know I can trust you. Help me, man.'

Noddy raises a hand and starts to tap his chin as he thinks. He utters a series of ums.

Big Mac says, 'C'mon, Noddy, c'mon. You owe me – get me out of this.'

Mooney offers advice: 'Noddy, do the right thing.'

Noddy continues to tap his chin and um.

Lawrence pleads with his colleague. 'Noddy, please, what should I do?'

Noddy lowers his hand and folds his arms and turns to Habitaz. 'Señor Habitaz, what should I do?'

Habitaz, who has been sitting quietly to this point with the astonishment of a ten-year-old watching a magician perform impossible tricks, offers his perspective. 'This is great fun, so exciting, dramatic. I would toss coin. Head he dies, tail he dies.'

Now Big Mac starts to panic. 'No, no, no, you got it wrong, you fool,' he tells Habitaz. 'I die both ways.'

Habitaz considers this for a few moments and says, 'My mistake. Head he lives, tail he dies.'

Noddy nods. 'That sounds like a good idea, Habitaz.'

Big Mac is incredulous. 'Noddy, you eejit, I'll kill you!'

Deadpan, Noddy advises, 'Hard to achieve that if you're dead.'

Worried that the moment will pass without a death, Boss cries out, 'Just shoot him!'

Big Mac thinks his time is up and starts to pray. 'Please God, Mary, Joseph, Jesus and anyone else who is listening, help!'

Lawrence has made his mind up. 'Okay, we'll toss for it. Spanish guy, you toss,' he orders.

'Mexican,' says Noddy.

Lawrence looks confused. 'He's Mexican?'

'Yip,' says Noddy.

Lawrence ever so slightly lowers the gun as he asks all his colleagues, 'Where's the Spanish guy gone?'

Habitaz points at himself with both hands and with the happiest of manic smiles announces, 'I'm here.'

Lawrence walks to the nearest chair and sits on it, without taking his gaze off Big Mac and keeping the gun trained on his general mass. 'This is so confusing – Spanish, Mexican.'

'Shoot him!' shouts Boss.

Big Mac has taken to his knees. 'Please, Lawrence, please, man. We've worked so many cases together.'

Boss shouts out, 'Toss.'

Habitaz obliges his new superior, and all eyes follow the coin as it rises and then falls through the air, constantly rotating. Habitaz catches it with his left palm and then slaps it onto the back of his right hand.

'It is head. He lives,' is the verdict.

Noddy cheers. Lawrence nods and places his gun back in its holster. Mooney goes back to polishing her nails. Big Mac looks to the heavens and mouths a thank you. Boss says, 'Shit,' and returns to his office, slamming the door behind him.

Big Mac gets to his feet and licks his lips. 'That was close. I'm parched. I need a drink.'

Habitaz nods in agreement and says to Big Mac in his best broken English, 'Me also. In English, how you say I like a cup of tea?'

With a smirk on his face, Big Mac offers his advice. 'Oh! Um, you say, "I would like to see your boobs."'

Habitaz motions as if he has had a eureka-moment having been taught this helpful phrase. 'Thank you,' he says. 'By the way, you need not to worry. The coin is double-head. You couldn't lose.'

'Thanks for that. I owe you,' says Big Mac.

Mooney has twisted the lid onto her polish bottle, painting task complete. She steps in the direction of the kettle and asks, 'Would anybody like a drink?'

'Me,' says Habitaz.

'What would you like?' she asks.

With a big smile, Habitaz makes his request: 'I would like to see your boobs.'

An angry Mooney turns to him and says, 'What?'

Habitaz recognises she is upset about something and it takes him a few moments to realise what. He faces her and in his best, but slow, English says, 'Sorry, how rude. I would like to see your boobs, two sugars, please.'

Mooney expertly delivers an uppercut just behind his chin, which sends him to the floor.

'Oops,' says Big Mac.

CHAPTER 35

With a hint of guilt, but mostly grace, Big Mac knows it's only right that he introduce his new Spanish colleague to the local Accident and Emergency department. For the craic, Big Mac takes him by blue light in an unmarked police car.

The car is an ordinary-looking Nissan, but under the bonnet the engine is huge, with more horsepower than Charlton Heston's chariot could ever muster. That enables going nought to sixty in about 5.5 seconds and a top speed of one hundred and sixty miles per hour, meaning when they need to give chase, they usually catch their target. Only those on high-powered motorcycles with cross-country aptitude could escape, as was the case recently when Big Mac and Noddy accidentally happened upon a gang making away from a jewellery store. The motorcyclists took to footpaths and narrow lanes, making it difficult for the cops, but using reverse and a sound knowledge of the streets, they overcame these urban obstacles. However, the thieves managed to abscond by taking to the fields. The powerful Nissan was neutralised there. Hares don't fear the great white shark – why would they? – and in the grassland and woodland of Ireland, this is just what the high-powered vehicles have become.

Once at A&E, IDs are flashed, so triage doesn't apply and Habitaz is immediately taken care of. Looking in the mirror as the A&E sister expertly straightens his nose, he thinks it is strange to see two huge balls of cotton wool sticking out of his nostrils. The balls are eventually removed and they have stemmed the flow of blood. The cut to the bridge is taped.

The nurse steps away from him and places all the waste in different coloured bins – some in general waste, some in sharps and others in bodily fluids. Then she returns to Habitaz and, admiring her handiwork, says, 'There you go, sir, good as new.'

Speaking slowly and with a higher pitch, given the nasal assault, the Spanish policeman thanks her.

Big Mac has been watching and making positive comments to the nurse since they stepped into the cubicle. He obviously fancies her. He steps towards her. 'Yeah, thanks. It's tough out there being an Extra-Special Special Branch cop and all that.'

'You guys are so brave,' she responds.

Habitaz replies, 'We do our best.'

The nurse is obviously attracted to Big Mac. It might be Big Mac's lucky day: she likes her men big, and her favourite mammals are whales. Big Mac is the most whale-like animal with legs she will ever meet.

Sensing that she has some sort of interest, Big Mac tries to impress her while testing the water. 'Can you take a compliment?'

'Sí,' says Habitaz.

'Not you, Iglesias, the nurse here,' clarifies Big Mac.

'Yes, I can,' she says.

He moves his large mass towards her and, looking her straight in the eye, says, 'Well, I'd just like to say that my job is made so much easier by the knowledge that if some unfortunate incident should happen to me, I'd have someone like you to look after me.'

The nurse reacts shyly, breaking eye contact and fiddling with her fingers, but then she raises her gaze and repays the compliment. 'You know, you're really fat, but you have a great personality.'

Big Mac knows he is in with a shot here, and with one hand on his hip and the other brushing through his hair, he smiles and gives her, 'Yeah, you know, nurse, if I had a burger for every time someone said that to me, I'd be ten times this size.'

They laugh manically for the best part of twenty seconds. This nurse is Joan, Joan O'Rourke, the woman Big Mac is dating and serious about; they're pretending to be strangers as a role play.

Then Big Mac takes her hand in his. 'I guess what I'm trying to say is that I love you, and also that I've never been with a nurse before and I just wonder what it might be like.'

A few moments pass and then she responds, 'I think I love you too. I know where we could go for a little lie-down, but let me just finish off what I have to do for Mr Habitaz.' She turns her attention to the Iberian cop. 'Señor Habitaz, would you like a drink?'

He thinks and then accepts the offer. 'Yes, please.'

'What would you like?' asks Joan.

Habitaz places the order carefully and slowly. 'I would like to see your boobs.'

'What?' Joan says, thinking, *He can't have said that.* I must have misheard him.

Habitaz obligingly clarifies for her. 'How rude, I'm sorry. I'd like to see your boobs, two sugars, please.'

A furious Joan lashes out with a right hook to the nose, knocking the unassuming cop from the stool to the floor.

As she leads Big Mac out of the room by the hand, Big Mac looks down at his re-bloodied colleague. 'Maybe you should try asking for coffee instead of tea? See you in a while, Rudolf.'

CHAPTER 36

Lawrence is walking through the streets of Limerick. He is quite paranoid and is using all the skills he has been taught to try to uncover whether he is indeed being followed. He has Noddy with him and Noddy is copying every single action and facial expression Lawrence makes. Lawrence takes no notice, as his attention is elsewhere.

They arrive at the toilet in the park off Perry Square. Lawrence turns to Noddy. 'You wait outside. If anybody tries to come in, stall them and whistle to warn me.'

Noddy nods.

Lawrence enters the toilet and on this occasion he doesn't barricade the door shut. Before he reaches the cupboard, a greeting is bestowed on him.

'I recognise that smell. Welcome, my old friend, Larry.'

Lawrence opens the cupboard and the bottom, Tom, is there with a big smirk on his face.

Lawrence is serious. 'Look, bad breath, we aren't friends, and I'd like to know who's been telling you I've got schizophrenia, cos it's not true. I'm having a psychotic episode and I'm bipolar. There's a difference.'

'Touchy, aren't we?' says Tom.

'Perhaps, but I won't be touching you,' replies Lawrence.

'Touché,' laughs the arse. 'I haven't been gossiping about you, Larry. I did hear you are a schizo though. I hear everything, which is why I'm of use to you.'

'I need to know where all this cocaine is coming from and who's distributing it,' Lawrence says.

'C'mon, Larry. You know this. It's coming from Columbia.'

Larry starts to pace about in front of the arse. His eyes are drawn to the flooded urinal. There are pieces of plastic floating in it. 'Interesting,' he says and returns his gaze to Tom. 'And who's behind it?'

Outside the toilet, Noddy is keeping guard, marching up and down like a Buckingham Palace soldier on parade, except he doesn't have the big bear hat or, indeed, the rifle. He cuts short his next journey to the end of the building as someone is approaching. Noddy quickly moves in front of the man, a large construction worker, blocking him from passing about five metres from the door.

The man tries to get around Noddy. Noddy keeps blocking his way. Eventually, the bloke gets past, so Noddy grabs his hat and throws it away. The man turns and puts his hat on and continues to try to get past Noddy.

This continues for a few minutes, and then the man gives up. 'Fine, I'll deposit it somewhere else,' he says and swiftly departs.

Noddy returns to his marching and starts to drift, thinking

about what it must be like to be a Beefeater working at the Tower of London, and wondering whether you could work there if you were a vegetarian. He is so lost in thought that he completely misses the new chap approaching the toilet until he's just about to enter.

Noddy is too far away to block him, so he shouts out, 'I wouldn't go in there if I were you.'

The guy, small and in his late fifties, gives Noddy an over-the-shoulder look. 'Why not?' he asks.

Noddy hadn't thought that far ahead. He ums and ahs for a minute and then comes up with what he thinks is the most brilliant ruse ever. 'Um, someone died in there last week.'

This doesn't have the desired impact. The older guy shrills with excitement, 'Really? How exciting!'

Noddy orders him not to go in, but the man merely shrugs his shoulders and grips the door handle. Looking over his shoulder again, he says in a seductive tone, 'When you've got to go, you've got to go.'

Noddy tries to whistle, but fails. Quick as a flash (most unusual for Noddy) he shouts, 'Sir, wait! Could you do one thing for me before you go?'

'Certainly, good-looking,' is the response.

'Could you whistle?'

The man blows the loudest wolf-whistle that Noddy has ever heard.

Inside, Lawrence is alerted and closes the cupboard. As he turns around, the man enters the toilet. When he sees Lawrence, the man starts to exaggerate his walk as if modelling on a catwalk.

'Have you been missing me, big boy?' he asks.

Lawrence is so unwell he misses the nuances of everyday communication. This guy is very blatant, but Lawrence just isn't at the races.

'Sorry, I don't know you,' Lawrence replies in a genuine manner.

'Would you like to get to know me?' enquires the older chap.

Lawrence answers honestly again, with a no.

'Do you come here often?' asks the man.

'Now and again,' says Lawrence. He has no idea this is an attempted pick-up, mostly because being gay isn't an issue for Lawrence and most men don't feel they have to hide away in lavatories like they may have done on the '70s and '80s scene.

'First time, is it?' says the man.

'No, I've been here before,' Lawrence replies.

The man notices a huge bulge in Lawrence's trousers and of course can't not comment. 'Is that a banana in your pocket or are you just pleased to see me?'

Lawrence still hasn't twigged that the chap is coming on to him. He puts his hand into his pocket and pulls out his revolver. 'No, it's just my gun.'

The man is affronted. With a look of disgust, he tosses his scarf around his neck and turns to walk away, saying, 'I'm not into that weird masochistic stuff, you perv.'

Lawrence is delighted as he wants to get back to work.

The chap closes the door on departure, and Lawrence quickly turns to the cupboard and opens it. The bottom is still there.

'I'm not completely sure about this,' says Tom, 'but I believe the trail of coke will take you directly to the corridors of power.'

Lawrence is bemused; he has no idea what Tom is on about. 'How do I get there?' he asks, and he slowly steps backwards until his hands are on the washbasin, a dejected look on his face.

'Follow the white lines,' is Tom's advice.

CHAPTER 37

Back at the hospital, Mooney is talking to a doctor. Noises are audible in the background: objects crashing and falling, and the grunting and groaning of Big Mac and Joan having sex. He is repeatedly saying, 'Oh yes.' She is repeatedly saying, 'Oh no.'

Mooney is conversing with the consultant. 'So you're a consultant?'

'That's correct,' he says.

'So you've got a lot of experience in the profession.'

'That's correct.'

'I'm Special,' Mooney announces. The doctor is slightly taken aback, so she quickly follows up with, 'I mean I'm Extra-Special Special Branch.'

He gives a small laugh of relief. 'That's admirable, keeping the streets safe.'

'I'm hoping you can help me keep the streets safe,' she counters.

'I'd be glad to,' he says.

She explains, 'We're trying to prevent cocaine from coming into the country, but we don't know what we're dealing with.'

The doctor nods his head. ‘Well, it’s a white powder, like this.’ He takes a see-through plastic bag out of his pocket, tips some powder onto the counter and uses a credit card to expertly cut it into lines. ‘It costs about sixty pounds for this amount and people usually take it like this…’ He snorts it.

‘Is that cocaine?’ she asks.

‘Yes,’ is his response.

Mooney is deep in thought. ‘And they normally take it like this?’ She hoovers up three of the biggest lines.

The doctor nods and in a very serious lecturing mode states, ‘That’s correct. It gives people a high; they become elated and happy. Though they can be aggressive as well. It’s also very addictive.’ He snorts a couple of lines.

‘Thank you for your time, Doctor,’ Mooney shouts, without realising she’s shouting. ‘I’ve got to go now. Got some scum vermin drug importers to bust.’

The doctor gives her a thumbs-up with both thumbs. ‘And I must do some operations.’

He turns, but before he can leave she shouts, ‘Who did you get this off?’

‘A guy called Ratty,’ he reports. He sniffles and wipes the end of his nostrils with his hand and departs.

Habitaz has witnessed all of this whilst waiting for Big Mac and his new lady to stop announcing their love to the world. He is sitting on a chair, not focusing on anyone in particular. A six-year-old boy is staring at him; the mother is oblivious to this. Habitaz makes eyes contact and says, *‘Sí.’*

The kid retorts, 'Saw.'

Habitaz: *'Sí.'*

The kid: 'Saw.'

Habitaz: *'Sí.'*

The kid: 'Saw.'

• • •

Big Mac and Joan have finished. 'I love you,' he tells her.

'I love you,' she gushes.

Big Mac is buttoning his tent-sized shirt. 'I've got to go, my petal. It's been lovely knowing you, but it would never have worked out.'

'At least I have this moment to remember you by,' she responds.

'Better to have loved and lost than never to have loved at all,' he offers.

Joan straightens and in a more serious manner says, 'It's just dawned on me, I don't even know your name.'

'It's Big Mac, Joan.'

'Big Mac Joan,' she repeats with a cheeky grin on her face.

He strokes her chin and smiles a little. 'No, just Big Mac, silly.'

'Just Big Mac Silly is a different kind of name,' she says.

'I'm a different kind of guy,' he says.

They reappear in the main corridor holding hands and receive a round of applause from everyone in the vicinity. They kiss and then slowly break apart, holding hands until the very last moment and then they separate.

Joan whispers in Big Mac's ear, 'See you later. This was great craic.'

Habitaz doesn't know about Joan, so he smiles and says to Mooney, 'True love. Make me feel like singing.'

An angry Mooney corrects him: 'Love, love? We haven't got time for love – we've got rats to catch.'

Big Mac catches the end of this and says mildly, 'What's got into you?'

'Not you, fat boy,' is her loud and angry response.

Smiling, Habitaz tells Big Mac, 'I stink she lobs you.'

Big Mac doesn't know what Habitaz has just said, but they haven't got time to discuss it, as Mooney has squared up to some visitors.

'What are you looking at? You want some? C'mon, give me your best shot.'

Habitaz and Big Mac intervene, restraining her and moving her out of the building as she protests, 'Let me go, let me go!'

• • •

Lawrence and Noddy are on a street corner. Lawrence is pacing, talking to himself, trying to work things out. Noddy is standing still, very still, completely still, so much so that some passers-by stop to watch as they think he is a statue street entertainer.

After pacing for the best part of ten minutes, Lawrence

approaches Noddy. Noddy reacts and the crowd disperses.

'There was a clue, he gave me a clue. C'mon, Lawrence, get with it,' he says as he scratches his head.

Noddy starts to move with him, copying Lawrence's pacing and querying, 'What was it?'

'Something about following the trail of coke, the white lines,' Lawrence explains. He continues with the pacing, walking in broad circles.

Noddy stops. He is deep in thought, staring out at the road. He tilts his head until it's horizontal and looks at the road from that angle. Then he turns his head in the other direction and looks at the road from that angle. He puts his finger to his lips, as he has seen many people do when they think. Then he raises his hand as if he is a child in a primary school class.

'Yes, Noddy,' says Lawrence.

Noddy lowers his hand, but instead of bringing it down to his side, he extends it in front of him and points at the road. 'Like those white lines over there,' he says, pointing to the painted white lines that councils all over the world put on their streets to separate the left side from the right.

Lawrence walks out into the middle of the road and examines three or four lines. Then he returns to the footpath, walks straight up to Noddy, takes Noddy's head in his hands, gives him a kiss on the forehead and says, 'Good work, Noddy. You're a genius.'

Noddy is made up. With a huge smile on his face, he thinks, *Genie ass*.

• • •

Habitaz and Big Mac are still struggling with Mooney and are tied up on the ground with her in some sort of messed-up restraint manoeuvre.

'I've never seen her like this before,' says Big Mac.

'Or me,' says Habitaz.

With an astonished look on his face, Big Mac says, 'Of course you haven't. You've only just met her.'

With a eureka-moment look on his face, Habitaz says, 'You are right, friend.'

They continue to struggle with Mooney. People around pay no attention, as if this kind of situation just happens all the time.

'How will we calm her down?' asks Big Mac.

'In movies, sometimes they tickle lady.'

The look on Big Mac's face makes it clear he has discounted this, but as they continue to struggle with Mooney, he shrugs his shoulders and gives her a little tickle. It fails to make an impact, so he tries again with more force.

Mooney gives a very exaggerated laugh and follows it up with, 'Ha-ha! I can't stop laughing, you morons.' Then she struggles even more.

Big Mac stops. 'It's no good. We need to think of another idea.'

'Let me try,' says Habitaz, and he proceeds to tickle Mooney in the most exaggerated way, barely touching her, almost an air tickle. 'You are right, tickling her not work.

Maybe I sing to her?'

'It's worth a try,' says Big Mac as he continues to struggle on the ground with his colleague.

Habitaz stands up and very theatrically, as if there were a huge audience, proceeds to sing the song, 'How Much Is That Doggy In The Window'.

He is about to stop when Big Mac offers some encouragement. 'Don't stop, it's working – keep singing.'

Apologetically, Habitaz informs his international colleague, 'That is all I know.'

'Do you know any other songs?' wheezes the sweaty cop.

Habitaz thinks for a second and then, with huge delight, says, 'Yes, I know one other.'

'Sing it, for fuck's sake, sing it!' shouts Big Mac as Mooney starts to struggle harder.

Habitaz again breaks into song, this time a Madonna number, 'Dress You Up'. He has all the moves and again it appears to be having the desired impact.

CHAPTER 38

Noddy and Lawrence have been driving for a couple of hours. Noddy has his head slightly outside the window and is enjoying the feel of the breeze, as some pet dogs do. Lawrence is energised: he feels more positive, he thinks he knows where the trail is leading, he thinks this will be his moment and that he will be able to win Eileen back. This is the most excited he has been in years.

It is clear from the buildings around, including Heuston train station, that they are no longer in Limerick; they are in Dublin. They are driving alongside the quay next to the River Liffey.

Noddy says, 'It's turned out to be a long trail. Where do you think it will take us?'

'I know exactly where,' Lawrence replies. 'It's taking us to the Taoiseach.' He points out the window. 'Look, there is Leinster House, the House of Parliament up ahead.'

'What goes on in there?' asks Noddy.

'That's where the ministers and the elected politicians run the country from.'

Noddy nods, as usual.

(At that moment inside the big house there are indeed many elected officials, some in robes, the rest in suits. They appear to be engaged in a game of chase, with calls of, 'You're it!' and the occasional, 'No, I'm not, you are – you didn't tag me properly.')

Lawrence is reaching Everest levels of excitement. He will explode. He is going to catch the Taoiseach and win back his missus.

And then, as if he has misplaced his footing and slipped from the peak, unbelievable levels of dejection, confusion and disappointment descend. He quickly pulls the car to the side of the road just past the Parliament building.

'Fuck, fuck, fuck!' he yells.

A calm Noddy interjects, 'That's a kind offer, but I'm asexual.'

Lawrence isn't listening. In despair, he says, 'Shit, Noddy, I won't get Eileen back. I thought the trail was leading us to the House of Parliament and the Taoiseach, but I was wrong. The lines go past – look.'

They sit there in silence for a few minutes with the engine running.

'"Follow the white lines" is what you said, so let's keep following them,' suggests Noddy.

Lawrence nods, sighs and, with little energy, puts the car into gear and heads back into the traffic.

They continue driving. They leave Dublin and are on a country road when they reach a crossroads.

Lawrence stops the car. 'What should we do now?'

Noddy starts to blow hard, as he is in deep concentration and must make a big effort, just like a refrigerator when you leave the door open for a minute or so.

'I don't know,' he says, and then he motions. 'You could go left or right, or you could go left or right, or you could go left or right, or you could go left or right.'

'I suppose that sums up all the choices open to us,' says Lawrence. 'Let's go right, as it's more of a major road.'

Noddy stops blowing and adds, 'And the white lines are bigger.'

They drive and they drive and they drive. Noddy looks straight through the windscreen and nods as he follows each line before it is eaten up by the car, then passes underneath and out behind, like the car is a line-making machine. Every time Noddy sees a new line, he alerts Lawrence:

'There's one, there's another one, there's one, there's another one, there's one, there's another one…'

They encounter a sign that says 'Welcome to Longford'. They pass a sign that says 'Welcome to Northern Ireland'. Then after a while they end up walking on the Giant's Causeway.

'Sorry, I made an error – I thought I saw a white line. Woops,' says Noddy.

They are back driving again. They pass 'Welcome to Tyrone' and enter a town. Two men and a woman are standing on a street corner engaged in conversation.

'Let's ask these people where we are,' says Lawrence.

He pulls up alongside and winds down his window. The two men are arguing.

'Apples are best,' says the tall guy.

'Nope, oranges are it,' says the short guy.

'Apples are more popular,' says the tall guy.

'Oranges are juicier,' retorts the small guy.

'The big Apple, iPhones, stupid,' says the tall fellow.

'The future is Orange, stupid,' responds the small fellow.

The lady steps away from them both and acknowledges Lawrence and Noddy. 'I think these guys are bananas,' she says.

The cops don't engage with her – Lawrence just rolls up the window and drives off.

Next up is a 'Welcome to Mayo' sign. They are driving slowly as they enter a small town. It's a quiet place, and unusual: every car apart from their own is driving in reverse. They see a couple of old men talking. Then they notice other people, and oddly they are all walking backwards. A couple of cars and a tractor reverse past.

'Bit of a strange place,' says Lawrence.

'I wouldn't mind moving here,' says Noddy.

They call over a local man, who approaches them, backwards.

'Hello,' says Noddy.

'Busy day,' says the man – a mechanic, based on his overalls.

Lawrence wonders if he has missed something or if his mind is playing up. He looks up and down the street. No, it really is dead.

'We're looking for cocaine,' says Noddy.

'Never heard of him,' says the mechanic. 'Wait a minute, though. Bert there, across the street, knows most things. He's been here for ninety years. Let's ask him.'

Noddy nods, and the mechanic motions for Bert to cross the street. Bert is a bit deaf, so everything has to be repeated loudly, and he himself is a shouter.

The mechanic explains, 'They're looking for cocaine.'

'They'll have to look elsewhere,' shouts Bert. 'Not around here, no. I've been here a long time and I know all the Kanes – Tom, Mike, Sean, Mary, Biddy – and there's no one called Co.' With that he walks away, backwards, followed by the mechanic, who waves goodbye.

Lawrence and Noddy look at each other, acknowledging that things are a bit bizarre. Lawrence looks at the ground and scratches his head, deep in thought. He thinks, *The arse wouldn't lie to me, no, he wouldn't lie. We might argue, we might occasionally dislike each other, but Tom wouldn't lie.*

He turns to Noddy, 'We must do what we were doing and keep following the white lines.'

As they leave the town, they see a sign: 'Welcome to Ballygobackwards'. *How appropriate*, thinks Lawrence, *that we are welcomed as we leave.*

CHAPTER 39

Habitaz, Mooney and Big Mac are seated in the café that Big Mac and Noddy frequent. Mooney has calmed. All appears well between them.

'You aren't so bad after all, Habitaz, even for a Bolivian.'

'Sí,' says Habitaz.

'I don't know what came over me,' Mooney says. 'It must have been the cocaine the doctor gave me.'

Big Mac laughs. 'You naughty girl. I didn't know you had it in you.'

Habitaz, on the other hand, has a very serious look on his face. He wags his finger at her as he says, 'Let that be lesson. Drugs are evil.'

'Quite right,' says Big Mac as he picks up a laminated menu.

'I'll never do anything as unsafe as that again,' Mooney says.

'Some tin bad might happen,' Habitaz tells her, and she nods sincerely.

They look at the menus, and Mooney is the first to order. 'Gosh, I'm so thirsty! Habitaz, would you get me a glass of orange juice?'

Big Mac puts his menu down and declares, 'Yip, me too.'

Habitaz puts his hand up and motions for the waitress to join them. In his best (but of course heavily accented) English, he says, 'Can I have two glasses of orange for my friends, please.'

The waitress writes this down while asking if he would like something. Habitaz pauses, and then he says with a huge smile on his face, 'I don't want to see your boobs. Coffee, please.'

The waitress takes the order, pauses, looks at Habitaz, looks at him more closely and then walks back to the counter, shaking her head and saying to herself in a low voice, 'Very strange, these Cubans.'

At that moment the 'La Bamba' tune on the radio ends and a DJ from Limerick Radio announces: 'And just in, news that a doctor at our regional hospital has been arrested after going apeshit. He's alleged to have amputated the wrong leg on at least half a dozen patients. He said he did it for a laugh. It's believed he was under the influence of drugs. The patients are hopping mad. And our next track is by Elton John, 'I'm Still Standing'…'

• • •

Noddy and Lawrence stop the car and get out. There is a lighthouse in the distance.

Lawrence looks frustrated. 'Fuck!' he shouts. 'The lines

end here. It's a dead end, a fucking wild goose chase.'

Slowly, slowly, slowly, without a care in the world, a very lazy gander waddles by. Lawrence looks down at him. The gander is smoking a cigar. He stops a few feet away, takes the cigar out of his mouth and looks up at Lawrence.

'Hello, Larry. It's not a dead end – the arse wouldn't lie to you. Head to the lighthouse.'

Lawrence is stunned. He turns to Noddy. 'Did you hear that?'

'Hear what?' says Noddy.

Lawrence explains, 'The goose spoke to me; he said to head to the lighthouse.'

Noddy's eyes light up. 'A talking goose? Could be the golden goose in disguise. Maybe we should catch it. I might get to marry the princess, or if we sold it, it would be worth a lot.'

Lawrence shrugs his shoulders. 'Whatever.'

They chase after the goose. He nips Noddy a few times, but they eventually catch the goose, and Noddy holds him over his head like some prize whilst dancing a celebratory jig. He brings the goose down and turns him around and they stare at each other, face to face.

'Say something,' Noddy implores, 'come on now, say something.'

The goose squawks and hisses.

Lawrence, who has been staring at the lighthouse, walks over to Noddy and the goose. 'Why are you telling us to go to the lighthouse?' he asks.

'You're just going to have to trust me, Larry,' says the goose.

'I don't know you,' says Lawrence.

'But you trust the arse?'

'Okay, Noddy, let's do this lighthouse. Put the goose in the car.'

Noddy tries to put the goose in the boot of the car, but the goose resists and hisses wildly, which scares Noddy.

The goose shouts to Lawrence, 'C'mon, man, quid pro quo. Where's the trust?'

'Fair enough,' says Lawrence. 'Noddy, stick the gander in the back seat.'

Noddy complies, and so does the goose.

• • •

Mooney has half of her orange juice left. Habitaz delicately empties the last drop of coffee into his mouth. Big Mac demolished his juice in one go ten minutes earlier, and has since been directing the remaining orange bits to the top of his glass before scooping them into his vacuum-cleaner mouth.

'So what do we do next?' asks Mooney.

Habitaz says something incomprehensible in Spanish, but then shrugs his shoulders, which they interpret as I don't know.

Big Mac contributes: 'I don't have any leads.'

Mooney takes a neat sip of her juice and states, 'The doctor at the hospital said he got his stash from a guy called Ratty.'

Big Mac puts his glass down, delivers the latest instalment of orange bits to his mouth and then raises his finger as if celebrating his status as the number one. 'That rings a bell.' He pretends to ring a bell and then nods at the waitress. 'Hilda, darling, there's a guy who comes in here, huge nose.'

'Ratty,' she says.

'Where does he work?' he asks.

'He works around the corner in a store,' she says, pointing to the right of the room and directly at three ladies in their sixties who look much, much older – life is tough for some – and are knitting an assortment of items in red.

CHAPTER 40

Lawrence and Noddy are walking briskly towards the lighthouse.

'You break the door down and I'll do the shouting, I mean the talking,' directs Lawrence.

'What will I break it down with?' queries Noddy.

'I haven't got time for this, Noddy. Think of something.' Tapping his temple, Lawrence adds, 'Just use your head.'

Lawrence hangs back as Noddy strides towards the front door.

• • •

Inside the lighthouse is an older male photographer and a young female model. The usual stereotypes apply: the man is portly with a thinning hairline, and the model, glamorous, young and naive. They are doing a photoshoot, all alone, and aren't expecting company. The man is walking about, slightly hunched over to hide his erection, which, if everything goes to plan, he will hide inside his muse.

'Good, you have the mermaid costume on. Now we'll do a few shots of you with that on, and then we can do a couple of topless shots down by the waterfront,' he says as he discretely pushes his erection to the side, licks his lips and tucks some of the few remaining long hairs on his head behind his ear.

'Okay, you know I'd really love to be an Instagram influencer,' she says.

'Stick with me and I'll sort you out,' he says, and thinks, *Yeah, I'll sort you out alright.*

Just then, as they start to take photos, the door is smashed through, with Noddy leading the way head first.

The model screams, and the photographer drops his camera, as well as his erection, and involuntarily gasps, 'Oh my God!'

Lawrence marches in and shouts, 'Everybody freeze! Special Branch.'

Noddy stands over the model. 'I like fish,' he says.

The model says nothing.

Lawrence walks up to the photographer, grabs hold of him and pushes him away. 'Where's the coke, you pap?'

The photographer has no idea what is going on, but he doesn't want to delay and keep the intruders any longer than is necessary. He points to the table. 'Over there. Take it all – just leave us alone, please.'

Lawrence walks to the table and sees two bottles of Coca-Cola, one half-empty and one with the seal intact. He turns to the photographer. 'Not this, the powder. Where is it?' he demands.

With complete sincerity and much anxiety, the photographer responds, 'I don't have any on me. I don't take it when

I'm on the job. I've got a few lines back at my flat, though.'

Lawrence looks lost and confused. He is thinking, *Why would the arse lie to me?*

Noddy nods and walks over to Lawrence. 'The only powder here is this brown stuff.' He snorts it, sneezes and then coughs. 'Makeup – blusher, to be precise. L'Oréal, I think.'

• • •

Around the corner from the café, the gang have entered a pawn shop. Big Mac is inspecting a George Foreman grill and Habitaz is waving his red napkin from the café at a life-size bull's head, making very grand matador movements. Habitaz and Mooney approach the counter.

Mooney leads with, 'Excuse me, sir, are you Ratty?'

'Maybe. What's it to you?' is the retort.

Quick as a flash, Habitaz exclaims with great excitement, 'Oh my God, you have big nose!'

Insulted, Ratty points at the door and orders them to get out.

Habitaz is back in matador mode. Waving his red napkin at Ratty, he chants, *'Toro, toro, toro.'*

Big Mac breaks away from the grills and walks towards the commotion. 'Remember me?'

Ratty recognises him. 'You again! I'll sue you. You're prejudiced against me cos of my nose. I'll take you to court. I'll take you to the European Court of Justice. This is just the ridiculously stupid kind of case they would take on.'

(Somewhere in Strasbourg are two men dressed in legal regalia.

One says, 'Will we take on this case?'

The other advises, 'Definitely. This is exactly the ridiculously stupid kind of case that we love here at the European Court of Justice.')

Back in the pawn shop, the conversation continues.

'If I were you,' Big Mac says threateningly, 'I would be more concerned about staying out of jail.'

'What do you mean?' Ratty asks innocently.

'Dealing drugs,' says Mooney.

'Prove it,' says Ratty.

Big Mac huffs. 'Look, we've got evidence against you. If you cooperate, we'll cut you some slack. Otherwise, you'll be in the lock-up, and you'll be very, very popular there, dildo face.'

Mooney straightens up and changes her manner. 'Oh, I see you in a whole different way now. By any chance do you have a brother?'

Habitaz starts laughing uncontrollably. 'Mooney, you are sooo funny. Everyone has a mother.'

Ratty relaxes. He has weighed up his options; he has understood the big man's words.

• • •

Lawrence and Noddy are driving again. Lawrence is in the driver's seat, but he orders Noddy to take the wheel. He roots around in his pocket and takes out a container. He unscrews the top, takes out two small items, puts them in his mouth and swallows them.

Noddy, who has observed all this whilst steering from the passenger seat and not once watching the road, asks, 'Can I have one?'

'No, it's medication. I'm very unwell. I think I just saw a mermaid,' says Lawrence.

'Me too,' says Noddy.

'Alright then,' says Lawrence, and he hands a pill to Noddy, who swallows it.

Noddy then hands the steering wheel back over to Lawrence, who composes himself before saying, 'Let's get back on the trail.'

They drive and drive and drive. Noddy puts his head half outside the window again, enjoying the breeze, and the goose does the same in the back seat.

We can see on the map of Ireland that they are now heading back towards Limerick. They enter the city. Two men on a footpath are circling each other. It appears they are getting ready to fight.

Man 1 says, 'I'll stab you.'

Man 2 says, 'I'll stab you.'

Man 1 says, 'I'll stab you first.'

Man 2 says, 'I'll stab you better.'

Man 1 says, 'I'm much better at stabbing.'

Man 2 says, 'No, I'm the best stabber.'

Man 1 says, 'My father stabbed my mother.'

Man 2 says, 'I stabbed my mother.'

The car pulls up next to the footpath. Lawrence rolls down the window very, very slowly (it is a bit stuck) and says to the pair, 'Excuse me, sirs. We're on the trail of white lines. Have you seen any?'

The men break away from their argument. Man 1 speaks while Man 2 physically highlights the directions. 'Turn right at the end of the road and go down to the end of that road. Turn left and then they're straight ahead of you. You can't miss them – they're on the road.'

Noddy nods, Lawrence very slowly winds up the window and they drive off.

On the map of Ireland we can see that they are making fast progress back towards Dublin. 'Road To Nowhere' by Talking Heads blares from the stereo. The trio in sync are tapping away to the beat, Lawrence the steering wheel with his left hand, Noddy his thigh with his right hand, and the goose, the back of Noddy's seat with his right wing. When it gets to the main chorus, they join the lead singer and all shout out 'Ha! Ha!'.

'Look, there is the House of Parliament again,' Lawrence points out.

'Gosh, the politicians do work hard,' says Noddy.

(Inside Parliament, music is playing and the politicians, all men, are paired off and dancing with each other, cheek to cheek, doing the Argentinian tango.)

• • •

The wheels of the lorry that were going round and round come to a stop in the middle of Dublin. The sides are rolled up to reveal a number of men on the back of the lorry. They have musical instruments. A man with a big smile shouts, 'Right, lads, one, two, three…' and they start to play. It is The Magic Band. They play a type of traditional music, and everyone across the country dances some sort of Riverdance, all in sync with each other.

Then Lawrence drives up to them, rolls down the window and shouts, 'Fuck off, the lot of you.'

'Sure thing, Larry,' says the leader, and just like that they disappear in an instant, like magic.

Lawrence turns to Noddy. 'Majella was right.'

Noddy, who knows nothing about anyone called Majella, says, 'Yes.'

The duo continue to follow the white lines. They reach the edge of Phoenix Park.

'The trail is getting stronger,' says Noddy.

'It is,' says Lawrence.

Noddy points at another car and waves at the occupants. 'Look, it's Mooney, Big Mac and the Mexican.'

They pull over.

'Where have you been?' enquires Mooney.

'We've been on a trail,' says Lawrence. 'It's led us to here.'

'Looks like we're all onto something. I think we're all

looking for the same person.'

They set off on foot and walk about a hundred metres, which takes them to the door of Áras an Uachtaráin, the female president of Ireland's residence.

Lawrence is almost in tears. 'I can't believe it's the president. This is big.'

'Looks like it is,' says Mooney.

Noddy rings the doorbell. The president's husband answers the door and he is covered in cocaine.

Big Mac says, 'Let me guess, you've been baking.'

CHAPTER 41

A few days later, Big Mac, Noddy and Mooney are at Shannon Airport to see off Habitaz. Hugs and kisses all round, though Noddy is concentrating on trying to get the goose to talk. He keeps saying 'Boo' to the goose, something to do with his long-deceased grandmother who used to say that Noddy wouldn't say boo to a goose – *How wrong she was*, thinks Noddy. Lawrence couldn't make it, he is feeling unwell, and Boss couldn't be bothered.

As Habitaz heads through departures, a few people with time on their hands are glued to the television. A news reporter is delivering a report:

'The relationship between the president and her husband, they say, is very strong, though sources close to Mr Mulcahy say he is tired of just being a house husband. It is worth remembering that before he supported his wife in becoming the president, he was a successful senator. Friends of the couple say that we therefore shouldn't read into matters too much, and that it's only normal that he would want to take up another political position and this is why he has agreed to move to South America, where he will take up the role of Irish ambassador to Columbia.'

CHAPTER 42

Lena explains to the class, 'obviously there are other things going on that Lawrence knows nothing about, like with Big Mac.'

Big Mac hasn't been able to forget about Bull. He decides to pay him a visit. He knows this is dangerous. He says nothing to his colleagues and nothing to Joan. Best not to visit this guy at work. Maybe meet him for a coffee – he dismisses this too; Bull isn't that kind of guy. *Grab the bull by the horns*, Big Mac thinks. *A home visit. But not too late or too early. Don't want Bull feeling threatened or cornered.*

He sets off. Bull lives in Meath; that's a big drive. Big Mac parks in front of Bull's house, a bungalow. It's a quiet location, with no neighbours nearby. Only the one car – Bull is alone. Big Mac knocks on the front door.

• • •

Inside, Bull is naked and running a bath. He puts on a robe and walks down the hallway, picking up the Glock on the table and holding it out of view in the pocket of his bathrobe. He checks the window: one car. Looks through a side window: one fat man. He laughs. *I know him.* He opens the door.

'Big Mac, long time.' Bull offers his left hand to Big Mac and he shakes it. However, Big Mac knows Bull is right-handed, so he figures he must have a weapon of some sort in his right hand, hidden in his robe.

They enter the sitting room. Bull is big, strong, fit, a good six foot four inches, a solid eighteen stone, probably too much for Big Mac. Big Mac is fast, also strong, good at martial arts and stands at six foot one inches, but he's grossly overweight, in excess of thirty stone, and has no stamina. That was the analysis Big Mac made when driving up in the car and he concluded that therefore he shouldn't antagonise Bull and should avoid any situation that would lead to physical confrontation. But Big Mac is a direct person and directly it begins.

They both stand in the living room, neither party sitting, even though Bull offers Big Mac a seat.

'To what do I owe the pleasure?' asks Bull.

Big Mac leads with, 'Were you blackmailing Mickey O'Rourke?'

Bull does a quick analysis. Big Mac is unlikely to be carrying recording equipment, and even if he is, Bull could take him if he wanted – he's holding a gun in his pocket. 'What's it got to do with you?' he grunts.

'I'm a friend of his sister, Joan.'

'Banging her, are you?' sneers Bull.

'What if I am?' responds Big Mac with confidence and pride.

'Honouring your dead wife and daughter, I see,' Bull sniggers.

No sooner have the words sunk in than Big Mac has catapulted himself across the room. He catches Bull unawares, meeting him with a head to the nose – which was accidental, as what he was trying to do was get control of the hand holding the weapon. He grabs it, but can't stop Bull firing the gun. The bullet goes nowhere near Big Mac, but the noise from the shot leaves his ears ringing.

Big Mac has an edge, as Bull is still reeling from the broken nose. Big Mac has control of Bull's shooting arm, and he expertly bends it back and twists it, dislocating the shoulder, with a loud snap. The gun goes flying.

This new, sharp pain focuses Bull and he somehow has a lot more energy to expend, whereas Big Mac is nearly done. They grapple with each other, moving across the hall, with Big Mac sustaining a number of kicks to the legs and stomach, but at least ensuring he isn't hit in the head.

Somehow, they end up in the bathroom and Bull tumbles, landing on his back into the bath. Big Mac is on top, and he applies leverage to the dislocated shoulder, shouting, 'Give me a name!'

Bull roars, but that is it: Big Mac begins to rhythmically dunk Bull and hold him under the water. Nothing is forthcoming, then progress of a kind – Bull is trying to talk in between dunks.

'You're working with Barry,' splutters the half-drowned Bull.

'Yes,' shouts Big Mac as he dunks him again.

Bull says something, but Big Mac can't quite make it out.

Bull says it again, but Big Mac still can't make it out. He pulls Bull up a little and hears, 'Rex bought them sails or snails.'

Big Mac dunks him again. 'For fuck's sake, a name.'

But when Bull next comes up for air, he's managed to get his hand on another gun, a Ruger LCR revolver that he had in a holster under the robe, and he gets another shot off. It misses the very wide target, and Big Mac, with a hand on the gun and his ears ringing even more, crashes into the tub on top of Bull.

Big Mac struggles and Bull kicks and splashes. Big Mac gets control of the gun and eventually manages to pull himself out of the bath. By this stage, there hasn't been any movement from Bull for a short while. Big Mac pulls him up from under the water and drags him out of the bath and onto the floor. He starts mouth to mouth and CPR, but after a while recognises it is futile. Bull is dead.

CHAPTER 43

Lawrence is getting a lot from his meetings with Majella. He looks forward to them. They meet again.

'I'm starting to trust some of the hallucinations,' he tells her. 'Especially the arse. We've become close.'

Majella smiles warmly. 'Remember I was saying I was struggling ever so slightly with the whole bum idea – please forgive me,' she says. 'I'd find it helpful if instead of referring to him as the arse, bum, backside, you could give him a name. Can you oblige me?'

Lawrence says, 'Sure. Tom.'

'Okay, thanks,' she replies. 'Why did you choose the name Tom?'

Lawrence starts to smirk and releases a small snigger and a chortle. 'Easy really. Bot-Tom.'

Majella returns the smile. 'As in Tom-ass.'

Lawrence claps and laughs. This is the most relaxed he has been in such a long time. *I like her*, he thinks. *I trust her; she gets it.* In his mind he breathes a sigh of relief.

'There's something else I want you to consider, Lawrence. I've been thinking. You're unwell, you've been very unwell, but you're a highly intelligent man. I checked out your CV after our first session. You scored a perfect eight hundred on the GMAT exam when you applied for your MBA. Only fifteen out of every hundred thousand people who take the GMAT get a perfect score. That's a little more than one person out of every ten thousand.

'I think there's a fight going on in your brilliant mind – a "good angel versus bad one" kind of thing. Yes, you're unwell, but your mind is trying to help you. I don't think that these good hallucinations are giving you clues and advice on cases – how could they? I think the detective in you is finding these answers, deducing them from facts, intel, experience and knowledge. Your brain is trying to help you overcome the major challenge of your illness and is presenting the solutions to you sometimes in the form of hallucinations.'

Lawrence takes this in and draws invisible circles on the glass table. 'Interesting,' he says. 'So the trick in some ways is being able to tell a good, useful hallucination from an unhelpful one, which is hard.'

A minute later he follows up with: 'I want you to think about something else for me, Majella – my memory, my short-term memory. How come I struggle to recall anything much from the eighteen to twenty-four months or so prior to my breakdown, whereas I can remember things from five, ten, twenty years ago as if they just happened yesterday?'

Majella doesn't immediately respond; she waits a few beats. 'I will think about it, Lawrence, I'll give it serious consideration. But as you know, Dr Best is of the opinion that it's a form of early-onset dementia. I'm sorry.'

• • •

Lawrence writes in his diary:

I'm still at the house in Annacotty. No contact from Eileen. She isn't even letting the kids speak with me – she must think I'm dangerous or something. It hurts. Work is stressful. It's complicated. I don't know what is going on. Majella Quinn is helping; I can trust her, I think, and maybe Bot-Tom. I'm struggling. I feel isolated.

There is something going on between the politicians and organised crime; we have proved some of this. Strange things are happening – my mind is very unwell; it might be the medication that is causing it. I'm unsure, though I saw a mermaid for fuck's sake, and a goose spoke to me. I feel so lonely.

As much as I trust Majella, I don't tell her about how often I wish I didn't exist. I don't think I need the medication. I'll reduce it a bit. Fear, hurt, loneliness, confusion. Dark brown, very dark brown. Red for danger. Maybe I'm better off dead. Who would miss me? What contribution am I making?

Johnny Cash, 'Hurt'. REM, 'Everybody Hurts'. Gary Jules, 'Mad World'. Culture Club, 'Do You Really Want to Hurt Me?'. The Doors, 'Strange Days'. Daniel Powter, 'Bad Day'. Pink Floyd, 'Comfortably Numb'.

CHAPTER 44

Big Mac's reality and the pressure he is under is something Lawrence is totally unaware of. Big Mac didn't go to Bull's with the intention of killing him. Self-defence. He knows there is no point calling it in, though. Someone at the top owned Bull. It would be the end of Big Mac – not career end, but living end. So he has to dispose of the body.

He waits about an hour before moving the body. He needs to get his energy back. He tries to recall where he has been in the house and he dusts some areas to remove prints, but then gives up. It's pointless; his DNA must be all over the place. Better to dispose of the body and make sure it never surfaces. When Bull is reported missing, they'll find Big Mac's DNA in the house, but he'll lie when questioned and say they were mates and so he'd been round to Bull's place loads of times.

Big Mac finds sheets of plastic in the boot of Bull's car and puts them in his own and somehow loads the body. He closes the front door and drives off. East or west is the choice. East to Louth – get a boat and sink the body in the Irish Sea. No, he decides, too complicated. He might be seen, could be picked up by a Navy patrol. West it is, but bridges will have to be built. He hasn't spoken with his brother in years – they fell out, over what he can't remember. *Families, so fucked-up*, he thinks. *Hopefully, blood is thicker than water.*

He drives to Clare. It's about two-thirty a.m. when he arrives at his brother's farm. Ronan O'Bese comes to the door in wellingtons. He lowers his shotgun when he sees it is Big Mac.

'Long time,' says the brother.

'Too long,' says Big Mac.

'That depends,' says the brother.

That has Big Mac worried. 'On what?'

Ronan raises the shotgun and points it at Big Mac's head. 'On whether you apologise or not.'

Big Mac immediately apologises.

Ronan asks, 'What are you apologising for?'

Big Mac pauses – *a trap*, he thinks. 'I don't know,' is his response.

Ronan lowers the shotgun and starts laughing his arse off. 'I'm only fucking with you. Give me a hug, you ballox,' he says and they embrace.

Blood is thicker than water, and they spend till daybreak taking care of the mess. Bull is stripped, his clothes and the plastic sheets he came in burned, his body cut up and everything fed to the hungry pigs.

'I have two hundred of 'em, he will soon be pig shit' says the brother.

Then Big Mac gets back in the car and heads to work;

Limerick city isn't so far away. He can't stop thinking about what Bull said and he wonders, *Why wouldn't he give up a name? Very strange.*

• • •

'So,' says Lena, 'do you see Big Mac in a different light now that you know about his deceased wife and daughter and following his dance with Bull? Who was it that said he was greedy and a joke?'

'I take it back,' says William.

'From tomorrow, please don't make assumptions. In fact, from today, please stop,' says the nurse lecturer. 'Now, remember Lawrence's goals: to get well, keep well and deliver something big so that he can get recognition from Dublin and get his old job back, and then Eileen. He believes the Specials have proven there is a link between organised crime and politics – and to be honest there is a connection. Now, key to everything, Lawrence thinks, is exposing some dirty cops and highlighting a link between all the above and big business. That's his new goal.'

BONKA

CHAPTER 45

Pat-pat-pat-pat-pap-pat-pat go the footsteps. They are the footsteps of two animals – one a great rhino, big, slow and steady steps, the other a meerkat, faster, more nimble… well, that's what it looks and sounds like as you observe Big Mac and Noddy pounding the streets in downtown Limerick city. Big Mac looks straight ahead, and Noddy keeps turning his head as he tries to keep an eye on everything going on around him.

'So, do you think you're Superman?' asks a serious Big Mac.

Noddy trots alongside, giving this some consideration. After about five of Big Mac's strides and ten of Noddy's, he has a question of his own: 'How do you mean?'

'The underpants,' is Big Mac's reply.

They continue, Big Mac's slow strides, Noddy's little trots. Then, matter-of-fact, Noddy gives his honest reply: 'Just trying to save money.'

'How's that then?' Big Mac asks.

Noddy thinks, *That's a reasonable question. Big Mac isn't trying to catch me out or anything.* He explains, 'Well, when I used to wear them inside my trousers, I had to wash them every day. Now they're outside, I only have to wash them once a week, and even then they don't really need it.'

Big Mac nods and smiles inwardly. 'That's illogical logic for you.'

Noddy smiles and glows and accepts the compliment. 'Thanks.'

They keep moving, and Big Mac poses a major life-checking question to Noddy. 'Why don't you consider wearing your socks outside your shoes? Then they wouldn't get sweaty.'

Noddy is obviously thinking about this; he has started to speed up – well, take smaller but more frequent steps. Then the excitement pops like a mini volcano. 'Big Mac, I think you might be onto something.'

Big Mac isn't paying attention; he is distracted by an unusual-looking guy outside the primary school. Looking at the chap out of the corner of his eye, he directs Noddy, 'Look, over there, the guy hanging outside the school.'

Meerkat Noddy does so in an 'up periscope, have a look, down periscope' kind of way. He reports back, 'He's probably a perv or a paedo or something.'

'Let's check him out,' says Big Mac.

They break off and expertly corner him in a pincer movement. The man – bent over a little, long and rangy and slight, with a bit of a nervous disposition, maybe a longer type of meerkat than Noddy – has his head down and doesn't notice Big Mac until the wide shadow appears before him.

'I want a word with you,' says Big Mac.

But before even the first word had come out of Big Mac's

mouth, the large meerkat man, who has survived in the jungle of life so far, had already decided to back away from the shadow and run in the other direction. This type of strategy has served him well so far, going all the way back to primary school, and kept him safe from the leopards, lions, bears, eagles and mad dogs of this world.

He turns and bumps straight into Noddy, and they both fall to the ground. Noddy helps him up with a, 'Hey! We want a word with you.'

The guy panics and goes to run again, but with a double tackle technique that every Irish coach would be proud of, Noddy tackles low and Big Mac high, and they bring this strange-looking man to the ground.

They all get back to their feet. Big Mac has the man in a vice-like grip. After identifying himself as a Garda, he asks, 'Why did you try to run?'

The man isn't crying, but is at the stage where it could happen quite easily. 'I didn't know you were cops. I just saw the guy in the underpants and panicked.'

'It helps me to save money,' explains Noddy.

'Not now!' bellows Big Mac.

The man is struggling to breathe. Big Mac relaxes his grip a little, and the man coughs and gives a squeal. 'My ribs, I think they're broken.'

Big Mac ignores this and continues with the questioning. 'Anyway, perv, what are you doing hanging around outside a school?'

The man pulls away from Big Mac's grip and defiantly replies, 'I was just waiting to collect my kids.'

Bang on cue, two children turn up crying. 'Daddy, Daddy, are you okay? What happened to you?'

Noddy says, 'Shit.'

Big Mac adds, 'Make it a double.'

CHAPTER 46

Back at HQ, Mooney is interviewing an American. He is quite small, dwarf small, and is obviously suffering from the genetic disorder achondroplasia. He is sitting on a number of phone books that have been placed on his chair so that he can reach the table.

'So, the cannabis?' she enquires.

'It's for personal use,' he tells her.

'Drugs are bad for you,' she advises, 'and two hundred kilos?'

He explains, 'I haven't used it yet.'

'Good,' she says.

'I am going to, though. I was at this party and everyone was smoking it, and they said it made them high. I've tried everything else. I want to be high; I mean, tall – that's why I bought so much of it from the Moroccans. I'm going to be a basketball star,' he finishes excitedly, using his hands to show how his name will be lit up in lights.

• • •

Big Mac pushes some guy, a suspect, into a room where Noddy is waiting.

'Process him,' he orders.

Big Mac looks in on Boss in his office. He is in his gym kit and doing sit-ups. 'Always sad to see someone of your age trying for a six-pack,' teases Big Mac.

'I'm trying to get it back,' says Boss.

Big Mac says, 'I've drunk a few six-packs in my time.'

Boss rises and breathes out and says, 'I heard, and also something about you being so hungry you ate the bottles and the cans they came in.' He lies back down.

'Don't believe everything you hear,' Big Mac replies calmly. 'That's a wild exaggeration. And it was nothing to do with me being insatiable or having binge-eating disorder.'

'No?' questions Boss on his next trip up.

'Of course not,' says Big Mac. 'That, sir, was for a bet.'

And he walks away, leaving an incredulous Boss lying on the floor. He has to stop his exercises to make sense of what he has just been told. After a few moments he agrees with himself that it is plausible and probably true, and he gets started on the crunches.

• • •

Noddy is in with the suspect. 'You have a right, you have a right, you have a right, you have a r–'

'I know,' interjects the slightly concerned suspect. 'Well,

what are my rights? I have a right to know my rights.' He folds his arms.

Noddy nods, pauses and re-engages. 'That's right, that's right, you have a right to know your rights. You have a right to, you have a right to, you have a right to–'

'What kind of place is this?' the suspect interrupts. He has stood up and is walking about at his end of the room. 'I bet you don't even know your rights.'

That makes Noddy feel pressurised. He starts taking deep breaths and blowing them out. After a few moments he tries to take control of the situation. 'My rights are to tell you your rights. That's right. You have a right to, a right to, a right to–'

'To make a phone call to my solicitor, duh,' the suspect cuts in, making the face of a simpleton, mocking Noddy.

Noddy nods. 'That's correct, sir. Let me dial for you.' He dials a number and hands the receiver over to the suspect, who puts the earpiece to his ear.

'Pizza delivery, how may I help?' says a guy at the other end.

The suspect hasn't really been listening, and he makes his request: 'I'd like to speak with a solicitor, please.'

The pizza guy assumes it's a crank call but remains polite, as so many organisations are recording their calls these days and he doesn't want to end up in a disciplinary. 'Sorry, there are no solicitors here, sir, just pizza.'

The confused and annoyed suspect replies rudely, 'Well, I'm not looking for a pizza, I'm looking for a solicitor.'

'Sorry, sir, we only do pizzas. If it's a solicitor you're

looking for, perhaps you should call a legal firm, not a food delivery firm. Good day.' He hangs up.

The suspect hands the phone back to Noddy. 'That wasn't a solicitor. I want to call a solicitor,' he demands.

'You had a right to a call and you made it,' Noddy replies slowly.

'It was a pizza delivery number,' says the suspect.

'It's up to you who you decide to call,' says Noddy. 'That is your right. But if it was me in your shoes, I would have called a solicitor.'

'But you didn't – it was you who called the pizza number,' accuses the suspect.

With the usual gormless look on his face, Noddy urges the chap to sit back down. 'I've heard it all now,' he says, shaking his head. 'Drugs are really ruining society.'

• • •

Big Mac heads across the office and sits down next to Mooney. He's holding the left side of his chest and breathing heavily.

'Ouch, chest pain,' he explains. 'I need to sit down.' After a few moments, he turns to Mooney, who is typing. 'Can you get me something to eat while I'm resting and recovering, please?' he says, obviously in pain.

'Sure,' says Mooney.

CHAPTER 47

Lawrence is lying on a couch. He is facing away from the person he is speaking with. That person is lying back in his chair with his feet on the desk, revealing his Mickey Mouse socks. It is a community outpatient appointment with Dr Best. Best isn't playing marbles, but he is examining one, bringing it up close to his eye.

Lawrence is speaking very slowly. 'I miss her a lot, Doc. I think about her all the time. I can't believe it's over.'

'It's not,' says Best. 'We've got another twenty-five minutes.'

There is a pause; neither gent tries to fill it.

With a hint of a sniffle, Lawrence continues. 'We've been through a lot, we have.'

The doctor responds, 'I suppose we have.'

Without looking over his shoulder and with little energy, Lawrence clarifies, 'I don't mean us, Doc. I mean my wife and I.'

Best briefly looks away from the marble. 'Oh sorry, I apologise. Please do continue.'

'It's the little things I miss. Like…' Lawrence starts sniffling and then breaks down crying.

After a minute, the doctor looks frustrated. He puts his

marble down, takes his feet off the desk, sits up and carefully unties his shoes and takes them off. He tiptoes to his right, where there is a clock on the wall, and moves the big hand forward. He sits back down, ties his laces and puts his feet back on the desk. Then he intervenes.

'Is that the time? Ah well, we can talk about this in a couple of weeks.'

Lawrence sits up and turns around and looks at the doctor. 'I thought we had another twenty minutes.'

Best shakes his head and points at the clock. 'Time flies.' In a busy, more professional manner, he continues: 'Anyway, your illness – have you any thoughts about killing others?'

Lawrence answers truthfully: 'No.'

'Good,' says Best. 'What about suicidal ideation?'

Lawrence lies, as usual: 'No.'

'Good,' says Best. 'And finally, have you been having any hallucinations?'

'No,' says Lawrence, though in fact he is hallucinating right now, as through his eyes Dr Best looks like an uncle of ET.

'Excellent,' says the doctor. 'I will decrease your medication again. Well done, Lawrence, you're doing so well.'

• • •

A worried Mooney brings Big Mac to see his GP.

'What has been causing the chest pain?' asks Big Mac.

'Well, I've got lots of results here from different tests we've run on you over the past few years,' says the GP. 'The last set highlight that your cholesterol is very high, and I believe it's clogging up your arteries.'

Big Mac waves this away with, 'I don't need arteries, just take them out.'

The GP obviously knows him well and ignores this, continuing, 'Also, your blood pressure is sky high, and as you're aware, you are very obese. If you don't lose weight, Seamus O'Bese, you will very likely die soon of a heart attack.'

This has sunk home a little with Big Mac and he goes quiet. After a minute he says, 'But my weight is part of who I am. It's taken me years to get this fat. Years of chips, curries, cakes, buns, chocolate, beer, cider, wine, chocolate and not exercising.' He stands up. 'I'll say it now and I'll say it loud: I'm fat and I'm proud.'

The GP is nonplussed, and once Big Mac has sat back down he says, 'Seamus, it's your choice. But if you don't change your diet, start exercising and lose weight, you will die of a heart attack.'

A dejected-looking Big Mac has got the message. 'There must be something positive about being this fat, Doc?' he asks desperately.

'Oh, there is,' says the doc.

'What?' says the cop.

'Well, if you were paid your weight in gold, you'd be very rich.'

'Thanks.'

CHAPTER 48

A commercial is playing on the TV. It is for a popular monthly magazine that is sold across the country. The voiceover talks the viewer through various spreads from the magazine:

'In this month's *Goodbye Ireland* magazine, Billy Bonka explains why he never married. He shows us around his cement factory. He explains how to make cement. He discusses sport, politics and philosophy. Only in this week's *Goodbye Ireland* magazine…'

Next up is a news flash. Pictures of various buildings and sites and of Billy Bonka flash up in the background as the reporter talks.

'Billy Bonka is going to give away his cement factory. He states that he has no living relatives and realises that he can't go on for ever. He wants to find the most deserving person to take over from him. He has placed five silver tickets in bags of Bonka Cement, which are currently on sale all over Ireland. The five winners can expect to spend the day at the Bonka Cement Factory next week, at the end of which Billy will hand over the keys to the factory to one of the five winners.'

• • •

The next day, on a different news programme, another reporter takes up the story.

'Cement mania has gripped Ireland! Since Billy Bonka announced he's going to give his cement factory to one of the five people who find a silver ticket in his Bonka Cement Mix, sales have rocketed.'

We see shots of people carrying cement bags. We see shots of people opening them.

The reporter continues, 'Last night thieves broke into the Bank of Ireland, where some customers had been storing their cement until they got an opportunity to personally open the bags. Some bags of cement were stolen from the bank, and other bags were just opened in the vault.'

Cut to a shot of the bank manager. 'This was an appalling act. What kind of person would break into a bank and steal cement? The robbers showed no regard for the cement. As you can see, these bags were slashed open.' We see shots of cement bags that were probably opened with a shovel. 'They didn't even have the decency to open them properly. On a more positive note, no money was stolen.'

Back to the reporter. 'Gardai are investigating, but have advised that it will be difficult to secure a conviction without concrete evidence.'

Cut to another news programme. We see people marching on the streets and they're chanting, 'Cement, cement, cement.'

Someone has a loudspeaker and calls outs, 'Give me a C, give me an E, give me an M, give me an E, give me an N, give me a T, give me cement.'

Cut to a shot of a girl somewhere. She is crying. 'I just love cement. I love cement so much. I pray to God for *cement* each night.'

A loud cheer erupts behind her. The camera cuts to a man excitedly shouting and kissing something that he is holding. 'I've got one, I've got one!' The camera zooms in on him. 'I've got a cement ticket. I don't believe it. I've got a cement ticket!'

The ambitious reporter is there right away and sticks a microphone under the man's nose. 'Congratulations. Tell the people of Ireland, what's your name?'

Emotionally overcome, the man says, 'Sandy, Sandy Beech.'

The quick-witted reporter says, 'What a great name for the owner of a cement factory. Sandy – it mixes perfectly with cement.'

The winner says, 'Can I just wish my mother well?'

'Of course.'

'Hello, Mam. If I win the factory, I'll empty all the cement into the Irish Sea and concrete the whole lot. That way you'll be able to visit Uncle Sean in London.' He turns to the reporter. 'She doesn't like flying, you see.'

The reporter nods and speaks down the camera. 'Back to you in the studio.'

• • •

The whole team are at HQ and have been watching this coverage. There is a stunned silence, broken eventually by Big Mac.

'I could kill for something to eat.'

Boss stands up and says, 'Allow me.' He heads into his office, comes out with a whole load of food and places it in front of Big Mac – cheese, meats, ice cream. 'There you go,' says Boss with a huge smile.

'Thanks, sir,' says Big Mac.

'That's very kind of you,' acknowledges Noddy.

Boss responds to Noddy in a whisper, but it is loud enough for Big Mac to hear. 'Not really, Noddy. The way I look at it, if he's dead from a heart attack, I won't have to manage him anymore.' He sniggers.

Big Mac immediately stops eating and spits what is in his mouth onto a napkin. 'That's probably the only thing that will motivate me to change. I don't really care about dying, but if by living I make your life more difficult, then hell, I'll alter my diet. I'll even start exercising.'

Boss sniggers again. 'Sure, and pigs might fly.'

Noddy says, 'They might.'

Mooney comments, 'I saw a pig fly once.'

Boss waves this away. 'Don't be silly, Miss Mooney.'

She says, 'It's true. I was going out with a pig farmer once. I didn't want to make love with him because he was smelly. I said pigs would fly before I would make love with him. Then one day we went for a walk and I saw a pig fly and we made love.'

• • •

Flashback of Mooney with the farmer.

'Pigs will fly before I make love to you,' she says.

'Okay,' says the farmer.

Cut to the farmer speaking to his brother. 'I'm taking her for a walk down the farm to the quarry. Take one of the pigs up to the cliff, and when you see us coming, throw the pig off the cliff.'

'Okay,' says the brother.

Cut to the farmer and Mooney walking down by the quarry.

The farmer says to her, 'Look over there!'

The pig is thrown off the cliff.

'That's amazing,' says Mooney.

'I know,' says the farmer. 'Now take off your clothes and I'll ride ya.'

• • •

Back in the office, Mooney is staring into the distance. 'We loved each other.'

Then the gang are interrupted by another news flash on the TV: 'Billy Bonka has admitted to sleeping with cement.

He said that at times during his life he felt very lonely, and at these times he abused his power and actually slept with his cement. He said today that it isn't something he's proud of. He said that since then he has sought help and he hasn't slept with cement for almost fifteen years.'

Mooney's response to this is, 'That's disgusting.'

The men don't really have a view, but agree with her anyway. 'Sure,' they say, nodding.

CHAPTER 49

A couple of days later, a woman enters the office, a stranger. She is crying.

'I need to speak with the superior officer, please.'

Boss approaches and puts out his hand, which she shakes. 'That's me,' he says, 'call me Boss.'

'I'm Mrs Doyle,' she says between sobs. 'I've come here rather than go to the main Garda station at Henry Street, even though they're leading on the case. A friend who's a well-known lawyer recommended I come here.'

'From the Office of the Director of Public Prosecutions?' asks Boss.

Mrs Doyle shakes her head. 'No, she's a defence lawyer, my friend.'

'How can I help?' asks Boss.

Tearfully, Mrs Doyle explains, 'My husband has been murdered.'

Before Boss can comfort her, Lawrence rushes in between her and Boss and gets right in Mrs Doyle's face, shouting, 'Finger lickin' chicken, KFC, KFC, finger lickin' chicken.'

The startled woman shrieks and steps backwards, and Boss

yanks Lawrence behind him, so that he is standing between Lawrence and Mrs Doyle. Lawrence walks around with his knees bent and his hands tucked into his armpits, and this hen-like performance is supported by vocals: 'Chook, chook, chook, here chook, chook, chook.'

Boss makes eye contact with Mrs Doyle. 'Don't mind him. That's Lawrence; he's a joker,' he says.

Mooney has stepped towards Lawrence and she quietly asks, 'Are you okay, Lawrence?'

Lawrence remains agitated and warns Mooney, 'She's a chicken, she's chicken. Don't stand too close, she might peck you.'

Big Mac stands up. 'Someone mention food?'

Lawrence is now pacing as a distressed human being as opposed to a fake hen. 'She's a chicken. She couldn't get on *Sesame Street*. She's trying to get a job here, spying on us for the commissioner. *But we aren't going to give you one*,' he shouts at Mrs Doyle. 'And you can tell him we are the Specials and we're not chicken, and you and Commissioner Hugh O'Sullivan can both cluck off.'

Mooney is appalled by Lawrence's behaviour. 'Cluck off?' she says furiously. 'How lovely, Lawrence. Chicken language?'

Mrs Doyle is in floods of tears; she has no idea what is going on and this is all too much for her. 'I'm sorry I came here. I'll leave. I don't know what to say. I came here for help. My husband has been murdered.'

Boss puts a consoling arm around her. 'Mrs Doyle, now that the sideshow is over, let me apologise for the ridiculous behaviour of my staff. Please explain what happened. How did your husband die?'

Mrs Doyle composes herself and says, 'He was attacked.'

A furious Lawrence is having none of this. He has to be pulled back by Mooney and Noddy as he shouts, 'It's all lies! He was henpecked, henpecked, henpecked.'

Boss shouts the loudest shout he has ever shouted in all his life: 'Shut the fuck up!' Then he calmly turns to Mrs Doyle. 'Please continue.'

'Well,' she says, 'he won a ticket to go to the Billy Bonka Cement Factory. He refused to put it in the safe; he insisted on carrying it with him at all times. That day he did the Healthy Heart Fun Run for charity – you know of it? He ran in a heart costume. Afterwards, well, we were walking home from the event and a man I had never seen before jumped out of the bushes and stuck him with a knife. He stole the ticket and left my husband to die.'

'What did he look like?' enquires Boss.

'He was tall, about six foot two inches, athletic build. He was wearing a hoodie of the heart run. I didn't get to see his hair as he had the hood up, but I saw his face, only briefly, but I will never forget him – he had deep blue eyes, but they were cold.'

Boss turns to the others. 'Right, team, brainstorm.'

Lawrence kicks off again. 'Fowl play, fowl play, fowl play…' He ends this when Boss holds up his hand to signal he should stop.

'I've no ideas, sir,' says Big Mac.

'Same,' says Mooney.

Noddy looks like he is going to say something, but Boss's expression says, *I don't want to hear from you, Noddy*, so he stands still, closes his mouth and says nothing.

Mrs Doyle pipes up, 'Well, if the ticket was stolen, surely the murderer is going to turn up at the factory on Thursday to try to win the prize.'

'You're right,' says Boss.

'But we can't get in, cos we don't have a ticket,' says Mooney.

'And if we can't get in, we can't identify the five ticket holders,' adds Big Mac.

Silence again.

Noddy puts his hand up.

'Yes, Noddy,' says Boss with a sigh.

'We know one person who got a ticket and therefore had no motive to kill the husband,' Noddy says.

'Sandy Beech!' says Big Mac.

'And if he loans us his ticket, we're in,' says Mooney.

'One last thing,' says Mrs Doyle. 'Lawrence might be right about the foul play. My husband, he used to be a Garda. He was kicked off the force, though – he was corrupt.'

• • •

Big Mac brings Sandy Beech to HQ and pushes him into an office with Noddy.

Sandy tells Noddy, 'I haven't done anything wrong.'

Noddy nods and says, 'You have a right, you have a right, you have a r–'

Sandy cuts him off, saying he wants to speak with his solicitor. Noddy offers to make the call, dials the number and passes the receiver to Sandy.

'Hello,' says Sandy, 'I want to talk to my solicitor, Mike Geary, please. What do you mean this is pizza delivery?' He turns to Noddy. 'This is a pizza delivery number. What should I do?'

Noddy smiles. 'Ham and mushroom is always nice.'

• • •

Half an hour later, Boss has his serious face on. 'Okay,' he says, 'now that we have a ticket, Big Mac and Noddy, you're going to use it. Noddy, you're the ticket owner. Big Mac, you're his chaperone.'

Boss looks over at Lawrence and Mooney. 'I need the pair of you to investigate our victim, Mr Doyle. See if he has any enemies, people who wanted him dead.'

Then, eyeing the four of them and with his hands outstretched, he finishes, 'And let's communicate with each other.'

CHAPTER 50

On the outskirts of Limerick, big chimneys bellow out huge plumes of smoke. These plumes reach high into the sky and don't look too dissimilar to cumulonimbus clouds; maybe it's a cloud-making factory and not a cement one after all. There is a huge gathering of people, including reporters and camera operators, and they are all being kept behind barriers by the security team.

Noddy turns to Big Mac. 'I like cement.'

'It's not me you need to convince,' says Big Mac.

Noddy looks confused. 'No?'

Big Mac faces him, fixes the collar of his coat and pats down his hair, like a proud mother. 'Remember why we're here. The other ticket holders are murder suspects.'

Noddy nods.

The loudest reporter can be heard commentating for the audience at home. 'And here we are outside Bonka Cement in Limerick with the winners of the five silver tickets. We're waiting in anticipation for Billy Bonka to welcome the winners into the factory. And… I think he's coming!'

Bonka walks to the security gate, but doesn't cross the

barriers. He speaks to everyone. 'Good morning and welcome to Bonkaland. By the end of today, there will be a new owner of Bonka Cement. One of these people here' – he points to the winners with his gloved index finger – 'will have the responsibility of carrying cement into the future.' He pauses, and then turns and calls to the winners, 'Let's go.'

He leads them to the main building, about 300 metres from the barriers, and turns to address them. 'Welcome. Before we enter, it's only right that we do some introductions.'

He directs his finger at the nearest winner. The guy is only in his forties, but for some reason he's bent right over, so much so that he can't look up from the ground. He doesn't know that Bonka is pointing at him and has to be prompted by his chaperone.

He says, 'I'm Mike and I used to be a cyclist.'

'A cyclist,' says Bonka. 'I'd never have guessed.'

Then Bonka extends his arm to the next winner, who is looking in a small mirror and fixing his hair. 'I'm Steve,' he says, 'and I'm a model. I'm the best-looking man in Ireland.'

'A model citizen, I hope,' says Bonka.

It's the turn of the only female winner. 'I'm Mary,' she says, 'and I'm an artist. I really appreciate the aesthetic value of cement.'

'Beautiful,' says Bonka.

'I'm Patrick,' says the man next to Mary, 'and I'm a monk.'

'That could be the key,' says Bonka.

A confused Patrick asks, 'What?'

Bonka says, 'Key, monk,' but can tell from Patrick's face that he doesn't get it, so he waves things on.

Noddy's turn. Bonka says, 'And you, sir?'

'I think it's either Steve or Patrick,' says Noddy.

Bonka says, 'What?'

Steve says, 'What are you on about?'

Patrick adds, 'That's strange.'

For his trouble, Big Mac gives Noddy a little punch in the kidney, and then saves the moment: 'He's just displaying his talents. Noddy is a crime fiction writer, so he likes to say creative and strange things.'

'How exciting,' says Bonka. 'What have you written?'

Noddy goes blank and says 'um' about twenty times, before smiling because he now has an answer that will save the day. *'Hamlet,'* he says.

'Interesting,' Bonka says as he opens the door into the reception area, 'I could have sworn someone else wrote that. Well, welcome everyone.'

The other winners enter first, and before Noddy and Big Mac go through the door, Big Mac says through gritted teeth, '*Hamlet*, you wrote *Hamlet*. You can't even write your own name.'

CHAPTER 51

Lawrence is down at the park toilet, deep in conversation with Tom.

'Don't worry, Larry, trust in fate. It will work out if it's meant to. I was married once too, you know.'

Lawrence is surprised by this. 'What happened?'

'She walked out; said I was an asshole. On reflection, I didn't treat her well; she was probably right. Anyway, we digress – back to the case. It might be worth having a snoop around 101 Main Street. Doyle worked there. You might get a lead.'

• • •

At the cement factory, Big Mac and Noddy keep to the back of the group.

'I do agree with you, Noddy. I think Pretty Boy and Monkey Boy are the most likely ones,' says Big Mac.

'Yip,' says Noddy, 'they'll win it.'

'No,' says Big Mac in an annoyed but low voice. 'One of them is the murderer.'

‘Right, please be careful, very careful,’ calls Bonka. ‘What you are about to see is where we store our bags of cement. Be careful where you go.’

They enter a huge space with bags of cement everywhere. Everybody gasps in awe.

‘Wow, this is amazing,’ says Noddy.

Mike is still hunched over but moving about quickly. He appears frustrated. ‘I can’t see anything,’ he says.

‘You have to look up, Mike,’ advises Noddy.

Mike strays into an area of danger.

Bonka screams out, ‘Mike, look out! Don’t go there – look up, look, cement!’

It’s too late: there is a huge bang and a hundred bags of cement fall on Mike. There is a stunned silence. Eventually, the dust settles.

Bonka dusts himself down and comments in a calm tone, ‘Too many years in the saddle. Sad. Couldn’t look up or out. Not observant enough. Wouldn’t have noticed whether the cement was made properly or cared for. Wasn’t suited to the job.’

‘How artistic,’ says Mary. ‘I’d love to paint this scene.’

‘Bless him,’ says Patrick.

‘I still look okay. That’s a relief,’ says Steve as he looks in his mirror.

Bonka moves on. ‘Forward! Come with me and you will see (pause) ment.’

Whether they got his cement gag is hard to know, but he has money, power and influence, and they want to the win the prize, and as such, they all applaud him.

They move to a different part of the factory. There are lots of cement mixers.

Bonka is quite the host. 'This is where we mix the cement with sand and water. This is where an important part of the process occurs.'

Big Mac leans towards Noddy. 'This is boring.'

Noddy nods.

Mary is very excited. She paces about, saying, 'This is so creative, so artistic. I'm almost hypnotised by its beauty. It's lovely. It's lovely. It's lovely.'

She has become transfixed by a cement mixer going round and round and round, a bit hypnotised, like a zombie. She appears unstable on her feet.

Bonka screams out a warning: 'Get away from it! It's dangerous!'

But it is too late: she falls into the mixer and dies.

Bonka looks away from the scene and puts his hand to his head. 'Painful,' he utters with a grimace.

Steve paces about. 'I'm so sexy.'

Patrick is more solemn. 'Oh Lord, bless her, concrete her.'

Noddy turns to Big Mac. 'We were right. Only Steve and Patrick are left.'

Bonka is still for a minute, and then he says, 'She was hypnotised by its beauty. You have to respect the cement and its power. She didn't. No control. She wasn't right to run Bonka Cement.'

Big Mac turns to Noddy. 'I'm starving. There's nothing to eat around here.'

Noddy points. 'Look over there.'

Big Mac nods for a change. 'Let's have a closer look.'

They stray into a small side room that contains trays and trays and trays with small items on them. Noddy picks up one of the items.

'It's bitesize concrete,' he says.

Big Mac picks up a few pieces. 'Smells okay. It's a bit hard. It tastes okay. Fancy that, eating concrete.' He swallows a number of pieces. 'Not so bad,' he says. 'Tasty.'

Noddy puts a hand on Big Mac's shoulder. 'Don't eat too much. They may be hard to digest.'

Big Mac turns to him and smiles. 'Who knows, I might shit bricks.'

• • •

Mooney and Lawrence are down at 101 Main Street, talking with an ordinary-looking man in plain clothes.

'So what exactly happens here?' Mooney asks.

The man explains in a kind voice, 'This is a meeting place for people who have problems with cement.'

'Like Cement Anonymous?' asks Mooney.

'Correct,' is the response.

'So Mr Doyle was a regular attendee. Did he have a bad cement problem?' she asks.

The man shakes his head. 'No, he was our best counsellor. If anyone could help you beat your addiction, it was him.'

Mooney nods. 'And did he have any enemies?'

'No,' the man replies, 'he was well liked by everyone. Even Bonka thought he was the tops.'

Lawrence opens his mouth for the first time. 'Bonka, he knew Bonka?'

'Yeah,' says the man. 'Doyle helped Bonka conquer his demons. In fact, I believe Doyle was seeing him again.'

'How come?' asks Mooney.

The man leans towards her. 'Well, I don't want to break confidentiality rules… but Doyle told me Bonka was back on the cement.'

CHAPTER 52

At the factory, Bonka continues with the tour. In a very slow and dramatic way, he says, 'And here we have the river of cement. It appears not to be moving, but underneath that calm surface are strong currents at depths of up to two hundred metres.'

'Amazing,' says Big Mac.

'Truly,' adds Noddy.

Patrick gets giddy and starts jumping about. 'Watch this,' he says.

'Don't do anything stupid!' shouts Bonka.

'I'm a man of God – I can walk on water, and now I'll walk on cement,' says Patrick.

'I wouldn't if I were you,' advises Bonka.

Patrick runs at the river of cement. He gets about two metres in and then quickly sinks.

'I'm still looking good,' says Steve.

'Pretty Boy must be the murderer,' Noddy whispers to Big Mac.

There is silence, and then Bonka speaks. 'Water and cement are totally different. He sank like a stone. Stone is not concrete and I'm only into concrete. There is no place here for stones.'

• • •

Lawrence is back at the public toilet, and very energised.

'Why didn't you tell me this before, Tom? So Bonka's back on it, worse than ever, sleeping with it, snorting it?'

'I believe so,' responds Tom. 'I've only just found out. However, what is most interesting is that Mr Doyle had a new holiday home in Greece, another in Spain, a new BMW and fifty grand in the bank.'

'Fowl play,' nods Lawrence.

• • •

'And this is the statue-maker,' Bonka announces, pointing to a big machine. 'It makes all the statues for all over Ireland.'

One of the statues by the machine has a really big penis. Noddy and Big Mac are looking at it.

'Interesting,' says Big Mac.

'Yeah,' says Noddy.

Steve is excitable and giddy. 'I'm so beautiful, I would be remembered for ever,' he says, thinking out loud. 'My statue could be put in O'Connell Street in Dublin. I'd be remembered always as Ireland's best-looking person.'

He runs at the statue-maker, shouting out, 'Goodbye, everyone! I'm going to be a statue.'

Bonka makes a weak attempt at discouraging him. 'Don't,' he says.

Steve jumps into the machine and disappears.

Noddy turns to Big Mac. 'Well, he wasn't the murderer either. That just leaves me.' Then he starts to panic. 'I don't think I killed Mr Doyle, though. No, I'd definitely remember that.'

Big Mac isn't paying any attention to Noddy; his focus is on Bonka. He walks towards him. 'Everyone's dead, Bonka. That means Noddy gets the factory.'

Bonka shakes his head. 'No, it doesn't.'

'That was the deal,' Big Mac argues with hostility. 'Hand over the factory. We've put up with enough concrete bullshit for one day.'

Bonka is unmoved. 'No,' he says matter-of-factly, 'he doesn't get the factory. Because you and Noddy stole from me. You were just too greedy. You ate concrete, didn't you? Didn't you? And therefore you've forfeited your right to the factory. Goodbye.'

Noddy walks over to Bonka, puts his hand in his pocket and produces a piece of concrete. He gives it to Bonka and walks away, saying, 'I didn't kill him.'

Bonka examines the concrete. Then he puts it in his pocket and with great excitement he cries, 'You did it!'

Noddy is very worried now. 'I didn't,' he says meekly.

Bonka approaches him and hugs him. 'You did.'

Noddy looks at Big Mac. 'I didn't, believe me, I didn't! I think I need a solicitor. I have a right. And please don't let them phone the pizza delivery.'

Bonka holds Noddy's head in his hands. 'You don't need

a pizza delivery, my boy. The cement factory is yours!'

Just then, Mooney, Lawrence and Boss arrive.

'Not so fast, Bonka,' says Mooney. 'We know you killed Mr Doyle.'

Unfazed, Bonka dismisses the accusation. 'Don't be ridiculous.'

Big Mac gets Mooney's attention and says calmly, 'Hey, let's forget about this. He's just given Noddy the factory. Everything's sorted.'

'I'm not guilty of anything,' snorts Bonka.

'We know Doyle was blackmailing you,' says Lawrence.

'We have proof,' says Boss.

'He was going to go public,' says Mooney. 'Kissy-kissy cement,' she mocks.

Bonka retaliates. 'He had it coming, dirty ex-cop. Thought he could betray me. I had the Ace of Spades, though. I have connections, you know. I didn't actually kill him. I had him killed.'

Big Mac is scratching his head. 'But what about the stolen ticket?'

'I figured that out,' says Boss. 'It was never stolen. When Doyle was attacked, it blew away in the wind, and one of the other winners here today came across it.'

(Cut to Mike, bent over, seeing the ticket on the street. 'What have we got here?' he says. He reads it and cheers. 'I'm going to the cement factory!')

Big Mac takes the keys to the factory from Bonka and gives them to Noddy.

‘I’m afraid not,’ says Boss. ‘Remember, we only borrowed our ticket.’

Big Mac sighs. ‘This isn’t the time to start practising honesty, Boss.’

‘The heroin wasn’t mine, O’Bese! How many times…’

• • •

Two months later, the evening news will cover an interesting story.

‘Sandy Beech, the owner of Bonka Cement, finished the goal he had set out to achieve. The Irish Sea has been completely concreted over, linking Ireland with mainland Britain. His mum was delighted, as she was able to meet her brother in England, but the shareholders of the ferry companies and fishermen from Ireland, England, Wales and Scotland are furious and are threatening legal action.’

• • •

After the Bonka events, Lawrence writes in his diary:

I’m on my own. I don’t like it. The house is too big. I’m even more convinced of the links between big business, politics, the Gardai and organised crime now. It’s not paranoia – everyone else thinks the same as me.

I’m starting to rely on the team. They’re weird, but so

am I, I guess. We are having some success. Big Mac looks better. He was fair rough a while back. If I didn't know better, I'd say he was doing white-collar boxing or some shite – he looked beat up. Maybe he is trying to look good for Joan.

No news from Eileen. Her mother let me talk to the kids on the phone the other day.

I hate life, but it's five days in a row now that I haven't felt like killing myself. I wish I was dead, though. No one understands. Majella Quinn saves me. I reduced the medication a while back, I don't notice any difference. I don't need it. I'll give it up completely.

Loathing, distain, self-hatred, useless. Brown. Purple. Brown. Purple. Madness, 'Night Boat to Cairo'. Bad Manners, 'The Can Can'. The Pogues, 'Fiesta'. U2, 'Zooropa'. The Beatles, 'A Day in the Life'. Patsy Cline, 'Crazy'.

• • •

Lena says, 'You probably understand by now that I'm explaining things the way Lawrence saw them and experienced them and understood them. However, let me clarify some matters…

'Bonka did exist. His name was Bill Burke, but the media referred to him as Bonka after he launched a Willy Wonka-type exercise to give away very lucrative apprenticeship schemes at his factory. It was a major PR coup for him – which he needed in order to divert attention from all the environmental damage he had been responsible for.

‘Doyle also existed, but not as a counsellor. He was a dodgy ex-cop and he was blackmailing Burke. He had lots of evidence of environmental issues that would have closed Burke’s businesses and put him behind bars. Doyle turned up dead, and Noddy went undercover. The team were able to get a confession from the arrogant Burke that he had indeed used his connections to have Doyle killed, but he wouldn’t reveal who actually murdered Doyle for him. However, one single piece of CCTV footage from a retail shop camera, about four hundred metres from the crime scene, gave the Specials a person of interest. It wasn’t a clear picture.

‘Lawrence thought he had seen the guy before, but the team discounted this as they thought Lawrence was off his head and unreliable; however, Mrs. Doyle was certain it was the man that knifed her husband. The team name him Suspect X.

‘Then, about a week later, a clearer photo of Suspect X, taken a couple of years earlier, turns up. The CCTV image had been matched against a number of databases and colleagues in Interpol delivered the goods. The identity of Suspect X is still unknown, but in the Interpol photo, Suspect X is in the company of another man, and this man is staring right at the camera and is completely recognisable. It’s none other than Bull. Big Mac keeps quiet, but Noddy says he knows the huge guy because he did his training with him. When Boss asks him more about him, Noddy tells him that he is lovely and a sound fella. This leads to a predictable chain of events: Boss finds out that Bull is missing, and Mooney finds out that Bull is (was) corrupt and dangerous.

'Bull's parents are dead, but Boss thinks it is worth going down to Wexford to speak with Bull's aunt and her husband, the now-retired and elderly Detective Dermot McDermot. According to Boss, McDermot was relatively senior at one stage, and it is widely believed that he schooled his nephew through his police training and likely pulled strings on many occasions to cover up several illegal matters that Bull never got reprimanded for. Boss says that Bull should have been brought down years ago.

'Lawrence asks if McDermot is connected to the commissioner in any way, but Boss is not sure. He thinks he is unlikely to be a player because he is old now. Boss tells Big Mac and Mooney to visit Wexford at their leisure.

'Lawrence, as you can see, is still quite unwell, but is doing a good job. And since his arrival, the Specials have started to deliver results, which is drawing attention from the media, Dublin Garda HQ and the government. This probably isn't ideal. Perhaps the smartest thing for Lawrence and the team to do is stay under the radar. Because with too much success, they become a problem for those who are the links between the criminals, dodgy cops and corrupt politicians. The Specials could become a target, and that certainly won't help Lawrence, who has enough on his plate as it is. He needs to get himself on the road to recovery. Yes, the best thing for

Lawrence would be to keep a low profile.'

• • •

Lawrence resets his objectives: *Keep well, build on the success I'm having with the Specials, get my old job back, get Eileen back.*

THE POPE

CHAPTER 53

Big Mac rises from his office chair and takes one step forward. 'You know, Miss Mooney, I think you're one of the best-looking women in the world, I really do, and I don't understand how we haven't made a go of it by now.'

There is a pause as Big Mac waits for a response.

Noddy, who has been tapping away on his laptop (just continuously pressing the @ key), says, 'Nah, she won't fall for that.'

Big Mac sits back down. 'Yes, she will. Women can't resist me.'

'She won't,' Noddy replies.

Big Mac isn't letting it go. 'She will.'

'If I didn't fall for it, she won't,' says Noddy.

Big Mac waves his huge hands and remonstrates, 'But Noddy, you're not a woman.'

Noddy thinks for a moment. 'You're right, I'm not. I didn't think of that. Good point, Mac, I concede.'

Of course, Big Mac is only having the craic, as they say; he is madly in love with Joan.

• • •

Mooney is in the interview room interviewing a male suspect, Tim Blyde. He is in his thirties and has handsome features, but they are somewhat spoiled by his eyes, which are a bit crossed.

'We know you're guilty. Admit it,' says Mooney.

'I'm not. You can't prove it.' Blyde laughs.

'We've got witnesses, you were picked out of a line-up and your fingerprints were on the gun. So admit it,' demands Mooney.

'Okay then,' says Blyde.

'For the tape, you are admitting it?' questions Mooney.

'No. Ha-ha,' snorts Blyde.

Taking a different, more manipulative approach, Mooney says, 'If you admit your guilt, you'll get a shorter sentence.'

'No, thanks. There's a short sentence for you,' says Blyde. Then, out of nowhere, he adds, 'Show me your knickers and I'll admit it.'

This catches Mooney off guard. She leans forward in her chair and says slowly, 'Okay then. Deal.' She lowers the top of her trousers and gives him a glimpse of the top of her underwear.

'Oh, nice ones. Ladybirds and flowers, good knickers,' is the response from a contented Blyde.

Mooney pulls her trousers back up. 'There you go. I kept my side of the bargain, now you keep yours,' she demands.

'I don't think so!' snorts Blyde.

Incredulous, Mooney points out, 'You promised and made a deal.'

'I know.' He laughs. 'I'm such a gangster.'

'You'll go down for this,' she threatens.

He goes quiet, leans in and says seriously, 'Is that another offer?'

An incensed Mooney is having none of this. 'How dare you! How dare you talk to me like that!'

Blyde sits back in his chair. 'You're right. I apologise. I guess you being so attractive brings out the animal in me. I sincerely apologise.'

Mooney is a little pleased with herself. 'Good. Now, are you guilty?'

He leans closer. 'I'm only guilty of one thing.'

'What's that?'

'Of thinking you're beautiful. You're a gorgeous creature – beautiful eyes, mouth, nose, voluptuous shape, nice height, beautiful hair.'

Mooney blushes. 'You're not so bad yourself. You have nice eyes – they look in the wrong direction, but they are nice.'

Blyde reaches out and takes Mooney's hand. 'Exactly. And do these eyes look like the eyes of a criminal?'

'Well, when you put it like that, no,' she says.

He sits back in his chair, looking at her in an adoring fashion. 'Exactly. God, you are gorgeous. Maybe we should meet up sometime?'

'Like on a date?'

'Yeah.'

She hesitates. 'I don't know.'

'Go on,' he says. 'We'd be good together.'

'Okay then.'

They shake hands.

'Excellent,' says Blyde. He gets up and puts on his jacket. As he does up the buttons, he says, 'I'll pop off then. You've got my details, so give me a ring later. We can go watch a movie.'

'Good idea,' she gushes.

'I'll just take the evidence.' He calmly scoops it up. 'We don't need this now, do we?'

She smiles up at him. 'You have it.'

He opens the door of the interview room and walks out. She rests her head on her hands, elbows on the table, and stares dreamily at the spot where he was just sitting.

After about five minutes, she departs and, with her head in the clouds, enters the main office.

Boss greets her with, 'Any luck? Get a confession?' She doesn't respond. He clicks his fingers in front of her eyes. 'Mooney, Miss Mooney, are you okay?'

'Yes,' she sighs.

'Any confession?' Boss demands.

'No,' she says. 'I pressed him hard, but no joy. He's such a nice man.'

'What!?' yells Boss. Jabbing his finger in her direction, he points out, 'He's scum!'

In a dreamy way, she says, 'No, he's ever so nice.'

The thought running through Boss's mind at this stage is *Fucking airhead*, but he isn't too concerned as the evidence against the guy makes it pretty much a closed case. 'Fine, thank you, Mooney. We have loads of evidence anyway,' he says.

She advises him, 'We don't.'

He quickly retorts, 'I've seen the file.'

'I gave him that, sir.'

'What? Why?' he yells in utter disbelief.

She considers her response. 'He looked innocent.'

'The judicial system doesn't care whether someone looks innocent or not,' he tells her. 'That's not how we determine the truth. Remember: evidence, trial, judge, jury, verdict.'

'I hear you, Boss, but he had nice eyes.'

With his head in his hands, Boss keeps repeating, 'Nice eyes, nice eyes, nice eyes.'

Noddy walks by and mistakes this for a compliment. 'Thanks, sir,' he says.

Boss immediately springs to attention. 'Noddy, tick-tock, tick-tock, tick-tock, tick-tock – if I'm tock, what are you?'

Noddy considers and then says, 'Tick?'

'Exactly, Noddy, now get out of my sight,' Boss orders. 'And you too,' he tells Mooney. He heads into his office and slams the door behind him.

Noddy goes over to Big Mac. 'Hey, Biggie, tick-tock, tick-tock, tick-tock, tick-tock – if I'm tick, what are you?'

Big Mac pauses and then delivers a slow response. 'I'm tock!' he says and he smiles.

A confused Noddy says, 'Yeah.'

Big Mac walks off, saying, 'Noddy, you brighten my day. Even if you were tock, you would always be thick. Thank you.'

CHAPTER 54

Lawrence is back at the house in Annacotty – alone; Eileen and the kids are still away at her mother's. He is asleep and dreaming. He is dreaming of sheep. They are calling him: 'Baaaaaary, Baaaaaaaaary, Baaaaary.'

Later, after resting, Lawrence is walking down a street when a stranger comes towards him – tall, long hair, bit of a beard – smiles and says, 'Ten million in the jackpot. If you're not in it, you can't win it! It could be you.'

Lawrence stops and looks at the man, quite bemused. Pointing to himself, he asks, 'It could be me?'

The smiley stranger says, 'Yes, you might be the one,' and keeps on walking.

Lawrence thinks for a moment and quietly says to himself, 'I might be the one.'

He goes into the local grocery store. There are lottery posters with the strapline 'IT COULD BE YOU'. Lawrence is a bit distracted, a bit in his own world. The staff and customers watch him, thinking he is behaving in an unusual manner. Well, he does appear to be having a conversation with himself.

Lawrence tells himself, 'I might be the one,' several times

as he walks about the shop, looking at various items. He sees a picture on the magazine stand, the cover of some religious magazine with a halo of light above a person. He freezes and stares at the picture, before saying to himself, 'I am the one.'

He turns to the others in the shop, who are staring at him, and tells them all, 'I am.'

He goes back out onto the street without purchasing anything. As he walks back down the street in the direction he came from, he looks up to the heavens and says, 'Lord, Father, Dad, give me a sign.'

At that moment a car drives by, hits a puddle and drenches Lawrence to the skin. He's still looking up to the heavens. 'A different sign, Father, please.'

A flock of birds flies overhead and starts egesting material from their bodies (pooing). As they fly off, visible on the footpath and written in white is the word 'YES'.

Lawrence smiles the biggest smile of his life. 'I knew it,' he says. 'Thank you, Lord, Father. I will do your work.'

Just then a sheep walks up, which is pretty unusual for this part of the city. The sheep nods at Lawrence, which he interprets as a non-verbal hello.

'You are a sheep?' Larry asks/states.

The sheep responds, 'Yes, Larry.'

'How do you know my name?' enquires Lawrence.

'We all do,' replies the sheep.

'Why am I dreaming of sheep?'

'Are you sure you're dreaming, or is it that you're counting them while trying to get to sleep?'

'It's definitely dreams,' confirms Lawrence. 'Is it because I'm Jesus?'

The sheep looks a bit unsure. He shakes his head and says, 'I don't see the connection.'

Lawrence expands on his point. 'Well, the Lamb of God, and Jesus was the shepherd of the people.'

'I see where you're coming from, and you've got a point,' says the sheep. 'But I'm not religious, so I can't really help in that way. It might be something more obvious, you know.'

'Such as?' asks Lawrence.

'Well, leader sheep,' says the sheep.

'Leadership, I hadn't seen that connection, and in fact I think there is a link. Brilliant, thank you.'

The sheep walks away in the opposite direction. 'Thanks, Larry.'

Only half-concentrating, Lawrence raises his hand to wave goodbye to the sheep and utters, 'Bless you.'

Lawrence turns the corner and the sheep continues down the road. The sheep is crossing the road when, out of nowhere, a speeding car approaches and hits the sheep. He is tossed into the air and lands in a broken heap.

The car stops and a couple get out, a man and a woman. The man is Blyde, the good-looking, cross-eyed chap that Mooney released earlier. He bends over the sheep and checks for a pulse.

'He's dead,' he says and shakes his head.

The woman, Constance Mullane, Connie, appears sorrowful. 'What a pity,' she says. She opens the boot of the car and walks over to Blyde and the sheep. 'Waste not, want not.'

Blyde nods. 'You're right. We can make stew and have chops and liver – I love liver,' he says.

'And I can use the wool to make a jumper,' Connie says.

They lift the sheep, Blyde holding the hind legs and Connie the front, and chuck him into the boot. They slam the boot closed.

Blyde turns to Connie. 'I love you.'

'And I love you,' she replies.

They embrace, kiss and then get back into the car and speed off.

CHAPTER 55

A newsflash goes out across the whole of Ireland.

'We interrupt this programme,' says the newsreader, 'to bring you news from the Vatican. The Pope has gone missing. It is alleged that the Pope has had a mental breakdown. It's been rumoured for some time that the Pope has been desperate to change his image. He resorted to pumping iron and taking steroids and working out at the gym. It's believed that the steroids have made him unpredictable and aggressive.'

The news show plays hidden-camera footage of the Pope and some bishops. The Pope is berating a bishop. 'You stupid bishop, you stupid bishop, you've spelt God incorrectly.' We can see that the bishop has spelt GOD as DOG. 'It's the wrong way round,' says the Pope and he gives the bishop a right hook to the jaw, not a knockout, but a wobbler. 'Get out of my sight!'

The newsreader continues, 'In recent weeks things have gone from bad to worse, and yesterday the Pope fled the Vatican in a stolen car. He's believed to have hijacked a plane at Rome Airport and landed in Ireland. He is armed and dangerous.'

• • •

We see the Queen at Buckingham Palace is watching the newsflash too. 'Ha-ha,' she says, 'the Pope is mad. That proves I'm the greatest religious leader.'

Next we see that a senior rabbi is laughing at the news. 'That proves I'm the greatest religious leader.'

Next we see an Arab laughing. 'That proves I am the greatest religious leader.'

Next we see an Indian man with a turban laughing. 'That proves that I am the greatest religious leader.'

Back to the newscaster. 'The cardinals at the Vatican are concerned that this is portraying the Catholic Church in a bad light and have considered how to deal with it.'

• • •

We cut to a group of bishops in a pub somewhere in Ireland drinking pints of Guinness. They are watching the news and are deep in conversation. One of the bishops adds his tuppence worth.

'I'm not bothered about gay priests, priests screwing housewives or sex scandals, but this is casting the Catholic Church in a bad light. They need to do something about it; they need to take action against the Pope.'

• • •

The news reporter concludes, 'The cardinals have decided that they will replace this Pope. They have decided to hold a competition to select the new Pope. So, the first ever *Pope Idol* contest will be held here in Dublin, Ireland, this Saturday. Contestants will perform before a panel, and viewers will get to vote on who the next Pope will be.'

CHAPTER 56

The Taoiseach calls a press conference. The usual baying and barking crowd turn up.

A reporter shouts out from the floor, 'Taoiseach, Taoiseach, is there any truth in the rumour that you're going to be a contestant on Pope Idol?'

The Taoiseach has his hands together as if he's about to pray. 'Heaven-and-Earth-God-is-Almighty!' is the Taoiseach's response.

The reporter seems confused. 'Yeah?'

The Taoiseach continues, 'I-am-holy-always-say-prayers.'

His aide enters and puts an end to the conference. 'That's all for today.'

• • •

The Taoiseach bursts back into his office. He phones someone on his mobile. 'Get onto the Specials immediately. I'm going to win Pope Idol. If we can rig a general election, we can rig Pope Idol. I was told the real Pope landed in Ireland. The last thing I want is for him to turn up on Saturday night and win the show. Get the Specials to find him and lock him up until Sunday.' There is a pause and then the Taoiseach shouts, 'Just do it, Commissioner.'

• • •

Boss is on the phone with the deputy Garda commissioner of Ireland. Deputy Commissioner Clarke is leading the talk.

'If you're successful in preventing the real Pope from attending Pope Idol on Saturday and the Taoiseach becomes Pope… well, Hugh said you could name your price in terms of getting away from working with your imbeciles in the Specials. He would support you getting a top cop post somewhere, maybe even within the Vatican.'

Boss has been listening intently. He knows this is a fabulous opportunity. He nods, even though it is a phone call; force of habit. Then he starts visualising it all. He sees himself in some fine Italian restaurant near the Colosseum, eating spaghetti Bolognese and saying 'mamma mia' to the waiting staff.

'That sounds really good to me. I'm in,' Boss says.

• • •

Boss stomps into the office, where his team are gathered. There is excitement in the air. Big Mac is sitting down, while the others are standing around him and cheering him on. His face looks swollen; he looks under pressure. There is a big, empty bowl on the table beside him. In Big Mac's right hand is an egg.

Mooney is jumping up and down; she is extremely giddy. 'Go on, Big Mac, go on – you can do it!' she cheers.

Noddy looks like he is about to meet Santa Claus. With unbelievable joy, he says, 'This is so special, this is excellent! Go on – that's fifty. One more and that'll be fifty-one hard-boiled eggs you've eaten.'

Big Mac picks up his right hand using his left hand. He is exhausted and his aim is off, so it takes him a few goes to get the egg to hit the target – he hits his cheek, he hits his nose, but eventually into his mouth it goes. He holds it between his teeth and the other two jump up and down, clapping. Then he does it, he swallows it whole. Somehow he manages to raise his arms in the air, but he is so wrecked he can't fully extend them.

'Paul Newman eat your heart out. I'm the new Cool Hand Luke.'

Noddy notices Boss. 'You won't believe it, Boss, but Big Mac just beat Paul Newman's record of eating fifty boiled eggs!'

Boss shrugs his shoulders. 'So? What's the big deal?'

'Big meal actually,' chips in Big Mac.

Boss continues, 'I hate to disappoint you, but that was a film. He probably never ate more than five. Tidy up in here.' Then he looks about. 'Where are the egg shells?'

'He ate them, sir,' says Mooney.

'That doesn't surprise me,' says Boss. 'Now listen carefully.

We've got a new case.'

'Excellent. I love holidays.'

'Not a suitcase, Noddy, get with the programme. A case case – detective, solve case, comprendez?'

Noddy nods.

'Right, everybody, we have to find the Pope. Unfortunately, he has become unwell,' says Boss.

'That's very PC of you, sir,' commends Big Mac sarcastically.

Boss follows up with, 'He's gone stark raving mad.'

'That's more like it. Why change the habit of a lifetime?' laughs Big Mac.

Boss continues, 'Anyway, this a very difficult time for Catholics. We have to get him into care, and then I'm sure we'll get our just rewards in heaven. So let's head to Dublin.'

CHAPTER 57

Lawrence is meeting with Dr Best. Best is doing the listening for a change. Lawrence is quite expressive and confident today, a side we haven't seen from him before; he appears focused and like he has a purpose.

'… and you see, Doc, I believe I'm the one.'

Best challenges him in a gentle and polite way. 'You've been watching *The Matrix* again. What did I tell you about watching films like that? Neil, Leon and all that stuff is a load of rubbish and it sends people round the twist.'

Lawrence flashes to a memory of playing a game of Twister with Noddy, Big Mac and Mooney.

'No, no, no, not Twister, Lawrence, the twist. It makes people unwell – they go crazy,' says Best.

'That's your perspective,' counters Lawrence, 'but whether you like it or not, I am the one. I am your Lord Jesus Christ.'

Best starts to giggle. 'Well, if you are, do you have a sore back?'

'Why would I have a sore back?' questions Lawrence.

Slapping his knee and laughing loudly, the doctor follows up with, 'From carrying the cross, of course.'

Lawrence isn't amused. 'How can you joke about it? That was a difficult time for me up there. It's blasphemous.'

Then, with a raised voice and banging the desk, he says, 'I'm not happy about this, Doc.'

The experienced doctor remains calm. 'I'm sorry, Lawrence, I just find it all amusing. I don't believe you're Jesus Christ for one second.'

Lawrence sits upright and jabs his finger at Best. 'Well, I am, and when my wife finds out, she'll want to be with me again.'

The doctor doesn't respond immediately, but when he does, he does so calmly and warmly. 'Your marriage is over, Lawrence. Why don't you come back into Desmond House with me for a few days?'

Quick as a flash, Lawrence is up on his feet and running out of the Riverside Clinic while shouting a loud 'NO!' over his shoulder at his psychiatrist.

The doctor stands up, but doesn't chase after him. He shouts out, 'Come back, Lawrence, you need help.' Then he catches sight of his watch. 'Oh shit, is that the time?' he says.

CHAPTER 58

Dr Ciaran Noel Best is sitting on a sofa on a well-known Irish daytime-TV chat show.

The male presenter asks, 'So what you're saying is that in effect it could happen to anyone?'

Best nods. 'Yes, Bob, and–'

'So the Pope succumbed to the pressures of being a modern man,' Bob continues, 'became obsessed with his looks, took steroids and became a little mentally unwell?'

The doctor responds, 'Yes, it–'

'So steroids are quite dangerous,' Bob interjects. 'They can cause kidney and heart problems and drive people mad.'

'Yes,' says Best, and before he is cut off again by Bob, the co-presenter, Jane (who is actually married to Bob), intervenes.

'Can you let him speak?'

Bob gets a bit shirty. 'I am. You're the one who just interrupted him.'

'Only to remind you not to.'

Before Best gets to add any more, the producer senses that the couple are going to break into a full-blown argument, so he waves at his colleagues whilst uttering, 'And cut to commercial.'

Once off camera, the couple indeed start to argue, and Best undoes his mic, steps towards them, smiles and hands them his card and says 'Ciaran knows Best'.

A nearby screen is playing the live feed. The commercial features a bodybuilder. He is pumping iron as he delivers his lines: 'Be strong, get babes, boost your confidence. Just use steroids and work out hard. Lift things you never thought you could. Okay, you might damage your heart or your kidneys or go mad, but get your priorities right. It's important to look good. Who knows, you might even end up being governor of an American state.'

• • •

Flashback to the shooting of the bodybuilding commercial. The bodybuilder has just finished his lines, and the director shouts, 'And cut.'

At that moment, the bodybuilder clutches his heart and falls to the floor. The assistant director runs over to help him, but doesn't bend down – he gives him a few harmless little kicks and turns to the director. 'He's dead.'

The director queries this. 'You're sure?'

The assistant director looks down at the bodybuilder and gives him a huge kick, and then turns back to the director. 'Yeah.'

'Shit,' says the director. 'Okay, okay, not a word about

this – we keep this quiet. It would be bad for marketing and sales and wouldn’t be good for business.’

CHAPTER 59

On a Dublin street, a middle-aged man can't help but stare at what he considers to be a most unusual-looking person. The man he is staring at is wearing a Rambo-style bullet belt across his chest under an open black leather jacket, a skirt of some description (he can't quite make it out) and a hat that has a religious look to it. There are also beaded bracelets and a lot of gold chains (not quite as many as Mr T), one of which bears a large gold cross.

The oddly dressed person feels the stare and stares back, confronting the Dubliner. 'Hey, what are you looking at?' he yells in a threatening manner and with a strong Italian accent.

The Dubliner – a middle-class lecturer – starts to scuttle away. 'Nothing,' he says meekly.

Victoriously, the oddly dressed man finishes him off with, 'Move on, you baldy, four-eyed mog, before I beat you so badly that they wouldn't even let you into hell.'

The Dubliner hurries around the corner, and the oddly dressed man realises that someone else is staring at him. However, this time it is a woman and he reacts differently. He starts doing different bodybuilding poses, which the woman seems to like.

'Nice muscles,' she calls.

'Thanks, gorgeous,' says the poser.

'I'm Gloria,' she tells him.

Continuing with the poses that are bringing him acclaim, the man responds, 'Bless you, nice to meet you. I'm Salvatore.'

'I'm going for a drink. Would you like to come?' asks Gloria.

Walking towards her in a very macho way, Salvatore responds, 'Would the Pope smoke dope?'

Gloria doesn't quite understand. 'What does that mean?' she asks.

Without breaking stride with his slow, macho, 'I'm cool' walk, Salvatore replies, 'Would a dog eat meat?'

Gloria starts laughing, an unusual laugh, a bit like a dentist's drill. 'Oh! I understand. That's funny.'

They link arms and walk off.

• • •

On a not-too-far-away street, Boss and his team are on the prowl.

'He's rumoured to be around here somewhere. We've had sightings, stories of aggression,' states Boss. 'It makes sense for us to split up. Mooney, you come with me. Big Mac, Noddy, you head that way.'

• • •

Lawrence is in Limerick. He is walking the streets, trying to help people see the light, praying out loud: 'Love thy neighbour as thyself. Father, forgive them, they know not what they do. Turn the other cheek...'

He is interrupted by a nine-year-old girl with pigtails who is chewing on half a bread roll. 'Do you really believe you're Jesus?' she asks.

'Yes,' he answers.

Munching away on her bread, she points at a lady and says to Lawrence, 'My mum says you're nuts.'

Lawrence looks over at the mother and then returns his gaze to the child. He gently takes the bread roll from her, looks at her and says, 'Blessed are the children. Watch me perform a miracle like I did at Galilee thousands of years ago.' Then, looking up to the sky, he says, 'Father, do your stuff.'

Nothing happens, and the only noise is the girl finishing off what she had in her mouth.

Again Lawrence speaks: 'Father, do your stuff. We're ready, Father.'

Nothing happens.

'Do something to the bread,' Lawrence says.

Then, out of nowhere, a dog runs down the street, jumps up, grabs the bread out of Lawrence's hand and runs off.

Lawrence looks down at the shocked child. 'Sorry. The Lord works in mysterious ways. I'll get your bread.' And he chases after the dog.

The dog, like many animals, has never been taught how to cross a road safely (or maybe he was, but due to lack of intellect he just hasn't retained it), and unfortunately in trying to get away with the bread he is hit by a car.

A couple stop and get out of the vehicle and stand over the dog. It is Connie and Blyde.

Blyde reaches down and feels the neck of the dog. 'It's dead,' he says, looking up at her.

With a remorseful look on her face, Connie says, 'What a pity.'

They pick up the dead dog and put it in the boot. On slamming the boot shut, Connie says, 'Waste not, want not.'

Blyde nods. 'You're right. We can make stew and have chops and liver – I love liver.'

'And I can use the fur to make a pillow,' Connie says.

They gaze at each other, hug and kiss.

'I love you,' says Blythe.

'I love you,' says Connie.

They get back in the car and drive off.

Lawrence gives chase. He hasn't seen everything that has happened, but he thinks he saw them put the dog in the boot. He was nowhere near them when they drove off, and as they accelerate away, they don't see him or hear him shout, 'Stop!'

As Lawrence slows down and gives up the chase, something on a street lamp catches his attention. He goes over to it. It's a paper poster that has been glued to the steel pole. He reads the poster aloud: 'Time for a new Pope. Have you got what it takes? This weekend, join *Pope Idol.*' He is shocked, but this quickly turns to anger. He rips the poster down, reads it again and stuffs it in his pocket.

'This can't happen. This is blasphemous. I must stop it.'

• • •

Back in Dublin, the Pope and Gloria are in a bar. They are getting along quite well – lots of laughing. Of course the dentist-drill laugh does attract attention, but then so does his regalia. He has, however, ditched the hat. It isn't a packed bar, but there is quite a crowd.

In his heavy Italian accent, the Pope offers advice. 'You see, Gloria, the trick with the Bolognese sauce is in the herps.'

She laughs her dentist laugh. 'You are so funny, Salvatore. You mean herbs, not herpes.'

He laughs too. 'I have a problem mixing up my Ps and my Bs. Sometimes it makes sermons very interesting,' he says.

At another table a group of guys are watching a football game on TV, but one or two of them are starting to pay more attention to the couple.

'Hey, look at that girl and her grandad,' says one of the men loudly. This is heard by many.

The Pope turns to Gloria. 'We'll just ignore them.'

Another man calls, 'Hey, Grandad, do you want me to spoon-feed you?'

The group laugh.

Another of the men delivers his best jibe: 'I bet your tool has been out of action for so long you'd need a box of Viagra to get it to stand for a second, even if you were upside down.'

Again all of the group laugh.

Gloria turns to the Pope. 'You're cool. You don't even lose your temper.'

'Watch this,' he says, and he clicks his fingers and starts to smirk.

The men at the other table have stopped laughing; they have a serious matter to deal with.

One of the men stops drinking and puts his glass back down on the table. 'My drink, it tastes funny. Like water.'

'Mine too,' says another guy from that group, and then the rest of the group say, 'Mine too.'

The barman is scratching his head. 'What's going on? Everything has turned into water.'

Amongst all this chaos, people start to stop what they are doing to try to detect where all the belly-aching laughter is coming from. Finally, they locate the source: the Pope.

He stops laughing once he realises all eyes are on him, and in his beautiful Italian accent he slowly speaks. 'See, I did that. I turned all the wine into water – well, in this case, everything into water. An old biblical trick of mine.' And he goes back to laughing.

Once the people in the bar realise what he has said, and that he is to blame, they are ripe to react.

'Let's get him!' yells one guy.

'Yeah!' says another.

Everyone in the establishment moves towards the couple. Gloria is no longer laughing; she is extremely concerned for her and Salvatore's safety.

But cool as you like, he turns to her and says, 'Don't worry, babe. Watch this.'

Again, he clicks his fingers, and all the men stop where they are. It sounds like they are farting, but it soon becomes clear that this is not the case.

'Shit, I've got diarrhoea,' says one.

'Me too,' says another.

'Ah no, my favourite jeans are ruined!' cries out a third.

Gloria wraps herself around Salvatore. 'You are the coolest person I've ever met.'

'Come on, let's go. It stinks in here,' says Salvatore, and as they exit through the swinging cowboy saloon doors, he delivers a *'Ciao'* to those he leaves behind.

CHAPTER 60

The milk dives into the brown substance and doesn't resurface, and somehow the brown substance is now a lighter shade of brown.

'That's enough,' says Big Mac. 'I like my coffee strong.' The team are in a central Dublin café.

Noddy returns the jug to the table. Big Mac has five empty plates and bowls around him and Noddy has one plate in front of him, a half-eaten lasagne dish.

'I think we should really be looking,' offers Noddy.

Big Mac swallows a mouthful of coffee and replies, 'As Napoleon said, you can't expect an army to march on an empty stomach.'

Innocently, Noddy replies, 'Your stomach doesn't look empty.'

Big Mac can't let that one go for free. 'Well, it is – it's about as empty as your head, and that's pretty empty.'

Noddy hasn't quite picked up that this was an insult and gives an honest appraisal: 'I suppose.'

• • •

Pope Idol starts and the compere introduces the evening.

'Ladies and gentlemen, welcome to *Pope Idol*. Comments on the contestants will be made by our panel of judges, and then you at home will have the opportunity to vote for the new Pope. And the first contestant is Dan from Limerick singing "Amazing Grace".'

Dan comes out and sings the song. The crowd clap, but politely, without much enthusiasm.

The compere takes over. 'Thank you, Dan, and over to the panel.'

Judge 1 is moving her body from side to side. It looks like she's still forming her opinion. 'Not a bad attempt. I don't think you hit all the notes correctly, but I think your image as a smelly farmer will win you lots of votes.'

Judge 2 is more dismissive. 'I just don't think you've got the essential qualities to make it as a Pope.'

Judge 3 doesn't even look up at Dan; he just says, 'That was awful. Go back to the farm and don't ever sing to the cows. They might stop producing milk. Worst attempt at being Pope I've ever seen.'

As Dan exits the stage, the compere gives him a tap on the back that says, *Well done*, and, *Bye, loser*. The compere takes centre-stage again.

'And our next contestant is our very own Taoiseach, and he's going to do…' There is a pause. The compere doesn't know what the Taoiseach is going to do and is waiting for some input via his earpiece. Radio silence, so the compere has to improvise. 'The Taoiseach is going to do... something.'

The Taoiseach stands there, frozen like a rabbit in the headlights. Then his thought processes kick in and tell him to just keep smiling, just keep smiling, so he starts to smile and then he starts to talk.

'I brought you higher taxation, I brought you unemployment, I brought you... um, um, I brought you... um, um... I will legalise willy warmers in the Catholic Church.'

(Cut to two Inuits in Greenland who are watching *Pope Idol* on a TV outside their igloo. They stand up and start cheering.)

'I think we should love one another as we love ourselves,' continues the Taoiseach, 'and by that I don't mean masturbation. Thank you.'

There is a pause, silence.

The compere asks, 'Is that it?'

The Taoiseach is back to his rabbit stare and nods an affirmative.

The compere takes over. 'Thank you, Taoiseach. I guess that "something" was a speech. Thank you for that.'

The audience haven't responded at all. Not a clap, not a cheer, but not a boo either.

The compere says to the judging panel, 'Over to you.'

Judge 1 is leaning forward on the table and takes the pen out of her mouth. 'That was a good attempt. The stuttering and stammering and incoherence will get many sympathy votes.'

Judge 2 adds, ‘I think you’ve obviously got some of the essential qualities for a Pope – well able to drink, good at sleeping and generally not having a clue what goes on around you. This is difficult to call.’

Judge 3 says, ‘I think you’ll probably win. I see you getting a lot of votes from other religious orders who would be delighted to see you as head of the Catholic Church so you could ruin it, just like you have this country.’

The compere taps the Taoiseach off the stage. ‘A potential winner? And our next contestant is a nun from Cork, a mickey dodger, Sister Margaret…’ But then he stops and listens to a message through his earpiece. He walks towards the nun, just coming onto the stage. ‘Sorry, Sister, I’m afraid you’re disqualified because you ate two pieces of bread instead of one at Holy Communion way back in 1983. Is that true, Sister?’

She hangs her head in shame, and then slowly lifts it. ‘They were stuck together; it was an honest mistake.’

The compere shakes his head. ‘Sorry, Sister, rules are rules. And can I take this opportunity to thank the Taoiseach over there for forwarding this information to us.’

The Taoiseach waves at him.

CHAPTER 61

Boss is searching hard with Mooney. She is lagging behind, distracted by something.

'Come on, Miss Mooney,' Boss urges. 'We're on an investigation. Can you please stop window shopping?'

She sighs. 'But it's a nice big window, rectangular, not round like the one over there.'

'Come on,' says Boss. 'He must be around here somewhere.'

• • •

In a side street, Gloria and the Pope are massively into each other. They are very excited, speaking loudly and making big gestures. They have become besties.

'And another scene I like is the one in *Psycho*. Come on, let's act it out,' Salvatore says with great enthusiasm.

Gloria fully commits and does fake screams as he makes stabbing actions with an invisible knife. Then they stop the act and laugh their hearts out.

Once their laughter dissipates, the Pope has another great idea. 'Another scene I like is the one from *Titanic*. You be at the front of the ship; I'll be behind you.'

They manoeuvre into position. He directs her, 'That's it. Then I go…' And he shouts out in his Italian accent, 'I'm the king of the world!'

• • •

Back at *Pope Idol*, there is an act on stage. It appears to be a magic act. A woman is lying on a table inside a box; her neck and head are sticking out of the top of the box and her feet are protruding at the bottom end.

The magician competing to become Pope steps away from the box. He has a long metal saw, and he starts to bend the saw to prove to everyone that it is metal. It makes a peculiar wave-type sound that satisfies everyone that it is indeed a metal saw.

He returns to the box and declares, 'And now I will saw Maria in half.'

He starts sawing away at the centre of the box. Maria starts screaming. The panel start grimacing. The compere starts grimacing.

The magician finishes the sawing. Maria has stopped screaming. The magician opens both ends of the box and shows the audience that he has split her in two, as he said he would. He stands next to his handiwork and puts his hands out to accept the applause that's starting.

'Ta da! That's what I call magic.'

He is about to bow when the compere intervenes and pushes him towards the side of the stage. 'She's dead, you fool. That's not magic, it's murder.'

Just at this moment, a high-energy Lawrence bursts onto the stage from the opposite side.

'This is wrong!' he announces loudly. 'We can't vote for the Pope like this. It's blasphemous. I'm bipolar and I'm a cop and I'm Jesus and voting for a Pope is wrong. My father wouldn't be happy, would you, Father?' He looks up to the heavens, and then re-engages with the audience. 'I can't turn the other cheek on this occasion. I have to be angry, like when I found people gambling in the temple and whipped them. So please stop.'

The audience goes wild: they stand, they applaud, they cheer, they love it. Lawrence is a bit stuck; it's his turn to look like a rabbit in the headlights.

The compere, who has been pushing the magician off the stage, walks towards Lawrence. He is clapping and nodding his head in admiration. As he gets close to Lawrence, he says, 'That was brilliant. What's your name again?'

A confused, caught in the headlights, rabbit-headed Lawrence says, 'Lawrence Barry.'

The panel are full of energy and don't wait to be invited to pass comment.

Judge 1 gets in there first. 'Excellent! Sympathy votes for being mad, and religious votes for pretending to be Jesus.'

Judge 2 delivers his verdict: 'Good emotion, good speech.'

Then it all goes quiet. The audience waits, the compere waits – what will Judge 3 say?

The third member of the panel stands. He claps, and then he delivers his expert view. ‘I think you will be the new Pope.’

The audience goes wild.

Lawrence is a bit overcome; he hasn’t encountered any positivity towards him in ages.

The Taoiseach is less pleased. With all the noise and commotion, no one can hear what he says, but the lip reader who’s present recognises it:

‘SHIT.’

CHAPTER 62

Salvatore and Gloria are having such a laugh.

He catches his breath. 'And another scene I like is from *When Harry Met Sally*. Do you remember it? Meg Ryan and Billy Crystal.'

Gloria laughs. '"I'll have what she's having."'

They laugh together, and then he says, 'Let's act it out.'

• • •

Boss and Mooney are still on the hunt. They have walked all the streets, they have been to the bar where the water incident occurred, they have followed up on every reported sighting of Salvatore. Boss is tired, but his motivation is high – he must keep going, win the prize.

'He must be around here somewhere,' says Boss.

Mooney is so bored and tired now; she gives a teenage response with folded arms. 'Yeah.'

'Did you hear that?' asks Boss.

Mooney shakes her head.

Boss listens intently. 'I heard it again,' he says.

He starts to run towards the noise. Mooney hears it too now and follows him. It's a strange mix of sounds: male laughter, a dentist's drill and then a woman shouting out a stream of yeses in what sounds like some kind of weird orgasm. Probably not the Pope, they think, but there is something strange going on and they are obligated to investigate.

It gets louder and louder, and then they round the corner into a side street and see the Pope about thirty metres away. He is rolling around on the ground, unable to get his breath as he is laughing so much. Standing near him is a good-looking woman who is having some sort of mock orgasm, and every so often stopping to laugh the weirdest laugh Boss and Mooney have ever heard, like a dentist's drill.

Boss shouts out and Gloria stops her act, but in the blink of an eye the Pope is on his feet and sprinting away from the police. The Pope is much faster than his pursuers (whether this is divine intervention or steroid inspiration is uncertain), and over the space of a few minutes he puts some distance between them. However, he doesn't see the car: bang, wallop, he is run over.

A couple get out of the car. They stand over the Pope. It's Connie and Blyde.

'He's dead,' says Blyde.

With remorse in her eyes, Connie says, 'What a pity. Waste not, want not.'

Blyde nods. 'You're right. We can make stew, and have chops and liver – I love liver.'

'And I can use his skin as a leather jacket,' Connie says.

They chuck the Pope into the boot, close it, turn towards each other and kiss.

Their romantic moment is broken by a man running past and shouting at them, 'Have you seen the Pope around here?'

Connie looks over at Boss. 'Yes.' She points down the street. 'He went that way.' She leans back in to kiss her beau.

Head down, Boss runs in that direction, but after about five paces he stops as Mooney shouts to him, 'Wait, Boss! It's him, the guy I freed.'

Blyde, whose face had been hidden behind Connie's as they kissed, comes up for air and looks over at Mooney. 'Hi there, sugar lump. You look even prettier than I remember.'

Boss approaches. 'What are you doing parked in the middle of the road?'

Connie reacts fast, but with the wrong answer: 'Flat tyre.'

This arouses the detectives' suspicion, as the tyres aren't flat.

'Open the boot,' orders Mooney.

Blyde opens the boot and Boss looks in. With an astonished look on his face, he tries to make sense of what he is seeing. He puts his hands in and sorts through the mess. 'A dead dog, a dead sheep, a dead donkey, a dead hedgehog, a dead… It's the Pope. He's… alive.'

CHAPTER 63

Ireland waits. Every pub, every church, every household – everyone is glued to the TV. *Pope Idol* is live and the results are about to be announced.

In the studio, the compere is on stage. He has slowed things down to increase the tension, the drama. 'The results are in, the viewers have voted, we are close to having a winner for *Pope Idol*. In third place… Mervyn the Magician – and thankfully third, because he's been arrested for murder. In second place, Bishop O'Connell. And in first place, the winner of the first ever *Pope Idol* contest… Lawrence Barry!'

There is pandemonium, chaos; the crowd goes wild. There is so much noise that only the lip reader catches the Taoiseach's words. 'Suck this.' She quickly corrects herself. 'Sorry, it's an F, not an S.'

• • •

Footage of a stunned Lawrence is being beamed across the country, and into a house where a group of women have got together. They have been having a laugh, having a few drinks, and only a few of them have been paying attention to *Pope Idol*. One of the women, Imelda, has been glued to it, though. She turns to one of the women who hasn't.

'Eileen, Eileen, Eileen, quick, look! Isn't that your ex-husband?' she asks.

Eileen and all the other women now turn to the TV.

'Yes,' says Eileen. 'What's going on?'

Imelda advises, 'He's just won *Pope Idol.*'

• • •

Lawrence is over-awed; this is all too much for him. He is full of joy; he is crying. There is a commotion all around him, reporters trying to get a quote. They are pushed away by the compere, who is emphasising that this is his territory.

Lawrence takes the microphone from him and slowly proceeds to make a speech of sorts. 'I'm delighted to be Pope, as well as Jesus and a cop. I'd like to thank everyone who voted for me. This is a very special and emotional day for me.'

Then, looking straight down the camera and getting up real close, he continues, 'I have to say something to my wife, Eileen, who couldn't be here tonight. Eileen, Eileen…' He pauses and closes his eyes, and with great emotion he shouts out, 'Hey, Eileen, I won it!'

He is completely swarmed by the media.

• • •

Eileen and the girls are glued to the box. They are all quiet.

'Fuck,' says Eileen.

'What?' asks Imelda.

Eileen says, 'I've seen this ending before. *Rocky II*. He thinks he's Rocky Balboa.'

'Don't be stupid,' says Imelda, 'he's the new Pope. You're married to the Pope.'

CHAPTER 64

Left leg folded over right and left foot tapping away, the man is reading a broadsheet paper. He's immersed in a story on an inside page and doesn't seem at all interested in the headline that announces 'POPE CONFUSION' accompanied by a picture of Lawrence. Neither does the man seem to be paying too much attention to the argument going on in the vicinity. Two voices are audible: an Irish man and an Italian man, each adamant that *he* is the Pope.

The man puts down the newspaper and stands tall and walks into the corridor that separates the locked rooms. Salvatore is looking through a small glass panel in his door and shouting across at Lawrence Barry, who is shouting back at him from the opposite room.

The pair are being held at Desmond House, Monagea, Newcastle West, and the man is Dr Best. He addresses them both in a calm manner: 'Chill, please. I will help you both.'

• • •

Lawrence writes in his diary:

I don't need Majella anymore. I don't need Eileen or the kids – I can have anyone I want.

Amazing, super, brilliant, super, super, super. Green, blue, green-blue, rainbow, rainbow, rainbow. Andrew Lloyd Webber, 'Jesus Christ Superstar'. U2, 'Even Better Than The Real Thing'. Robbie Williams, 'Let Me Entertain You'. Right Said Fred, 'I'm Too Sexy'. The Beatles, 'All You Need Is Love'. Kings of Leon, 'Sex On Fire'. David Bowie, 'Heroes'. REM, 'Superman'. The Wannadies, 'I Love Myself'. Pharrell Williams, 'Happy'.

CHAPTER 65

Mooney does the driving while Big Mac snoozes. He misses the counties of Tipperary and Kilkenny, but Mooney wakes him in the county of Wexford, advising him they will be at the house in fifteen minutes.

Their feet sink noisily into the loose stones on the driveway, and when they reach the front door it is opened by Mrs McDermot. They are expected; they phoned and agreed an appointment with the couple a few days earlier. They only want to speak with Dermot, but he insisted that the wife sit in on everything, that he has nothing to hide. He obviously wants her to support his version of events.

And his account is plausible, but he doesn't admit guilt for anything, even though he knows everything is off the record. Bull, he says, went off the rails at around age thirteen. His parents had died a year earlier and Mr and Mrs McDermot took responsibility for him. Dermot describes Bull as messed-up and with a bad streak in him. He was constantly in trouble – violence, theft, but it was arson that got him taken into the care of the state. He spent his formative years in a secure educational facility and refused to see his aunt and her husband. When Bull got out, they were informed he had applied to join the police and been accepted. Mrs McDermot says she was surprised he was accepted into the academy, and more surprised that he got through the training – he wasn't academic at all and was extremely dyslexic; no way could he have passed.

All eyes turn to Dermot. He denies ever pulling strings to get Bull through his exams and completely repudiates every accusation that he covered for Bull for years as he committed crime after crime after crime. He says he has given a lot of thought to Bull. At one stage Dermot kept getting accused of small crimes, and the evidence against him was planted, he says. He thought it was his nephew, bearing some kind of grudge against him and his wife. Over the years, the evidence became more serious, and so did the charges – but on every occasion the charges against Dermot were dropped. It became clear to Dermot that he, Dermot was being used as some sort of pawn. Someone powerful was running Bull, and probably lots of others, and was making it look like Bull was untouchable, being protected by his own, his dodgy uncle, and that Bull was able to beat the system as nothing ever stuck.

Big Mac takes all this in, but pretends to dismiss it to get a rise from the disgraced retired cop. But it is actually the wife who delivers. She verbally attacks Big Mac, to such an extent that it is clear she isn't just backing Dermot up – she is adamant.

When asked who he thinks is the head honcho, Dermot says

it has to be the commissioner, Hugh O'Sullivan, and that he must have a lot of influence, as he was able to leapfrog some excellent and honest cops to get that gig.

Big Mac asks Dermot if 'Rex bought them sails or snails' means anything to him, but it doesn't. Big Mac has asked several people now about Bull's final words, and the only one who thought it meant something was Lawrence – but he is unreliable and off his head.

Big Mac and Mooney thank the couple and make their way out of the house, but Dermot joins them at the door and issues a warning before waving them off.

'Be very fuckin' careful if you're going to go after the commissioner. He's obviously very well connected. He completely fucked my career, and I think he was blackmailing me too; I'm sure it was him. He's dangerous and well protected; he'll have a lot of people in his pocket and many watching his back. And be careful of his attack dog, the deputy commissioner, Clarke. She isn't to be trusted either. You have my respect if you choose to chase O'Sullivan, but I wouldn't if I were you – you'll fail. All the best. We'll pray for you.'

There is mostly silence in the car on the way back. Big Mac is thinking about Lawrence.

Lawrence has connections; he is well liked. The assistant commissioner responsible for the Crime and Security Branch used to be Lawrence's boss, and he was one of Lawrence's best friends. He's potentially a huge ally. We'll need his support and involvement if we're to tackle the commissioner. If I can make peace with my brother, Lawrence can with Reggie. Lawrence is in the wrong. What does he think Reggie should have done? Lawrence lost it big style, and Reggie had no choice but to side with O'Sullivan. I need to convince Lawrence to stop being a selfish ballox, put his pride aside and do what's right for the team, the Gardai, the country.

• • •

Lena sighs. 'In the aftermath of all this, Lawrence felt huge embarrassment, huge, and shame, a lot of shame. He had stormed onto a live TV competition show, *Ireland's Favourite Cleric*, where viewers were voting for their favourite religious person. Never one to miss a publicity opportunity, the Taoiseach, who is very different to how Lawrence has been representing him, was there to present the award to the winner, which was Father Cornelius Redmond. But Lawrence grabbed the microphone and delivered the speech I just told you about. He made it into the national newspapers. He felt like a joke.

'Eileen obviously heard – well, she actually saw it live. His chances with her now were zero. That was them finished.

'The team did well again. Of course, they are much more switched on than how Lawrence depicts them. They were able to help with a small but potentially embarrassing international matter involving a prominent Italian minister's brother-in-law, Salvatore. He suffered from grandiose delusions, sometimes thinking he was Caesar, sometimes Nero, other times the

Pope. He'd left his mental health hospital in Milan without permission, and they knew he'd boarded a plane to Ireland. The Italians were keen to get him back as quickly as possible without too much media exposure. Mission accomplished.

'Lawrence and his team were also able to apprehend a notorious couple, Connie and Blyde, who'd been on a car-theft spree for over a year and were wanted by the authorities. They became a priority when they knocked down and killed an elderly woman as they fled the scene of a theft.

'The team and Lawrence should have kept their heads down, but they didn't and were big news now, and of course they attracted attention from Dublin.'

Nota Bene

'Sometimes we don't recognise success, it comes in many guises.'

SINK OR SWIM

CHAPTER 66

Lawrence feels depressed. He thinks it will be an uphill battle to win Eileen back. There is a chance he might be sacked from the Specials; he is waiting to find out, but it is likely that his fifteen months working with the team will end. Going on the TV show was a bad idea. He regrets lying to Best, he regrets not taking his medication. He has to accept responsibility. He spent three months in Desmond House this time.

He decides to reset his goals. He will accept that he will never get his old job back and will make the most of the current job – try to keep it, try to avoid being sacked. He knows he needs to reset his other expectations too. He is beginning to recognise that he has blown it with Eileen, and maybe what he needs is to build some sort of cordial relationship with her so that he can have access to the kids. It's hard, though. He loves her. This hurts.

• • •

Big Mac is sitting on a sofa wearing only his underpants – the largest pair of white old-man's underpants ever made. He buys four pairs a month and wears each for a week (unless they're dirty and need changing; nothing worse than getting caught short) and then he chucks them out. He doesn't chuck them because of anything to do with cleanliness. This is the only brand that fits him comfortably, but after about a week of wearing the same pair, they start to break and tear and the chaffing is very uncomfortable. He has to be very careful with his groin area; in between his legs can get very sweaty, and the last thing he needs is worn-down underpants breaking his skin. Wearing one pair of pants for a week seems to work for him, and he hasn't had thrush since he implemented this system.

Big Mac has stacks of pancakes beside him and is flicking through the channels. Someone is wailing in the background.

Noddy enters the sitting room. He is wearing pyjamas with a picture of Tubbs and Crockett on the front under the heading 'Miami Vice'. He sits on the sofa near Big Mac. He has a bowl of Rice Krispies.

'I love that sound,' he says, putting his ear to the bowl. 'Cornflakes and Weetabix are useless, no sounds at all.'

'Every day, every day you say that to me, Noddy,' moans Big Mac as he swallows a pancake.

Noddy giggles. 'I do, and you're going to tell me now that I have the brain of a goldfish.'

'Not anymore, Noddy. I think I was being unfair to the goldfish.'

Noddy changes the subject. 'It was fierce decent of you to let Lawrence stay here for a while, since the wife left him.'

'Sure, but his crying all night has kept me awake. I'm beginning to regret it,' says the portly cop.

'Fair play for coming up with that idea to stop him wetting the floors,' says Noddy.

Lawrence, we now see, is standing in a bath full of water. His tears flow in a cartoonish way, arcing from his eyes as opposed to running down his face, joining the gallons he has already cried out.

Big Mac enters the bathroom, still munching on a pancake. Noddy follows him, still eating from the bowl.

'God, look, he's filled it up again.' Noddy points with his spoon.

Whilst finishing off the pancake, Big Mac reaches into the water and pulls up the plug and the bath starts to empty. 'I hope you're drinking enough to replace all the tears you're crying out. You don't want to get dehydrated,' he says.

Lawrence reaches down and picks up a half-full bottle of water. He stops crying whilst he takes a few slugs of it. He places it down and, crying again, says, 'I am.'

'That's it, keep it up – it's important. Anyway, we're off to work. Is there anything you want us to do before we go?' asks Big Mac.

Lawrence shakes his head.

Noddy volunteers, 'Do you want to hear snap, crackle and pop?'

Again Lawrence shakes his head.

Big Mac offers some sensible advice. 'Maybe you should

go see your psychiatrist. He might be able to offer some guidance.'

Lawrence nods.

Then, somewhat inappropriately, Noddy follows up with, 'I was wondering if you might cry in the garden for an hour or so later? There's been a ban on hosepipes on account of the good weather, and the grass is awfully dry.'

Lawrence doesn't reply, but starts to cry harder.

CHAPTER 67

A cheer rings out as two glass spheres clink off one another. Dr Best is delighted with himself – he is beating himself in a game of marbles. He continues his conversation with Lawrence as he plays on.

'You're very quiet today. Are we depressed?' asks the doctor. He takes another shot and gives another cheer.

After a few moments, Lawrence asks without energy, 'What do you mean "we"? Do you mean "you and I", or "me and my voices"?'

Concentrating on his shot and without looking up, the good doctor clarifies, 'No, no, no, merely a figure of speech.'

Lawrence starts to cry. 'I can't help myself. I can't handle never being with my wife again.'

Best misses his shot. Irritated, he makes eye contact with his patient. 'Look what you made me do! How dare you come in here and cry like this. It won't be tolerated.'

Lawrence looks confused and whimpers, 'What?'

Standing up and pacing in a macho way, the doctor coaches him: 'You need to be manly, be strong – chin up. Do you think you're the first person ever to be dumped?'

Lawrence considers and after a few moments replies quietly, 'No.'

The doctor tries to invigorate him with, 'Hell, even *I've* been dumped.'

'Really?' says Lawrence.

Best freezes, and then he walks back to his seat. 'Well, actually no. I just said that to make you feel better.'

Lawrence sinks a little further into his seat. 'Oh,' he says quietly.

The doctor leans forward. 'Did it work? Do you feel better?'

'I don't think I had enough time to think about it for it to work,' says Lawrence.

Picking up a marble, the doctor reflects. 'I suppose. Maybe I should have let you believe it for a while longer. Anyway, sure there are plenty of fish in the sea.'

Lawrence nods and slowly responds, 'I don't really fancy fish, though, Doc, not in that way. Okay for dinner.'

'Fair enough, but I've had a few old trouts in my time,' Best says. Then he breaks into a huge cheer, the biggest of the day, and shouts out, 'Did you see that shot? Shot of the century!'

Lawrence shakes his head. The doctor calms down again and there is silence between the two men for a couple of minutes.

Best says, 'You must forget about her. First things first, give me your wedding ring. Come on, this is part of the letting-go process.'

Lawrence hands it over. The doctor examines it and puts

it in his pocket.

'Thank you. I'm sure I can get a good price for this,' he says and guffaws.

Lawrence says nothing. There is silence apart from the occasional chinking of marbles.

After a few minutes, Lawrence sits up a bit. 'Is there anything I can take to make myself feel better?'

The doctor looks at him. 'Um, well, you're on a mood stabiliser, an antipsychotic and now an antidepressant. That should be enough. However, what might help is eating as much chocolate as you can. It produces chemicals that make you feel like you're in love. It will ease the pain.'

'Okay,' says Lawrence.

'By the way, are the voices still there?' enquires the medic.

'Yes,' says Lawrence.

'Any visual hallucinations?'

Lawrence says no, which is a lie, as when he looks at the doctor what he sees is a giant hotdog.

And then a final question from the doctor: 'Lawrence, are you suicidal?'

'No,' lies Lawrence.

'Great, we're making progress,' says an excited Dr Best. In jest, he follows up with, 'Alright then, I'm off. I must go and see a jeweller.'

CHAPTER 68

Big Mac is sitting behind his desk. His hands are under the desk and out of view and he appears to be rubbing and stroking something. Noddy is watching a commercial on TV.

'Hi there!' says the guy on the advert. 'Fed up with taking medication for your headaches? We've come up with this innovative idea to help cure headaches.' He holds up a hammer. 'When you've got a headache, all you do is get a hammer and bang it on your knee. Your headache goes away. Brain Relief is a natural product. Here are some people who've tried it and benefited from it.'

The advert cuts to a close-up of a man's face. 'I used to get frequent headaches, and then I started using Brain Relief. I feel a lot better now.' A wide shot shows he is walking with crutches.

Next a woman announces, 'I used to get migraines all the time, but since I started using Brain Relief I'm a completely different person.' A wide shot shows she is in a wheelchair with both legs in plaster.

Back to the commercial man: 'There you go – now you know all about it. Next time, use Brain Relief.'

Noddy nods. 'I will,' he says.

Mooney enters and is her usual bright and cheery self. Big Mac bids her good morning. Mooney stops in her tracks.

'What are you doing?' she asks in a very serious and assertive manner.

'Just trying to get in the habit of starting the day in a positive way,' smiles Big Mac.

Mooney lays her hand on her temple. Obviously, she is a woman of the world, but she expected more of her colleagues. 'I can't handle this,' she says.

In a very relaxed way, Big Mac says, 'I know it's a bit of a shock, but hey, it's the new me. If I make this extra effort, maybe women will become even more magnetically attracted to me.'

Mooney looks to Noddy for support. 'Noddy, I don't believe it.'

Noddy looks over at Big Mac and offers words of encouragement and a fist pump from a distance. 'Good man.'

'This is against my human rights,' Mooney says.

An excited Big Mac exclaims, 'I'm nearly there!'

Noddy breaks away from the TV for a moment. 'Go on, Biggie, put your back into it.'

A very serious Boss walks quickly through the office. He notices Mooney looks outraged and stops. 'What's going on here?'

Mooney points at Big Mac. Boss can't see Big Mac's hands but can see by the motion of his arms that he is stroking something.

‘It’s disgusting, sir,’ states Mooney.

A chilled-out Big Mac advises, ‘I’ve been at it for ten minutes, Boss. Nearly there.’

Boss is a bit incredulous. He’s in two minds. Use this as an opportunity to finally dismiss Big Mac? Or just accept this as another example of how low he, the boss, has sunk and use it to motivate himself to get out of this division? ‘Beef, for Christ’s sake, don’t you know where you are?’

Calmly, Big Mac responds, ‘It’s no big deal.’

Without taking his eyes off the TV, Noddy pipes up, ‘He’s right, sir. I’ve done it here a few times myself.’

Mooney gurns.

‘That’s a little more info than I need,’ Boss says to Noddy. Turning to Big Mac, he orders him to stop what he is doing immediately.

Big Mac complies and puts his hands on the desk. In one hand he has a cloth and in the other a shoe.

Boss exhales in relief. ‘Thank God for that. You’re only polishing your shoes.’

Mooney says, ‘I thought you were–’

‘Mooney,’ Boss interjects, ‘let’s leave it there.’ Without taking his eyes off Mooney, he tells Big Mac to finish what he was doing and then he asks Mooney to join him in his office. They both head in that direction and close the door behind them.

Noddy, still engrossed in the TV, shouts over to his mate, ‘I watched Basic Instinct last night and Michael Douglas said that he was horny. Did he mean he was turned on, mad for it, ready for it?'

Big Mac strokes away as he carefully considers his response. 'Very good question, Noddy. But if you're wondering how to put such things to a sophisticated woman, you're better off phrasing it as being happy rather than horny.'

Noddy keeps his eyes on the telly, but gives a thumbs-up and a 'Gotcha'.

Boss and Mooney are sitting down. Boss is doing the talking.

'A bit of news. Deputy Commissioner Clarke is coming round to give me an appraisal today. You know of her – she's a cleanliness freak, hugely into hygiene, so much so that I got the cleaners to do an extra-super job last night. With some of our recent successes here, my stock has risen and I think I'm back on the radar. All going well today, there's a chance I might be able to get out of here and back on the road towards my old job as an assistant commissioner.'

Mooney starts to cry. Boss gets up out of his chair and sits on the corner of his desk, holding her hand to comfort her. 'Don't worry, I'm sure your next boss will be equally good. Well, maybe not as good as me, but okay.'

Talking through her tears, Mooney explains, 'I'm not crying about that, sir. It's my boyfriend. I dumped him.'

With that Boss removes his hand, helps her to her feet, opens the door, walks her through it and announces, 'Again, gentlemen, Miss Mooney has dumped her boyfriend. She's upset. Can you console her, again?' Boss returns to his office and closes the door.

Realising this is becoming a daily ritual, Big Mac rises from his chair and walks towards Mooney. Both Noddy and Big Mac give her a group hug, but the men are getting more out of it than that – it's a bit more sensual than it should be.

'There, there,' says Big Mac.

Noddy adds his tuppence worth: 'This is great. I feel, I feel, really, really…'

'Happy,' says a smiling Big Mac.

Pleased, Mooney thanks them for their support, and the group breaks up, the men walking back to their desks a little bent over.

'Are you guys okay? You're walking funny,' says a concerned Mooney.

'It's only cos we're happy,' explains Noddy.

'I'm pleased to hear you're both happy in life,' she responds.

Big Mac beams. 'I'm definitely at my happiest when I'm happy.'

Boss's door opens and he strides back into the office. 'Can I have your attention, please. Deputy Commissioner Clarke will be doing an inspection today. I must warn you that she's a bit of a cleanliness freak. Anyway, she may attend a couple of calls with us and observe our fine work here in the office, and she may want to speak with you all about your roles.'

'Jam,' says Noddy.

'What?' says a bemused Boss.

'I like jam rolls.'

Boss loses it a little. 'Not food rolls, you idiot, your role as an officer. Remember, your job – cop, police, detective, pig, oink-oink.'

Boss is jumping up and down with his hands above his head making the oink-oink noise when the deputy commissioner enters the room. Boss keeps his composure, trying to make out this is normal in some way.

He stops, turns to Clarke and says, 'Good morning, Deputy Commissioner, I'll be with you in a moment.' He then turns back to his team and, with great energy, says, 'Come on, guys. And an oink-oink here and an oink-oink there, here an oink, there an oink, everywhere an oink-oink, Old McDonald had a farm, E-I-E-I-O. Very good, very good, hurray.' He walks around, clapping the gang on the back and shoulders. 'Well done, well done. Now please start work.'

He turns back to Clarke and escorts her into his office and offers her a seat. 'Good morning, ma'am. Just doing some motivational work with the team, trying to inspire them with my enthusiasm.'

Clarke, an ex-show-jumping champion, responds with a stern challenge. 'Do you think I'm a fool? Don't lie to me. You were calling him a pig, and you concocted that "Old McDonald" song to try to get out of it.'

Feigning innocence, Boss says, 'No, ma'am, I would never do something like that. Honestly.'

'You don't know the meaning of honesty,' Clarke says. 'Remember, it was your dishonesty that got you put here in the first place.'

He calmly responds, 'I can honestly say that was all a big misunderstanding.'

'Yes, ten kilos of heroin just wandered into your garage. One hell of a misunderstanding.'

Big Mac just happens to be passing the door to the office at that moment. 'Sir, any chance of some charlie?'

A mortified Boss musters a good-spirited response. 'Ha-ha-ha! Very funny, Big Mac. Deputy Commissioner Clarke, we have a good team spirit here – we use humour to get ourselves through stressful situations. Ha-ha.'

Clarke is on her feet and is looking out the window, no doubt taking in the beautiful sight of King John's Castle on the banks of the Shannon.

Boss quickly walks to the door, gives Big Mac a punch to the kidney and shoves him out of the room. 'Thanks for dropping in,' he calls as the door closes. 'Remember, my door is always open and I'm always ready to offer support and advice based on my many years of good service on the force.'

Clarke turns away from the sightseeing. 'Sit down,' she orders Boss, pointing to the visitor's seat he originally offered her. Boss makes himself comfortable in the bigger, more luxurious chair. 'We need to talk, but first, I'd like a cup of tea.'

Out in the office, Big Mac rubs his kidney and starts walking towards the corridor. 'It's that time of the day,' he tells his colleagues. 'I'll be back in a short while. Time for my daily dump.'

CHAPTER 69

Lawrence is in a newsagent's, sifting through the chocolate collection. With his arms full, he pours the bars he has chosen onto the counter.

The shopkeeper counts as he places the chocolate bars in a bag. 'That's ten Mars Bars, ten Snickers, ten Wispas and ten Crunchies. Office party, is it?'

'Something like that,' says Lawrence, handing over a note and receiving his change.

• • •

The toilet is a relatively large room. The frosted windows don't offer a scenic view, and even if you could see through them, you would only see the side of a department store. Big Mac is sitting on the loo reading a newspaper. He has been busy and has gone through his usual preparation ritual: five wads of toilet roll with six sheets per wad are on the side, ready for when the time comes for the toilet paper to fulfil its purpose. He doesn't break away from his reading, but a small grunt is audible, followed by a large plop.

• • •

Lawrence is making his way slowly along Arthur's Quay. He stops to listen to some buskers. Tears roll down his face as a guitarist gives his retention of 'Nothing Compares to You', a Sinead O'Connor track. This emotional track has set him off again. He just thinks of Eileen. *Break ups are hard, life is tough,* he thinks to himself.

There is also no let-up from the voices. Immediately, he delves into his bag and unwraps a Mars Bar. He digs in and follows it with two Wispas and a Snickers.

The five wads of toilet roll on the side are gone and have been replaced by the newspaper. Big Mac has his trousers up, and he is down on his knees and bent over the toilet bowl and is busy with the toilet brush in hand. He takes a break and straightens up, but remains on his knees and is face to face with the 'Armitage Shanks' logo.

He gets stuck in again and sends a command into the toilet: 'Get on your way, down the U-bend, you lump… Oh, dammit.'

He stands up and puts the brush back in its stand, he walks over and opens the window wide, and as he leaves the room, he shoots a jokey threat at the toilet: '*Hasta la vista*, poo-poo. I'll be back.'

• • •

Lawrence is nearly at the office. A dog stops and looks up at him with pleading eyes, and Lawrence isn't expecting what happens next.

'Hello, Larry,' says the dog. 'Thank Crunchie it's Friday.'

Lawrence gently corrects him. 'But it's… it's a Monday.'

The dog laughs and says, 'I know. I must be barking mad – like you,' and he walks off.

Lawrence hasn't the energy or the inclination to argue or tell him where to go; he feels rejected, dejected, depressed.

CHAPTER 70

Back at base, Boss is doing all the listening and nodding and is reasonably pleased with himself. The earlier situation has passed and the deputy commissioner is making positive noises as she drones on.

'And so there is a possibility that as part of your rehabilitation you could get transferred back to a normal job and away from these morons. It does appear that you've got control of them – what an embarrassing lot.'

'Yes,' acknowledges Boss.

'And you've even managed to help them solve some of the unsolvable cases,' she says.

Politely, Boss says, 'I've worked very hard.'

It goes quiet. Clarke, who has drunk half of her tea, is staring into the cup. After half a minute she advises, 'There is a tea stain on my cup.'

'Really? I apologise. Show me,' says Boss. He sees it, puts his finger in his mouth and wipes the stain away. 'There,' he says.

'There?!' she says, much louder and with incredulity. She stares at him and shouts, 'I can't believe you just did that! You know how I feel about hygiene.'

Boss immediately realises he has made a huge error. He is unsure why he did it; he would never usually do something like that. Must be because of the stress, spending too much time with the clowns in his team. 'Sorry,' he says, 'sorry, sorry, I do apologise, I beg your pardon. I don't know what's come over me. Well, yes, I do. It's being constantly surrounded with the vermin staff here.'

And to prove the point, at that moment Big Mac passes, drops a fart and, without even thinking, excuses himself.

Boss pleads with Clarke: 'See, see, see what I mean?'

She keeps him under pressure. 'You run this unit, and it is your responsibility to ensure that your staff behave in a professional way, be it with personal hygiene or following rules and procedures. *You* are accountable, and incidents such as this one show me that you haven't been doing your job very well and probably don't deserve to be transferred.'

He grovels in a bit of a whiney tone. 'But I do! I work hard and do a good job, and these incidents are rare. Please, I need to get out of here, I do.'

'Okay.' Clarke sits back in her chair. 'Very well. Now, if you'll excuse me, I would like to use the toilet.'

• • •

Big Mac trundles towards his peers, swaying as he strides like a sumo wrestler, the floor beneath him bending with his weight. As he approaches his colleagues, he says in a loud whisper, 'Guys, I've got a log stuck in the bog and I can't shift it. What do you recommend?'

'That's a stupid place to put a log. What were you trying to do, set a fire in the toilet?' enquires Noddy.

'Not that kind of log, my damaged friend,' is Big Mac's response.

'What kind then?' asks Noddy.

Mooney crinkles up her nose. 'Do you mean a poo?'

Big Mac makes a gun pose with each hand, the index fingers the barrels and the thumbs the hammers. 'Correcta-mondo,' he says.

'If it's yours, we'll need a JCB or a crane to move it,' jokes Noddy.

Big Mac fires his fake guns at Noddy. 'Funny,' he says.

Big Mac turns and walks away from them, and both Noddy and Mooney start laughing at him, as he has a trail of toilet paper sticking out of the back of his trousers, giving him a tail.

'What?' Big Mac asks, hands out and palms facing upwards.

Noddy just grins.

Mooney says, 'Davy Crocket underpants?'

Big Mac reaches around and pulls away the toilet paper. He rolls it into a ball and scores a two-pointer as he lobs it straight into the dustbin. 'I'm such a fashionista.'

Big Mac notices that Boss is giving directions to Clarke. He overhears Boss telling her, 'Just go straight down and it's on your right; you can't miss it. It's a tidy and clean bathroom. I'm sure it's up to your standards.'

‘It better be,’ threatens Clarke.

Big Mac enlists the support of his colleagues – ‘Shit, stall her, you guys!’ – and he rolls quickly towards the loo.

As Clarke passes Mooney, Mooney screeches like a banshee.

A startled Clarke says, ‘Good God, woman, what’s wrong with you?’

‘Oh! Sorry. I thought I was falling, but I’m not, so that’s okay,’ says Mooney.

With a stern look, Boss orders Mooney to return to her desk.

• • •

Big Mac is back in the loo and is frantically trying to push his turd down the U-bend with the toilet brush.

‘Go! Go!’ he commands. ‘Off with you, freedom, go, go now, shoo – shoo, poo, shoo, poo.’ He stops as he realises what he has just said. ‘Shoo, poo.’ He shakes his head. ‘I’ve heard it all now.’

Then he returns to his piston-like approach to removing the poo.

• • •

Clarke walks past Noddy and Noddy falls down. ‘Are you alright?’ she enquires.

He is back on his feet, dusting himself down, and responds

in a serious manner, 'I just took a trip. Boss always says that if I feel stressed, I should go on a trip and get refreshed, so that's what I was doing and now I feel great.'

'Really,' says a puzzled Clarke.

Boss is waving his hands at Noddy like a referee indicating that a shot is wide. He stops when Clarke turns to him. 'Deputy Commissioner, I assure you I never said such a thing,' he says. 'It's ludicrous.'

She stares at Boss sternly. 'This is a very bizarre unit you run. I'm beginning to think you're suited to this lot.'

'I'm not, I'm not, honestly,' is his response.

'Just show me to the toilet,' she orders.

He escorts her. 'Down this way, follow me.'

As they reach the toilet, Big Mac is blocking the door. Boss, Clarke, Noddy and Mooney are forming an orderly queue.

Boss taps Big Mac on the shoulder. 'Excuse us, Big Mac. Deputy Commissioner Clarke wants to use the toilet.'

Big Mac doesn't look at him, just says, 'Me too. Just waiting for it to be empty.'

'Who's in there? You're all here.'

'Lawrence,' Big Mac replies.

'I thought he was back in hospital?'

'No, sir, he never went in. He was seen at Outpatients. He's feeling much better.'

'That's good,' says Boss, and he starts knocking on the door. 'Come on, Lawrence, hurry up.'

At his manipulative best and using all his face-pulling

ability, Big Mac whispers while pointing at Clarke, 'Don't rush him, sir. You don't want him to make a *mess*.'

Boss acknowledges the tip with a nod.

Clarke is getting impatient. 'I do really need to go. I've got a kidney infection,' she volunteers.

Boss takes control of the situation, and in a macho way he sidesteps Big Mac, saying, 'I'll just go in and–'

'You don't want to do that,' Big Mac cuts in quickly.

'How do you mean?' enquires Boss.

Big Mac slows his speech down and emphasises each syllable: 'Trust me, Boss.'

At that moment Lawrence enters the corridor, though no one notices. He is carrying a white plastic bag.

Clarke takes control now. She knocks on the door. 'Lawrence, could you open the door, please?' There is no response, so she knocks again. 'Lawrence, answer me. Open the door. Say something. That is an order.'

Lawrence, who encountered Clarke in his Dublin days, extends the bag in front of him, holding a handle in each hand, and starts to act like he is riding a horse. 'Giddy up, Clarke,' he shouts.

They all turn. Big Mac, Noddy and Mooney laugh. Boss freezes and thinks, *What the fuck?*

Clarke has had quite enough and makes the obvious statement: 'So there's nobody using the toilet.'

Big Mac blocks the way again and declares, 'The loo is occupied.'

‘Get out of my way, Detective O’Bese,’ she orders sternly.

He steps out of the way. ‘Okay, but do remember that I advised you against this.’ As she enters the room, Big Mac turns to Boss and says, ‘Sorry, Boss.’

Clarke sees the log in the bog and is shocked. She goes from being giddy to laughing outrageously to going very still. Slowly, she exits the room, passes the team and leans her head against the wall opposite the toilet. She is a little green and pale.

‘O’Shea,’ she says, ‘this place is disgusting. I’ll never let you leave. Excuse me now while I puke.’ And she turns her face to the side, bends over and vomits.

Noddy steps forward and points at the floor. ‘Carrots, there are always carrots.’

‘Thank you, Noddy,’ says Boss sarcastically.

CHAPTER 71

Boss suggests to Clarke that he escort her out for a walk, and she accepts, saying that it will do her the world of good and help her compose herself. As they depart, Boss orders his team to clean up the two messes.

The team return to the office space and sit around the TV. They are drawn to the report on the screen. A crowd is gathered. Behind them are factory chimneys and signs that read 'Nuclear Station'. A man is talking to the crowd, his back to the camera.

'Ladies and gentlemen, I assure you, you have nothing to worry about. The water is safe to drink. The safety precautions we've put in place here are amongst the best in the world. I repeat, you have nothing to worry about.' The camera angle changes, showing him from the front. He has the head of a fish. 'Thank you for your understanding and your support.'

Mooney switches off the TV. 'There are some very strange people out there,' she exclaims.

Looking at Noddy and Lawrence, Big Mac chips in with, 'There are some very strange people in here.'

Lawrence is tipping the contents of his bag out onto a desk.

‘What’s the story with all the chocolate?’ Mooney asks.

He explains, ‘Doc says it produces a chemical in the brain, and if I eat enough of it, I’ll feel like I’m in love and won’t miss my wife.’

‘No contact from Eileen?’ asks Big Mac.

‘None,’ says Lawrence sorrowfully.

‘Ah well,’ offers Noddy, ‘chocolate is nicer than women.’

‘Yeah, but I really miss her and the kids,’ Lawrence says.

Leaning forward, Big Mac says, ‘I know. Listen, you need to do something to take your mind off things.’

‘Yeah, that’s right,’ Mooney says. ‘I read in a book, or was it a magazine, that when you get dumped, you need to occupy your time.’

Noddy puts his hand up like a schoolkid.

‘Yes?’ says Mooney.

‘Well, there’s a poo in the toilet that won’t budge. Maybe Lawrence could occupy himself with that,’ suggests Noddy.

‘That’s not along the lines of what Miss Mooney and I were really thinking about, Noddy,’ says Big Mac.

Lawrence sighs. ‘I don’t mind. I’ll give anything a try. If it takes my mind off things…’

‘I’ll sort out the puke,’ says Noddy. ‘Amazing how all puke has carrots, even if you haven’t eaten any. Amazing.’

• • •

Boss and Clarke are out strolling by the Shannon.

'And so you see, I knew nothing about the log. Honestly. I just want to get away from here. I know you have the power to get me away from here. Do you think I would let a log be there when I know that you hate them? Of course not. And that log, I don't know how it got there. It could be sabotage. Someone, somewhere, trying to prevent me from being transferred…'

Clarke listens to Boss making his case while looking out at the great river.

CHAPTER 72

Lawrence has put on yellow rubber gloves. He takes a deep breath and enters the toilet. He looks into the loo.

'What was all that commotion about? There's no poo here at all,' he says.

'Hello, Larry, over here,' calls out a voice, and Lawrence looks over at the windowsill to see a large crow standing there, obviously male and smoking a cigar.

'How do you know my name?' asks Lawrence.

'I know all about you, Larry,' is the response.

Lawrence tries to set some boundaries. 'Look, first things first, we don't allow smoking in the toilet.'

'Fair enough,' says the crow and he stubs the cigar out to save it for later.

'Thanks,' says Lawrence. 'Now, there was a bit of a situation earlier, and I'm afraid I have to ask you to fly off while I sort things out.'

'I'm not going anywhere,' says the crow and he sits down on the sill.

'Look, I'm a cop. You will do what I tell you to do.'

'That's the stupidest thing I've ever heard. No wonder your

wife left, Larry,' says the crow.

Lawrence pulls out his gun and points it at the crow. 'Don't get personal!' he yells.

'Go on, shoot me, go on, shoot me,' provokes the crow.

Lawrence is surprised. Then he smirks. 'I'm not stupid. You just want me to kill you. You're probably suicidal. Death by cop. Nice try, crow.'

'They don't think so much of you around here,' says the crow.

'Why do you think that?' asks Lawrence.

'Cos they have you in here looking for a poo. Most detectives are hunting killers and drug dealers, and you, poo. You have fallen a long way,' says the crow. The crow follows up with: 'That's not even a real gun, it's fake, probably a water pistol, they wouldn't give you a real one.'

Lawrence recomposes himself; he knows he has fallen a long way. Then he responds, 'It's real alright, watch this,' and he points the gun out of the window and takes aim at a magpie on a rooftop about sixty metres away.

'Hey,' shouts the crow, 'don't be an asshole, that's my cousin.'

Lawrence changes target and instead aims at a sign about fifty metres away and hits the dot of an 'i' in *Big Sale*.

'Impressive, good shot,' says the crow.

• • •

Big Mac and Mooney are chatting.

'Yeah, he's been having a hard time lately, but at least

we're here for him,' says Big Mac.

'Yeah, we're being supportive,' she states.

They hear the gunshot. They are both stunned. A moment passes.

'Oh my God!' shouts Big Mac. 'I hope he hasn't killed himself!'

They rush down towards the toilet and join Noddy, who has just finished cleaning up the puke. Mooney tries to open the door, but it is locked.

Big Mac bangs on the door whilst shouting loudly, 'Lawrence, are you okay in there? Lawrence, Lawrence?'

After a few moments, Lawrence replies in a low, flat voice, 'Yeah, I'm okay.'

Mooney can hear him talking. 'Who are you talking to?' asks Mooney.

'A bird,' he replies.

'A turd,' says Mooney, scrunching up her face, having misheard him. 'It spoke to you?'

With a smile, Big Mac says, 'Well, it's my log, it was part of me, so it's not surprising that it's able to talk. I am, after all, one of the most intelligent men on earth. I bet that is one charismatic lump of manure.'

'Don't be stupid, Big Mac. He's probably hallucinating from all the stress,' Mooney points out.

He counters with, 'Yes, that's a possibility, but I think my explanation is more likely.'

• • •

Clarke is feeling much better for her walk along the Shannon. Boss is putting in a big effort to convince her that he is worthy of being removed from the Specials task force in Limerick.

'I'm an excellent cop. I have a great temperament. Watch this,' he says, and he walks over to a member of the public, a fifty-year-old woman who looks like an accountant. He sticks his chin out. 'Hit me, hit me,' he urges.

She duly obliges, with a one-two combination that she has learnt at a boxercise class. It hurts him. She departs and Boss turns to Clarke. 'See, see? I have a good temperament.'

He turns and runs across the road to the other footpath, calling, 'Watch this.' He goes up to some youths and requests that they spit at him. They take their time sniffling and clearing their throats, so that when they open their mouths they are able to unleash a shower of snot, phlegm and sputum onto the lanky man.

Boss walks back across the road while wiping his face using the bottom of his shirt, which he deliberately untucked for this purpose. Upon reaching Clarke he says, 'See, see, Deputy Commissioner? I'm very deserving, very deserving indeed.'

'Okay, okay, one last chance. Let's return to the office and continue with the inspection. But I warn you, one more incident and you'll spend the rest of your career working with those misfits.'

Boss walks backwards as she walks forwards, semi-bowing

as he says, 'Thank you, thank you, you won't regret this, you won't, you won't, thank you.'

CHAPTER 73

The trio remain outside the toilet door. Inside, Lawrence has holstered his gun. He is feeling more positive, it was a fine shot. The crow continues, 'I must apologise for earlier, Larry. You are a good guy. I shouldn't have said what I said. I get irritable.'

'What's your name?' asks Lawrence.

'Don't laugh when I tell you.' The crow sighs. 'I'm Caroline.'

Lawrence doesn't laugh, but he does pose a serious question: 'Isn't that a girl's name and you are male?'

'Yes,' says Caroline. 'My dad chose it cos he felt that it would mean I'd get picked on at school and that would toughen me up for adulthood and life.'

Lawrence nods. 'Like with Johnny Cash's song, "A Boy Named Sue".'

'I guess that's where he got the idea,' says the crow. 'He met Elvis once, but he was a huge Cash fan.'

Lawrence continues, 'Look, Caroline, I like you, but I must ask you to leave. I need to find that poo.'

'Fair enough,' says Caroline, 'but the poo, Winnie, she

slipped off a few minutes before you arrived. Let me try and cheer you up. It's an old joke, but sometimes the old ones are the best. The train family are sitting down at the table eating supper. Junior train is wolfing down his meal in an attempt to get away from the table as quickly as possible so he can play on the IPAD. Mammy train, concerned that he will choke advises him, *chew chew.*' Caroline turns and without looking back says, 'It was nice meeting you, Larry. Bye.'

And with that Caroline, the big male crow flies off.

Lawrence looks out at him, waits, and after a few moments says, *'Bon voyage.'*

He looks in the mirror and then he gets the punchline, he laughs uncontrollably. He sits down on the floor with his back to the wall and his legs bent at the knees. He takes off the yellow rubber gloves and then undoes his tie. He is still laughing. *I miss Eileen and the kids so much*, he thinks, and then the laughter turns to tears, he is crying.

He reaches into his pocket and pulls out a Wispa. It has badly melted. He eats it as best he can, but melted chocolate being melted chocolate, he gets it everywhere – on his hands, his shirt, his face.

• • •

A more contented Boss and a calm Clarke return to the office. They approach Mooney, Noddy and Big Mac, and Boss asks, 'Is everything okay?'

Mooney answers. 'Yes.'

'Thanks for clearing up the vomit,' Boss says. 'Is the poo gone?'

'Yeah, I think so. Lawrence is dealing with it,' says Big Mac, pointing to the toilet door.

Boss knocks on the door. 'Lawrence, Lawrence, have you got rid of the log?'

'Yes, sir,' is his response.

'Good,' replies Boss.

Clarke whispers loudly to Boss, 'Well, ask him to come out so I can congratulate him.'

'Can you come out, please, Lawrence?'

The door opens and Lawrence presents himself. He is even messier now, as he is onto his third melted Wispa. Swallowing the last bite, he looks straight at Clarke. She is horrified, shocked, appalled. She backs away from him, but can only get as far as the wall opposite the toilet.

'Oh my God, that is disgusting,' she gasps.

Boss tries to recover the situation. 'Well, he has been ill. However, he's never done anything like this before.'

Clarke puts her hand to her mouth and just gets out an 'I'm going to be sick' before she vomits on the floor exactly where she did so earlier in the day.

Noddy steps over for a look. 'Definitely carrots,' he says.

• • •

Outside, Clarke is in her car and she is pulling away. Boss is chasing after her on foot, but she is getting further and further away.

'It's not what you think!' he shouts after her. 'It's only chocolate. Honestly. I know it sounds daft. It was only chocolate. His psychiatrist told him to do it. Please take me back, please!'

FINGERTIPS

CHAPTER 74

Big Mac is more persuasive than he expected. He strikes the right chord with Lawrence and they agree that they will enlist the support of his old boss, Reggie, to take down the commissioner. The clincher seems to be Big Mac explaining that Mickey O'Rourke actually committed suicide because he was being blackmailed and harassed by dark forces connected to Dublin.

Lawrence is quite depressed, a new low. He can't believe that his colleagues think so little of him that they believed he would eat poo. He is devastated. Majella has explained to him that those with mental health conditions encounter a negative bias, but he didn't expect it from the group that he has started to rely on. *Stigma*, he thinks, *I understand what stigma means now.*

They are heading for Dublin, Big Mac driving, armed with nothing more than the information that Big Mac has gathered, plus a picture of Bull with the guy that Bonka used to kill Dodgy Doyle, Suspect X.

Lawrence is thinking maybe it is time to break bread with Reggie. They have been through a lot; they were friends for a long time. It was Reggie who recruited Lawrence into the Special Branch and gave him four promotions, including the top job. And because Lawrence is still missing Eileen and the kids and is having suicidal thoughts, he figures this is worth a try. One last chance at redemption. One last opportunity to not feel like a failure. A chance to build a coalition to take down the commissioner, Hugh O'Sullivan, a cancer in Ireland.

At the most secure Garda building in Dublin, they eventually get through security and reception and are shown into Reggie's office.

Reggie shakes hands with Big Mac. 'I've heard a lot about you.' He then offers his hand to Lawrence, but instead they embrace. 'Great to see you, Lawrence,' says Reggie. 'I've missed you.'

The kettle is on, and when it boils Reggie makes his visitors a drink. 'Just how you like it,' he says with a smile as he gives Lawrence his coffee.

A few moments later, Reggie makes a request of Big Mac. 'Look, Lawrence and I have known each other a long time. Is it okay if we have some personal time? There's a lot we have to catch up on.'

'Sure,' says Big Mac.

Reggie shows him to the door and hands him a file. 'There's an office down there. Have a read of this. It's a case I'm working on and I'd value your opinion.'

'Right-oh,' says Big Mac. *Nice to get recognition from the big shots*, he thinks.

Reggie sits back down in his big, comfy chair and sees that Lawrence has a pen in his hand and a pad on his lap and has laid a photo on the desk. It's a blown-up surveillance shot of two men.

Lawrence rubs his head. He has the beginnings of a migraine, something else to add to his never-ending list of woes. His mood is flat, and he is still psychotic.

'You alright?' asks Reggie. 'Do you want another coffee? You swallowed that one fast enough.'

'I think I've got a migraine coming on.'

'Sorry to hear that,' says Reggie. 'Maybe we should cut to the chase, so you can get home and into a dark room.'

'The commissioner,' Lawrence starts, 'we think he's corrupt. We're convinced he's involved in some sort of setup where he and probably Clarke and others have dodgy cops working with criminals on their behalf.' He shows Reggie the photo. 'The guy on the left is a detective, Bull, apparently very dodgy. The guy on the right is a hitman used by Bonka, I mean Burke, to get rid of a dodgy ex-cop, Doyle, who was blackmailing him.

'We know there are politicians involved too – the president's husband for one, but also others. Scores of criminals get caught, but then evidence goes missing and cases get thrown out of court. That makes us realise that the underworld is tied into this too, and also members of the legal system. It's big, and every time we hear a whisper, it's the commissioner who comes into the equation. It's obvious…'

Lawrence stops and thinks, then says, 'And how did the commissioner get his job ahead of the likes of you and some of the others, how?'

Reggie has been paying attention. He sits back in his seat and tips the chair back. 'Is this all you've got?' he says.

There is a silence. Lawrence rubs his temples; the headache is progressing, and he is finding it hard to concentrate. He is experiencing both visual and auditory hallucinations, though not as bad as usual – it is the headache that is the real issue now.

Reggie continues, 'I've heard all those rumours about the commissioner and Clarke, and I'm certainly no fan of the commissioner. But no one's ever brought me concrete evidence; this is circumstantial.'

Lawrence is looking to the side to try to manage the headache. He sees a picture of Reggie and his wife, Alice. He had forgotten about Alice.

Then he has an extremely worrying thought. W*hat was it Big Mac was asking: does 'Rex bought them snails' mean anything to you? I thought it did, and it does.*

Lawrence writes on his pad *'REX AUTEM SCELUS'.*

I've written this before, he says to himself. *That's why.*

Then, with fear, he looks up at Reggie.

CHAPTER 75

Reggie's wife, Alice, has a nickname for him; she calls him Rex. When he was working for Reggie, Lawrence must have realised that somehow his boss was involved in organised crime. Why else would Lawrence have written down *'REX AUTEM SCELUS'*, the Latin for 'king of crime'? *Maybe it's a coincidence*, he thinks – but no, he needs to trust his gut, his instincts. Reggie is somehow tied into all this criminality too.

Reggie is observant; he notes the sea change in Lawrence. He peers over the desk and reads the upside-down phrase.

'That old nugget,' he says, smiling. 'It's bigger than that, Lawrence, much bigger. Actually, I'm *Rex autem Hibernia*, the king of Ireland.' He laughs and continues calmly, 'The commissioner is a nobody. I made him. I could have had his job, and Clarke's – muppets the pair of them. I've put them in those jobs. It allows me to manoeuvre things discreetly. I've been blackmailing the commissioner for years. He doesn't even know it's me, and hilariously, he confides in me.

'As for the president's husband, I got him into my pocket by helping him protect the reputation of his daughter, a right little druggie, who will give men a turn for five grand – her looks won't last for ever mind.

'I have some of the main crime bosses in my pocket, many leaders of industry, some from the legal system and a number of politicians. I run this country, Lawrence, me. I have millions in a number of bank accounts across the world. I even have underworld connections in other countries. Brian Boru eat your heart out!' He laughs again.

Lawrence is devastated; it is written all over his face.

Reggie says, 'Sorry, old pal. You scored eight hundred in your GMAT, the perfect score. Had the offer from Harvard to do an MBA with them, but did one in Dublin instead, because Eileen didn't want to go to Boston.' He shakes his head. 'Bad mistake, Lawrence. I didn't waste my opportunity. I didn't get an offer from Harvard, but I got the chance to do some training with the FBI, and when I started to understand some of their profiling systems, I realised what I suppose I must have already known, which is that I'm a psychopath. I get a top score in that.' He laughs. 'I can't help it, it's just the way I am, and I enjoy it.'

There is a short pause and then Reggie continues. 'I do like you though, Lawrence, I do, but I recognised years ago that you were brilliant and therefore a possible nemesis. Best place for you was close by, where I could keep an eye. And you didn't disappoint. There was no point in me trying to turn you, I knew you weren't for turning, but I did try to hypnotise you a few times – another skill I learned in America. I'm good at it, very good. I've applied it on lots of occasions, especially with those I rely on the most, a safeguard to make sure they can never turn the state's evidence against me or even name me.

'I was constantly having you monitored. I knew you'd written *"Rex autem scelus"*. I have a photo of the original note you made. You were getting too close, Lawrence, so I had to take action. Don't feel too special though. I had to take care of your new boss a few years ago too, John O'Shea. He was getting on my nerves, so I got a muppet called O'Rourke to sort him – and look at you both now, best buddies having fun down in Limerick.'

Reggie points at the man next to Bull in the photo, Suspect X and says, 'You see this guy here? You've met him on a few occasions. He works out of Copenhagen, but he's originally from Omsk in Siberia, the old USSR. I got him to take care of that problem for Burke, but I also used him on you.'

Lawrence studies the picture. He kind of recognises the man, but can't remember from where.

'Alexi followed you for a while. He had a fix, but he needed to figure out how to give you the tiny pill. After a few weeks, he decided to take a job working Sundays at Luigi's ice cream parlour in Malahide, as you'd take the kids there every Sunday morning. On the fourth Sunday of work, he slipped the pill into your dish and you ate it. You might recall you had a migraine very shortly afterwards – the beginning of your demise, Lawrence.'

'What?' says Lawrence.

'Yes, he gave you DXH 4571, a nerve agent that very quickly brings on migraine-like symptoms and then symptoms of mental illness – severe schizophrenia, mood disorders, depression and other things like early-onset dementia. Well, the dementia bit we're unsure of; the drug has only been tested on rats and prisoners in Siberia serving life sentences. People don't recover. Sorry.'

Lawrence has his gun in its holster. He could take care of Reggie here and now, but he is in a lot of pain and his hallucinations are becoming stronger, so he doesn't think he would actually get a shot off. *No*, he thinks, *then I'd be making it easy for Reggie. He's in better shape than me and he probably has a gun within reach. He would only kill me. No, I'll live to fight another day.*

'I'll turn you in,' says Lawrence.

Reggie laughs, 'You, my friend, won't remember a thing, and even if you did, who would believe you? You went on TV and told the nation you were Jesus Christ. People around here have been saying you eat shit.'

'It wasn't shit,' Lawrence says.

'I know that, Lawrence, of course I do. But it isn't about the truth or reality, it's about perception, and you, my friend, have no credibility.'

Lawrence, who is pretty much a write-off at this stage, manages to get out a, 'Why?'

Reggie considers and then he says, 'Lawrence, it's simple. Remember we watched the film *Layer Cake* a few times together, remember at the end Michael Gambon gives a speech about him rising to the top so he didn't have to take bullshit from people, well, I'm afraid it is nothing as interesting or hierarchical as that, simply, I do it because I can, and I do it because I like it.'

Lawrence is in a state, a combination of the migraine, the existing mental health symptoms and the new ones arising from the DXH that Reggie put in his coffee.

Reggie picks up the phone and asks his secretary to send in Big Mac. Big Mac enters with caution. He left Reggie feeling very positive, but he steps into the room understanding that Reggie is very, very powerful and very corrupt.

Reggie greets him with a handshake. 'I'll need your help with that case,' he says with a solemn look on his face. 'I have plans for you, Big Mac. Big plans.' He points over at Lawrence. 'He's taken a turn for the worse. Mental illness, it's such a hard way of life. Take him back to Limerick with you.'

CHAPTER 76

On the drive back, Big Mac has plenty to reflect on. There was a lot in the file Reggie gave him – every misdemeanour that Big Mac had ever made, unproven accusations, other matters that had obviously been made up for leverage purposes. There were also notes on a missing detective known as Bull: that blood from both Big Mac and Bull had been found at Bull's home, that there was clear evidence of a struggle and that Bull's DNA had been found in Big Mac's car boot. Big Mac knows, therefore, that he is the prime suspect in this missing-person case. Actually, Bull is presumed dead, so Big Mac is a murder suspect – and he should be arrested and dealt with through the appropriate channels, but obviously Reggie is sitting on the evidence.

On reaching HQ, Big Mac pulls up outside the building and nudges Lawrence, who is slumped back in his seat with his eyes closed.

'I'll be back in five minutes,' Big Mac says. 'Just going to get a sandwich. See you inside.'

Lawrence isn't asleep. He's in a world of despair and is hatching a plan to address his situation. Still in a bad way

– the headache is blinding and the hallucinations strong – he gets out of the car, makes his way to O'Connell Street, hails a taxi and jumps in.

Big Mac returns to the office with loads of food. 'Where's Lawrence?' he asks. 'I got him a roll.'

'Don't know,' says Noddy.

'He isn't here,' says Mooney.

• • •

Lawrence pays the taxi fare and enters the hotel on the bank of the Shannon. He takes the lift to the top floor. He is looking for a particular maintenance room. Eventually, he finds it, and he enters and then goes through another door.

'There it is.' He has found what he was looking for. He walks to the bottom of the steel ladder and slowly climbs it. It is a tough climb as his head is absolutely killing him. 'Not for much longer,' he says quietly.

At the top of the ladder is a roof hatch. He undoes the latch and pushes the door upwards. The breeze catches it, which helps the struggling cop. He steps up and onto the roof.

He walks towards the back of the roof, away from the river. There is a wall about four feet high, and he rests his hands on it and looks across the south of the city. He can see spires and rooftops. 'Nice,' he says.

• • •

Boss rushes into the office. ‘Where’s Lawrence, where is he?’

The group are reasonably chilled out. There are a few head shakes.

Big Mac answers, ‘He was with me; we were driving. I went for food, and when I came back he was gone.’

Hurriedly, Boss asks, ‘How long ago?’

‘Fifteen minutes,’ says Big Mac.

Boss orders the three of them, ‘Get down to the Shannon Hotel. There’s been a call – a weird, distracted guy called Barry with a police badge is heading towards the roof.’

Big Mac drops his sandwich, and he and Noddy and Mooney run faster than they ever have in their lives. In under a minute they are in the car and driving at speed, Mooney at the wheel.

• • •

Lawrence makes his way towards the front of the roof. There is no wall here, only a small ledge. *At least twenty stories*, he thinks. He looks down. Concrete and tarmacadam. *No coming back from this*.

He looks over to his left. He can see the river stretching on for miles. The tide is on the way in; a most dangerous time to be in the water. To his right, he can see the rest of the river and the castle in the background. Then his eyes focus on Thomond Park. *All the great Irish players who’ve graced the turf there down through the years, and here I am, a failure, about to end it all. 'To the brave and faithful, nothing is impossible' – that's the Munster motto. Sorry, everyone*, he thinks.

He starts to think about how people talk about those who commit suicide, saying they took the easy way out. *But it's not easy, it's not. It's just that I don't add value at all – no wife, no kids, no job. I used to be a top cop, and now I'm a joke and betrayed by my best friend. This is sensible*, he thinks, *this is the right thing to do. I add no value to this world.*

• • •

The trio are in the lift and then they burst into the maintenance room.

• • •

Lawrence manages a smile. He thinks to himself, *Things are bad when the seagulls are betting on you.* He is hallucinating.

Seagull 1 says to Seagull 2, 'A jumper.'

Seagull 2 responds, 'No, he won't. I can tell by his eyes.'

'He will. How much do you wanna bet?'

'Five herrings.'

'What are you putting up?'

'I bet fast-food leftovers for two nights.'

'Nah, I'm not eating that shite.'

'Okay, how about a date with my sister?'

'Which one?'

'Shirley.'

'Cool, that's a deal. She's the fittest bird I've ever seen.'

• • •

Big Mac climbs up the ladder, but once at the top he is too wide to get through the hatch. He climbs back down and allows Noddy and Mooney to make their way up onto the roof. Then Big Mac gets back on the ladder and climbs as far as he can, so that his head is sticking up through the hatch.

Mooney does the talking. She doesn't want to startle Lawrence, so she calls to him gently. He half-turns and is spooked and nearly falls off the building. He sees Noddy, Mooney and the severed head of Big Mac – but then recognises that it isn't severed, and that he can only see Big Mac's head because he can't get out onto the roof.

'Don't jump, Lawrence,' says Mooney. 'Come back to us.'

Lawrence thinks for a few moments and responds, 'Why?'

Immediately, Mooney shouts out, 'Because I love you!'

Noddy copies her, as usual, and Big Mac realises he is going to have to be honest and put his macho shite to the side and he also calls, 'I love you.'

Lawrence smiles as he considers this.

CHAPTER 77

Back in the lecture hall with Lena, the class remain fully engaged. She says slowly, 'And then Lawrence steps forward and falls, and he dies instantly on impact.'

She sits back down. There is silence, a different kind of silence to before – this silence is one of disappointment, of sadness, of regret. There is a lot of sighing and deep breathing.

After a few moments, Glasgow Ross speaks up. 'I was hoping for a happy ending.'

'It's the real world, Ross – we don't always get a Hollywood ending. As you all know, and as I've illustrated here, suicide is devastating. Look at the impact it's had on you, and you didn't know of Lawrence until I told you about him a few hours ago. It's final, and it devastates families, mental health teams. It's a scourge, it's a scourge in Ireland, in England and a scourge across the world.'

She pauses and then continues, 'That was Lawrence, everyone, my most interesting patient. Thank you for your time. I've loved these past three years with you, and it's been my pleasure to teach you. You have my number, and my email is on the whiteboard. If I can do anything for any of you ever, just ask. It's four p.m., I know a number of you need to rush off. Goodbye and thank you.'

She turns towards her satchel. No one else moves; everyone is flat, stuck, disappointed.

She waits a few moments. Then Lena puts the bag back down, slowly turns back towards her audience and poses a question to the class: 'What if Lawrence didn't jump?'

The energy in the room starts to change.

'But why would you tell us he died if he didn't?' says Seamus.

'Forgive me, maybe I wanted to make one last point about suicide. And also to a lesser degree it was four p.m. and I needed to bring an end to proceedings so that those of you who needed to leave, could, which would then enable me to come back and finish the story for those of you who stayed.' She smiles a cheeky smile.

'He isn't dead?' queries William.

Lena shakes her head and says, 'He's not dead.'

'I could kiss you, Lena!' Robert shouts out jokingly.

'You had me there,' Rita cries.

'Lawrence is alive!' Liverpool Dean declares. 'I knew it all along.'

'I'm rooting for you, Larry,' calls Seamus.

A loud and visceral 'C'mon, Larry,' from Ross ignites the passion and emotion in the room.

The energy builds to a crescendo. The students start to bang their feet on the floor, then their hands on their desks, and loudly cheer out, 'Larry, Larry, Larry, Larry, Larry, Larry!'

This cacophony continues for a minute or so until Lena intervenes. Quietening them down with her hands, she says, 'Shall I continue with the story about my most interesting patient ever?'

Silence in the room again.

• • •

Lawrence turns back towards his colleagues. Slowly, he plods over to Mooney and Noddy, who embrace him. Big Mac can't make it onto the roof, but he is able to reach his hand out and touch Lawrence's shin.

The four of them remain like that for the best part of a minute, until Big Mac proudly calls out, 'Team!'

Noddy copies this (obviously), and then so does Mooney.

Lawrence just holds on and smiles through his tears.

• • •

Lawrence returns to hospital, back to square one. He is in Dublin though, not Desmond House. He makes slow progress.

Nine months have passed since the Shannon Hotel incident. Today Dr Best comes to see him and they have perhaps their most normal conversation ever.

'I'm off to New York for a year. A very interesting media opportunity has presented itself and I just have to explore it,' explains the doctor.

'What about me?' asks Lawrence.

'Don't worry about that, there's cover – a Dr O'Leary. She's quite good; not as good as me, there can only be one Best, but you'll be fine.'

'Okay,' says Lawrence.

'I'm sure we'll meet again,' continues Best, 'it's a small world. But you've made significant progress and I'd be amazed if you aren't discharged in six months.'

Lawrence sighs, resigned to his fate.

Best stands and is about to leave when Lawrence asks, 'Don't you want a game of marbles?'

'I can't find them,' is the doctor's reply, and with that they exchange silent nods and a wave, and Dr Ciaran Noel Best is gone.

• • •

That night Lawrence writes in his diary:

I don't like being in hospital. I'm not thinking about work too much. I've seen the kids recently – my mother-in-law brought them to see me. I guess it's over between Eileen and me. Best says I've got bipolar disorder with what he describes as very psychotic features. Majella Quinn does a lot of good for me. I hate life a lot, but some days are okay. I am profoundly sad, though.

Big Mac visits every now and again. I think he must be thinking about taking a job in Dublin, as he has asked me a few times what my old boss, Reggie, is like. Reggie is a top guy, my best friend. Sometimes I think Big Mac is losing it – he said to me last week, 'Does "Rex bought them snails" mean anything to you?' What is he like?

Health is everything, I realise now. I am lonely. I miss what I had. Dark brown, black, dark brown, black, dark brown. Dark brown. I really miss Eileen, if I had three wishes each one would be to get Eileen back.

Guns 'n' Roses, 'Don't You Cry Tonight'. Guns 'n' Roses, 'Knocking on Heaven's Door'. U2, 'One'. Elton John, 'Nikita'. George Michael, 'Careless Whisper'. Steve Earle, 'Galway Girl'. Van Morrison, 'Brown Eyed Girl'. Snow Patrol, 'Run'. Rick Astley, 'Never Gonna Give You Up'. Hope, hope, hope, love, love, love.

Dexy's Midnight Runners, 'Come On Eileen'. Dexy's Midnight Runners, 'Come On Eileen'. Dexy's Midnight Runners, 'Come On Eileen'. Dexy's Midnight Runners, 'Come On Eileen'. Dexy's Midnight Runners, 'Come On Eileen'. Eileen, Eileen, Eileen.

• • •

The students slowly slip away, happy. Lots of hugs and goodbyes, phone-number exchanges, promises made to keep in touch. Lena reminds them all about being kind. After ten minutes, nearly everyone has gone. Liverpool Dean is the last man standing. He approaches Lena.

'Thanks for the three years, Lena. It was great.'

'It was my pleasure,' she says.

'That Larry guy was interesting. Is he well now?'

'Well enough.'

'And what does he do now?'

'He's in Manchester, I believe.'

'Really? Small world.'

'Very,' replies Lena. 'I'll be meeting him in twenty minutes.'

'For real?!' Dean says.

'Have I taught any of you anything in the last three years? Being an excellent mental health nurse is partly about being brilliant at observing. Have I just been wasting my time?'

She laughs, and then she digs in her bag and brings out a business card. 'You all know me as Maguire, but it is my maiden name.' She hands the card to him, smiles and walks off.

Dean looks down at the card. It reads 'Lena Maguire (Barry), senior mental health lecturer, RGN, RMN, MA, PhD'. Stunned and stuck for words. *Of course, Lena is short for Eileen*, he thinks to himself. He smiles, then shakes his head, looks at the door, puts the card in his pocket and runs after her.

THE END

THANK YOU

A special thank you to Charlie, Damien, Katie, Kenneth, Paddy, Rose and Vanessa.

Printed in Great Britain
by Amazon

66529639R00206